An Allie Babcock Mystery

TERRIER TERROR

by

Leslie O'Kane

Book Seven in the Series

Copyright 2019 by Leslie O'Kane

This book is a work of fiction. The names, characters, places, and incidents are a product of the author's imagination or have been used fictitiously and are not to be construed as real. Any additional resemblance to people living or dead, actual events, locales or organizations is entirely coincidental.

All Rights are Reserved. No part of this book may be used or reproduced in any manner whatsoever without written permission from the author.

Dedication

To Gus

You will always have a special place in my heart.

Books by Leslie O'Kane

Life's Second Chances:
Going to Graceland
Women's Night Out
Finding Gregory Peck
By the Light of the Moon
How My Book Club Got Arrested

Molly Masters Mysteries:
Death Comes eCalling
Death Comes to Suburbia
Death of a Gardener
Death Comes to a Retreat
Death on a School Board
Death in a Talent Show
Death Comes to the PTA

Allie Babcock Mysteries:
Play Dead
Ruff Way to Go
Give the Dog a Bone
Woof at the Door
Of Birds and Beagles
Dog Drama
Terrier Terror

Leslie Caine Domestic Bliss:
Death by Inferior Design
False Premises
Manor of Death
Killed by Clutter
Fatal Feng Shui
Poisoned by Gilt
Holly and Homicide
Two Funerals and a Wedding

Chapter 1

"We'll get right to the point," Kiki Miller said as she took a seat on our living room sofa. "We need your help, Baxter." She was eying my boyfriend with unmasked appreciation. That was more than a little inappropriate under the circumstances, especially considering her father, Davis Miller, was sitting right next to her. Davis was the president of the Fort Collins Dog Club, which automatically put him in charge of the annual show this weekend. The show drew dog owners from the entire state of Colorado.

Baxter glanced at me. His half-smile was an acknowledgment that I'd been right about the reason for the Millers' sudden need to pay us a house call today.

"Allie filled me in on your troubles last year in the Terrier division," Baxter said. "But isn't it a little late to be looking for someone to help you put out fires? The show opens this Friday."

Kiki and her father exchanged glances. I got the feeling they were delivering their own silent *I-told-you-so*.

"Troubles" was an understatement. Last year, someone brought a female Airedale in heat to the benched competition (a show-dog term that means dogs are on display to the public throughout the event). Her crate and a male Airedale's crate were subsequently shoved together, either by one of the owners, or by the determined dogs rattling their cages. A family became unwitting witnesses to the dogs mating and were now demanding restitution for post-traumatic stress of their children. Additionally, a seemingly endless stream of rancor, accusations, and various claims of damage to reputation and personal finances sprang forth between the two Airedale owners. A boycott of the event was then organized, and the majority of Terrier breeders in Colorado were drawn into the controversy.

"As the saying goes, Baxter," Kiki finally replied with a big smile, "better late than never."

"In this case, I think it's *too* late," Baxter countered. "If I'm suddenly thrown in the middle of this, I'm guaranteed to rub the managers and the judges the wrong way."

"We realize you'd be in an awkward situation," Davis Miller replied. "This year the competition will be unbenched, so we can avoid a repeat of last year's incident. Originally, we decided to refrain from stirring the, er, boiling pot. We thought we'd merely incite negative attention by making public statements."

"Our business-as-usual policy hasn't worked," Kiki interjected. "We've had way fewer Terrier entries than usual. The furor didn't die down. We underestimated just how big this tempest-in-a-teapot could get. Valerie Franks is known as Colorado's Terrier Tyrant—"

"Kiki," Davis interrupted, making such a vigorous "stop" gesture that his hand was almost in front of her face. "No need to get into who did what."

Kiki glared at her dad's hand as he returned it to his lap. "First things first," she said. "Baxter, we're desperate. We'll make it worth your while financially, and we'll praise you to the sky to all of our club members. This will boost your career."

The Millers stared at Baxter, awaiting his reply. I, in turn, stared at *them*. They made an interesting duo. If Davis was Kiki's biological father, the glamorous blonde must have gotten her looks from her mother. He was a puffy-looking man with sagging jowls, wearing a brown suit and a brown-and-black plaid bowtie around the collar of his starched-white shirt. All told, he was not unlike a balding Saint Bernard. Kiki, on the other hand, was tall, thin, and immaculately coifed—more of a personified Poodle.

With Baxter still not responding, Davis said, "We unanimously agreed that, if we can publicize your taking over that entire branch of the conformation class—"

"By 'unanimously,' do you mean all of the staff?" Baxter interrupted. "Including whoever was overseeing the Terrier class?"

"The, er, person who had been in charge of the Terrier class resigned," Davis replied.

Baxter peered at him with raised eyebrows. "Ah. So *that* explains why your offer is coming to me so late in the game."

"His departure was a mutual decision," Davis explained. "I'd told him we needed a steadier hand."

"Right," Kiki said, "and we'd already realized we should have ignored Cooper's long history with the Fort Collins Club and hired you."

"Cooper Hayes?" I asked, surprised. Cooper was a good presenter of dogs in local conformation competitions. He was always the first to volunteer his help and declined to take sides in a controversy. But he did not strike me as confident and decisive enough to want to be running a large division of the show, even during smooth-going times.

Ignoring me, Kiki leaned toward Baxter. "We also unanimously agreed that, due to the chaotic state of the Terrier class, plus our last-minute-itus, we need to give you complete autonomy." She winked at Baxter. "Whatever you say goes."

"But couldn't that make him the fall guy for anything that goes wrong?" I asked.

Both Millers widened their eyes. "Well, er, I am still going to be Baxter's supervisor," Davis said. "By autonomy, we simply mean we won't be micromanaging. We will have faith in Baxter's skills in managing events such as this. His record speaks for itself."

"If you're willing to take charge," Kiki quickly added, "Valerie Franks has agreed to enter her dogs."

"She *agreed*?" I blurted out. Valerie had been keeping me—and in turn Baxter—up to speed with the goings-on for months now. "The Fort Collins

Kennel Club voted to *bar* Valerie Franks' dogs and Jesse Valadez's dogs, due to their Airedales mating last year."

Once again, the Millers exchanged glances. Kiki lifted her chin in a tacit agreement to have Davis answer field that question. "That was a rash decision, which we now regret. They are now unbarred. And don't forget, we'd allowed them to enter the agility competition all along. Just not conformation." (*Conformation* is what a typical dog show is actually judging; how well the contestants conform to the AKA standards for their breed.)

"Valerie directed all of her clients to boycott the conformation show unless she was allowed to enter her dogs," I retorted, "which is why your enrollment is so low."

"Indeed," Davis said. "But the point is, she's now happy to enter her dogs. Jesse is still mulling the decision."

"I'm working with Valerie's Westie, Sophia, in the agility competition," I said. "She told me she found it puzzling that nobody minded what dogs she or Jesse entered in agility. In fact, prior to the boycott, Jesse enrolled the very same Airedale from last year's incident."

"Because we've never held a benched tradition for the dogs in the agility," Davis replied, spreading his arms as if his statement hadn't begged the question: *So?* "Those dogs aren't in it for their looks." (Again, my thought was: *So?*)

"Also, her dogs have done remarkably well in that particular area, considering they aren't Border Collies," Kiki interjected. "We didn't want to undermine the national attention she gets. But this is where *you* come in, Allie. Valerie specifically asked us to tell you that *Jesse* will enter his dogs in the conformation competition as well, on the condition that *you* will agree to handle his Airedale in the agility competition."

"Valerie Franks told you that?" I asked, surprised. *Valerie had not kept me informed with all the shows' gyrations, after all.*

Kiki nodded. "And I called Jesse myself to verify."

I looked at Davis. "You just got through saying that Jesse was still mulling the offer to enter his dogs in conformation."

"Right. Yes. Exactly. I meant that he was, er, waiting until you gave your answer to working with his Airedale in the ring." Davis was squirming in his seat as he spoke and sending the occasional glare at his daughter. He couldn't have made it more obvious that Kiki's statement had come as a complete surprise to him.

"He typically handles his own dog in all agility trials," Kiki said, "but he fell recently and broke his leg. That's why he agreed to Valerie's proposal to hire you. They wanted to even out the competition between them. Plus the top-notch agility handlers are already spoken for."

"Oh. I see," I said, less than gleefully.

Kiki chuckled. "No offense, Allie. Valerie told me you were aware of that."

"I'm fully aware that I'm inexperienced at agility training."

"Kiki, we've said all that needs to be said." Davis handed Baxter a folded piece of paper. "This is as much as we can afford to pay for a week of your time. Assuming you start tomorrow, it includes all the overtime you'll need, which is inevitable at this late juncture. We'll give you both the opportunity to discuss our offer, but we need your answer first thing tomorrow morning."

"Thanks, Mr. Miller," Baxter said. "This is going to be tough to take on at this point. I haven't had the chance to talk to the judge of the Terriers, or to see..." His eyes widened as he looked at the figure. He held the paper out to me, and my eyes widened as well. It was a generous sum. So generous that alarm bells were going off in my head.

"The judge, Julie Cameron, is beyond capable," Davis said, "and it's been slim pickings with the judges this year."

"She was judging a competition in Greeley last year. For Labs, I think. Point is, she told me she owned a Bull Terrier, so that should eliminate her from judging Terriers."

"That dog died three years ago," Kiki snapped.

"Which doesn't mean she won't wind up judging dogs from her former dog's breeder's."

"That's true. But, fortunately, keeping or replacing the judge falls in the realm of *Baxter's* autonomy," Kiki said.

I grimaced despite myself. This was feeling more and more fishy. I'd managed to have a peaceful eighteen months living out here in Dacona with Baxter. But the previous couple of years prior to my moving here had been a string of my canine clients leading me into murder cases. My experiences led me to develop a radar for potentially dangerous scenarios. The Fort Collins dog show now was dead center in my stay-away blip. I wasn't even sure I could handle it if I wound up with yet another murder investigation swirling around me. Baxter and I were already stressed out by a lawsuit a cat-loving neighbor had brought against us, which forced us to close the kenneling portion of our business until the issue could be adjudicated. Baxter, however, welcomed challenges. A glint in his gorgeous, dark brown eyes spelled trouble.

"Allie and I will have to think it over and discuss this, of course."

"I'll have to speak to Jesse and meet with his dog, etcetera, before I can let you know if both Jesse and I agree to my handling his Airedale," I said. "But I have to say already that the idea of handling both Valerie's and Jessie's dogs makes me uncomfortable."

"They're in different size categories," Kiki said glibly.

"Yes, but dogs competing in the twenty-inch jumps usually win the overall prize. Valerie's Westie winning Best in Agility last year was astonishing. She already warned me that she considers Jesse's Airedale her biggest competitor for that prize."

"Right. And with you as the handler for both, they will be equally unlikely of falling prey to biased judging."

"Biased judging? This is a *timed* event. It's not a matter of personal preferences. Even the faults are assigned according to measurable data. It isn't the *judging* we have to worry about. It's how Jesse and Valerie behave around each other and, more importantly, while each other's dog is on the obstacle course."

"Precisely," Davis said, wincing and putting his hand on the small of his back as he stood. "And they are certain you will notice if one of them is distracting the other during the trials."

Kiki rose as well and touched Baxter's shoulder. "You have my number. Please let me know as soon as you can. It's going to be such an honor to work with you." Her smile faded a little as she turned toward me. "You, too, Allie. I really hope you'll agree to help us." She sent a longing glance in Baxter's direction. "The more the merrier when it comes to us dog *lovers*."

Chapter 2

While Baxter walked the Millers to the door, I remained seated. Kiki's final remark had left me nonplussed. Maybe she hadn't meant to imply she was going to try to vie with me for Baxter's affection. On the bright side, her obvious attraction to the love of my life might be all that was setting off my alarm bells. *That* I could handle—she wasn't going to be able to steal him from me—I just dreaded the possibility of this simmering animosity erupting into violence.

Baxter returned and gave me a big smile. "You were right. They gave me a generous offer."

"Which I'm not sure you should accept. For one thing, Kiki has the hots for you."

"I suspect she's just a compulsive flirt."

"Maybe so. But I'd prefer she be 'compulsive' with someone else."

He chuckled. "No worries. If she puts her hands on me, I'll step on her foot. That always works with dogs."

"I wish we knew why they hang onto Cooper till the last possible moment. They haven't taken the common-sense steps to assure Terrier owners that the judging is going to be impartial. Judges are not supposed to judge the class of dogs that they own themselves."

"Right, but if Julie has a good reputation—"

"They easily could have hired another respected Terrier judge from Utah or Kansas, for example. And they could have courted other less-popular breeds of Terriers by offering lower entry fees. Instead, they claim to have struck some sort of *mutual agreement* to get rid of Cooper. If anything, that will have enflamed the situation. Furthermore, they didn't allay my fear that they're setting you up as the fall guy. Nothing's to step them from throwing you under the bus when *their* lack of due diligence bites them in the rear."

Baxter's posture spoke volumes. His arms were crossed, and he was glowering at his feet. "I can help them set better boundaries. I'll start by talking with the warring parties. Jesse and Valerie are already willing to agree to hire you as their handler, in order to keep the peace."

"By making a totally illogical decision to have the girlfriend of the man in charge handle both dogs. They're putting us front and center, and they're doing this so late in the game, we'll be everyone's bad guys."

Baxter held my gaze. "On the other hand, Allie, we need the money."

I winced. *There it was again—Eleanor McCarthy's lawsuit. Were we ever going to get out from under that curse?* "You want to say yes."

"Yes. Besides, you said you were really enjoying working with Sophie at improving her speed."

I grinned a little in spite of myself. The Westie's full name was Sophie Sophistica the Third. Running around on the agility course with her was fun and brought out my competitive spirit, like in my old college-basketball days. I was able to compensate for my lack of height by being agile and quick-footed. "I've never met Jesse's dog. Valerie has basically gotten volunteer spies to time his practice runs. If the dog and I don't click, it's going to put a kink in their strange little peace pact."

"It isn't really all *that* strange."

"The Fort Collins Dog Club is embroiled in a lawsuit that involves the biggest Terrier breeder in the state and an up-and-coming Airedale breeder. They're allowing those breeders' dogs to compete against each other, even though both breeders are currently suing the other. And they're suddenly asking me to be the handler for both dogs."

Baxter gave me a comical grimace. "Okay. When you spell it out that way, it does sound odd. But you're perfect for the job. You're a former college athlete. You're a dog whisperer."

"I am not a dog whisperer."

"Okay. You're a dog...cooer."

I laughed.

He wrapped his arms around me. "It's all going to be good. We can handle anything they throw at us."

"I don't like the way Kiki Miller keep giving you googly eyes."

He chuckled a little. "She did seem to stare at me. She probably does that to all men. In any case, it doesn't matter. She's not my type. She isn't *you*."

My heart made a little thumpity thump. "I only have googly eyes for you," I replied.

After a long phone conversation with Jesse Valadez, I drove to his house in Table Mesa, located in a southern quadrant of Boulder. My knocking on his door set off a cacophony of dog barks, which lasted so long that I knocked a second time.

"Coming," he hollered. The door slowly opened. Jesse was a nice-looking, compact, fortyish man with dark hair and the beginnings of a dark beard. He was on crutches, a cast on his left leg. I had been mentally prepared for the cast. I was not, however, prepared for his knitted brow; he looked ready to bite my head off. Six Airedales trotted into the spacious great-room behind him, observing me from a distance. One of them came up beside Jesse. Most likely, he was the alpha-dog of the pack.

"Hi. I'm Allida Babcock. You can call me Allie."

"Jesse Valadez. In case you hadn't heard, I broke my leg by falling off the dogs' seesaw in my back yard." He turned around awkwardly to get away from the door so I could enter. "Hopefully, it was an accident. The motion detectors failed to pick up anyone breaking into my backyard," he continued, speaking over his shoulder at me. He rotated again on his good leg. "But it could have been sabotaged."

"You really think Valerie Franks would booby-trap an obstacle in your yard?"

"Valerie will sink to any level to thwart me." He tried to spread his arms despite holding onto his crutches, one of which hit an Airedale in the chin. The dog made a small yelp but clearly one of surprise, not pain. This second dog was a female—smaller than the likely alpha-dog. "These damned things!" He shifted one crutch to his left hand and hopped to a mustard-colored stuffed chair nearby.

"She wouldn't have wanted to hurt your dog. She's just not like that."

He shrugged. "No, but I weigh a lot more than my dog. The teetertotter snapped apart when I stepped on a spot that was halfway to the ground."

Jesse wiped some sweat off his brow. He truly did seem to be in serious pain. "If you don't mind, go ahead and grab your new charge and head out back yourself. A generic course is set up, with both weave poles and a pause table." (Both of those obstacles were never in the same competition course, but that made little difference for training purposes.) He pointed at the male Terrier I'd labeled as the alpha. "That's Dog Face right there."

Surprised, I looked at the handsome, mostly grey Terrier. "Is Dog Face his actual name?" Most breeders followed the AKC practice of giving their purebred show dogs the same first initial to keep track of the lineage, and typically it was grandiose or a person's name.

Jesse chuckled. "It is *now*. I changed it and registered it. He's the infamous sire of Valerie's litter from last year's competition." He paused and grinned. "I just wish I could've heard her voice when she had to tell her hoity-toity clients that the puppies were from 'Miss Bella Beauty...and Dog Face.'" He started laughing so hard he had to dry his eyes. "Anyway." He made a couple of air-sweep gestures to indicate the route to the back door. "Take as long as you need, then report back to me if it's a go or not."

"Okay, Jesse, but I feel like I should say one last time that agility training isn't one of my specialties, and this show will be my very first competition."

"And I just want to assure you one last time that my options were limited. So I'm truly fine with hiring you as Dog Face's trainer and handler."

I studied him. He was brusque, certainly. For all I knew, he could be either a fabulous person or a complete louse. I'm much better at picking up on dogs' personalities than I am at people's. Yet here he was, with the crushing disappointment of having a broken leg and being unable to handle his own dog in the competition. If I were in his shoes, that would have stuck in my craw for a long time, too.

"I am really sorry this happened to you."

"Especially since it happened just four days ago. No time to sign anyone up. Other than you." His expression softened. "No offense. Kiki Miller told me she watched you work with Sophie once. She said that, even though you use the chase technique, she thought you had extraordinary potential."

I used the "chase" technique of encouraging the dog to chase me only infrequently, but that was beside the point. That Kiki had seen me training Sophie was news to me and unsettling. "It's strange that Kiki could have seen me train Sophia. Valerie's exercise ring is under lock and key. She explained that she didn't want the competition to get a leg up on her." I winced a little as the inappropriate image of a dog lifting his leg popped into my head.

"You'll have to ask Kiki. Or Valerie. Maybe Kiki was lying. Although, believe me when I say it's a given that Valerie would've lied to *you* if that's what served her purposes. Such as claiming I pushed those cages together when she did it herself. Valarie's way too on-the-ball to miss all the signs that Bella was in heat. She just didn't want to concede her obligation to give me the pick of the litter for owning the sire."

Last year, I hadn't known which one to believe and still didn't now, nor did I need or want to take sides. Even so, I felt obliged to say something kind about Valerie. "She's been really nice to work for."

"Yeah? Well, wait until it's show time. That's when her 'Mr. Hyde' comes out of her Dr. Jekyll shell."

Not wanting to continue the conversation, I turned and headed toward the sliding glass back door. Dog Face responded to my casual, "Come on, Dog Face, let's go."

"One more thing," Jesse said. "I fixed the seesaw. It's safe for Dog Face to use. Just don't try it yourself."

"Got it," I said as I let the dog trot outside ahead of me. It was far too late in the dog's training to be on the actual obstacles myself, which begged the question of why Jesse was on the seesaw four days ago. Just then, however, I thought of a more pertinent question about Dog Face's training. "Have you been varying your course direction every couple of days or so?"

"Yeah. Every other day. Hope this goes well. I'll hobble out there myself after you've had a chance to get accustomed to each other."

With that, I shut the door behind me, walked across the concrete patio, and surveyed the obstacle course. I had a little shiver of delight. Although I tried to convince myself otherwise, I'd found agility training to be the most enjoyable, natural-to-me task of my career. Having been a guard in basketball, I was perfectly happy to lead dogs through any of their challenges. It was not unlike leading my teammates down a court and dodging as competitors tried to steal the ball from me. Yet trainers weren't allowed to even touch an obstacle or the dog in a competition, so the bulk of the training was dedicated to the dog understanding and obeying my commands, especially when I was pointing at one of two side-by-side apparatuses and instructing which one to attempt first and which direction to go.

Dog Face had been trained exclusively by Jesse. Not only did the dog and I need to establish a fruitful camaraderie, but Dog Face would need to be able to concentrate solely on me, despite his owner and established coach watching from outside the fence at the event itself. Sophie Sophistica, for example, had grown accustomed to me handling her with Valerie watching from the actual arena she'd built in her barn. Valerie also frequently recruited an audience so that dogs would grow accustomed to noise and distraction in the show arena.

The longer I worked with Dog Face, the more attached to him I became. Certain dogs are just so overjoyed to do what you've asked of them, you can read in their eyes that *you* are just their all-time favorite companion *ever*. Admittedly when I was training for agility, I totally let my hair down and raced around the course myself as fast as I could, and mimicked the body motions the dogs would have to use as closely as made sense to up their pace.

One of the downsides of being so physically active myself on the course was I could get thrown off my game by the judge standing in my way. Competitors never know in advance where the judge would be standing on the course. The judge would intentionally stand in front of the dog's logical path to *one* of the obstacles, and it would be my job to show the dog which side of the judge to run past. Because I sometimes ran backward for a few steps I needed not to bump into the judge and essentially end the dog's chances.

Dog Face was great at leaping over the various jumps, weaving through the posts, and racing through the tunnels. He was beginning to pick up on my cues nicely and was giving me an excellent race time overall. If my calculations were correct regarding the speed handicapping for small versus large classifications, Dog Face could really give Valerie's Sophie a good run for the money. He frequently missed his foot placement as he took his last step down from the triangular "bridge," however. That fault was a three-point deduction—meaning three seconds were added to the dog's race time. He also tended to leap sideways off the see-saw, a second three-point deduction. I retrained his foot-placement by yelling "pow" as I slapped the spot I wanted him to step and acting happy. He quickly got the message as I said "pow" and praised him when he stepped on the same spot.

I was unabashedly gleeful as he recorded his best time with no foot-faults. I knelt and held up my had for a high-five and said, "pow" as he slapped my hand. I hugged him. "You are just the best dog!" My definition of "best dog" was always fluid and applied to many, many of these wonderful animals I'd had the enormous pleasure to know. "Yes, you are."

My smile faded when I caught sight of Jesse, glaring at me through the window with an expression of utter contempt. The instant our eyes met, he ducked out of sight.

Deciding it was best to confront Jesse's reaction promptly, I led Dog Face and back to the house. He was still standing near the kitchen window. "Is something wrong, Jesse?"

He grimaced. "Not really. Sorry if you caught me at a bad moment just now. My leg was hurting."

I saw a pill bottle by the sink, along with an empty water glass. "Can I get you anything?"

"Nah. I just took a dose now. I can't take strong pain killers. Not even Ibuprofen. I used to have a problem with alcohol. Anyway. I just...got an attack of the green-eyed monster."

"From seeing me hug Dog Face?" I asked, already feeling sympathetic.

He nodded. "I've been working with Dog Face for just under a year. Started right after last year's show...when they gave my dog and me the boot. You know, Allie, even if none of my dogs were any good at agility, I'd have trained one of 'em as best I could and entered the contest." He shrugged with the one shoulder that wasn't above a crutch. "It keeps me fit. Gives me a sense of purpose. Not to mention joy and exercise." He glared at his left leg. "Not no more, though."

"You'll be able to compete again next year, right? This hasn't been an incapacitating injury, has it?"

"Yeah, I should be all right in another year. It's just that...." He let his voice fade.

"You wanted to compete against Valerie's dogs?"

Again, he nodded. "To be honest, Valerie and I have had a feud going for five years now, ever since I moved here and started breeding Airedales. There's like a hundred types of Terriers out there. But she wants the whole AKC class, all to herself, in the entire state."

To the best of my knowledge there were only thirty types of AKC-recognized Terriers, but I wasn't going to quibble with him. "You've decided against entering the conformation competition?"

He shook his head. "I'm on the fence." He peered at me, still not giving me the impression that he wanted to be in my company. "I don't see the judges giving me much of a shot after last year's scandal. I've only got him and one other three-year old that are up to AKC standards. One's too young. One's too large, one's ears are too floppy, and Chelsea there has knee problems." He gestured at the female he'd bopped with his crutch earlier; hopefully she didn't now have jaw problems, too. "I'm not going to enter Dog Face in conformation, and I would just be putting the three-year old in for the experience. It kind of feels...I dunno. Like I'm conceding that this was my fault. You know?"

"By entering a dog to gain experience in the ring?" I shook my head. "You should do whatever is best for you and your dogs. No matter what, Dog Face and your three-year old won't be going head to head with Valerie's bitch from last year." Valerie had told me she would never even *think* about showing a dog less than a year after she'd had a litter. I assumed Jesse had also heard her stance on that matter.

"All I asked for in my counter-lawsuit was the pick of the litter. She, on the other hand, insists on a guarantee that I won't sell any puppies for the next five years. It's vindictive and just plain nasty." His knuckles were turning white while he gripped the kitchen counter.

I forced a smile. "So, are you ready to come out and time us and stand in for the judge?"

He managed a small smile. "Sure thing. Looked to me like you were doing as good a job with my buddy as I could have. And it sure would be satisfying if I got to see Dog Face smoke Valerie's Westie. Even though I can't be the handler. That's the only means I have to get a little revenge." He snorted. "The only means that's *legal*, that is."

Chapter 3

My thoughts were in a whirl as I drove to my standing daily appointment at Valerie's house that afternoon. Jesse's explanation that he'd been forced to hire me due to a dearth in available handlers made sense, but why Valerie had suggested the idea to Kiki and to Jesse was beyond me. I couldn't shake the feeling that something underhanded was happening, and that I would ultimately take the blame.

Like Baxter and me, Valerie owned a large parcel of land east of Boulder—a former ranch. She'd built her Terrier empire there, and the woman knew her stuff. Jesse was right about one thing. It was really hard to fathom that she unknowingly brought a dog in heat to the show. She had explained to me that a hired hand, since fired, had gotten confused between which of two female Airedales she was supposed to bring to the show. The employee had assumed the dog's diaper was for a costume competition, and then compounded the mistake by removing the "diaper." That Valerie was willing to relate such a seemingly far-fetched explanation made me inclined to believe her.

I pulled up to the front door in Valerie's circular driveway. Her property was nothing short of stunning. Very little was left of the old farmhouse that used to be here. She had flattened all but one brick wall with a fireplace in the back and built a columned Georgian-style house around it. I sat still, looking at the grandiose front door, trying to psych myself up for conversing with her about Jesse and Dog Face and how I fit into the picture.

I climbed the steps and used the old-fashioned brass doorknocker. Valerie answered the door herself. We both stared at each other for a moment. She was wearing slippers and a gray sweat suit and was leaning on her cane—she said she had bursitis in her hip. She was also without her makeup, which made her look much older. The effect was slightly disconcerting. She was roughly my height—a tad over five feet—but she usually wore leather boots with two-inch heels and bold colors, which she had told me helped her to make a larger impression on people. I had always assumed she was in her late fifties, but maybe I was off by ten years, even.

"You're early," she said.

"Yes, I am. By five minutes. I wanted to talk with you about the show and my handling both Jesse's Airedale and your Westie."

"I could have guessed as much." She held the door for me and I dutifully entered. "I'm assuming you don't understand why I encouraged a competition between D.F. and my lovely dog, Sophie Sophistica the Third, with you controlling both dogs."

"Precisely. Nobody discussed it with me first, even though I was the one who got volunteered for the job."

She cocked an eyebrow. "That's true. I should have consulted you. But I've been getting worried by the information I've heard from my...sources. He's even faster than I've anticipated."

"Yes, he's got an excellent command of all of the obstacles, and we were in sync today from start to finish."

"Drat!" She grimaced. "That's exactly what I was afraid you were going to say. This means *you* must work all the harder with Sophie Sophistica the Third. You need to go into the ring with the attitude that SST cannot lose."

Uh, oh. Whenever she called Sophie "SST," as if she were a jet, she was edgy and would watch me like a hawk and find fault with my every move.

She took a step toward me and pointed at my face. "Can. Not. Lose." I had to battle back the urge to snap at her finger.

"The thing is, Valerie, *every* dog can have a bad day, or bad luck. I assure you that I will expect Sophie to be at the top of her game and to win. If she doesn't, I'll be disappointed. But you have to know, Valerie, I will be putting in the same amount of time and energy into both dogs. If you can't accept that, you can still handle Sophie yourself."

She snorted. "You're twice as fast as I am. We'll lose. You're our best chance."

"If you think I'm your best chance, why did you encourage *Jesse* to hire me?"

"Because he *will* lose, and I don't want him to claim his injury deprived him of his victory. He doesn't have the sense of purpose or the passion he needs. He's half-committed to breeding dogs. He's half-committed to agility trials. He's half-committed to being a software consultant. He's half-assed. It's one thing to lose to a breeder who is dedicated to this pursuit of bringing brilliant, beautiful animals into the world. But I cannot and *will* not lose to a backyard breeder who just fiddles with breeding Airedales. Let alone one who connived and conspired to breed my dog with his! He bribed my new hire last year to bring Bella to the show. Nobody with half a brain could have believed the story she concocted! Claiming that she thought the doggie diapers were a costume? If I hadn't been under the weather at the time—" She broke off and made a dismissive gesture.

I hadn't heard anything about Valerie having been ill at the time, but before I could ask about that she plunged farther into her diatribe. "Honestly, Allie! You're young, but you weren't born yesterday. You knew from the start that I demand excellence from my personnel and my dogs. I want Dog Face and his dog-faced owner to lose in such a way that he can't blame his handler. Or blame *anything* other than the *fact* that *I* have the superior dog."

Yikes! She was turning red and was literally spitting mad. I was going to have my head on a platter if Sophie lost. "Um, okay. I get it, and I'll do my level best with both dogs." I paused. "Although, Valerie, if you're trying to intimidate me so that I'll work harder to have Sophie win, that won't work. As far as I'm concerned, I want both dogs to tie for first place."

"I understand. That's what I expect from you. You're very consistent with how far ahead of the dog you are, how and at what point you give commands, verbally and nonverbally. I also know that the arithmetic the AKC uses to even out the sizes of dogs is flawed. The twenty-inch class wins best dog some ninety percent of the time. And guess what size class DF is in."

"Twenty inches. I just got back from—"

"Twenty inches," she repeated. "Yet my SST took the crown last year and is nationally ranked. DF is a rookie."

"But even so—"

She waved at me with both hands. "I know. You're working with the dogs' different temperaments and what not. And sometimes rookies win."

"Right. I'm a little surprised you didn't scarf up the most-experienced and highest-ranked handler for Sophie...Terrington Leach."

"I did. Then he backed out. He decided to limit himself to presenting in conformation alone this year. Didn't I already tell you that he was the one who recommended you?"

"No, you didn't. And I'm really surprised. I don't know why he would recommend me. We've only met a handful of times...most recently at the Denver show last spring. He didn't even recognize me."

"He said he knew you by reputation as a dog whisperer."

"Ah." I held my tongue and smiled a little, remembering Baxter teasing me by calling me a "dog cooer." I considered myself a dog therapist, not some kind of a Shaman who could peer into a dog's eyes and communicate nonverbally. However, as someone who wears many hats within the canine world, I really shouldn't worry about how others chose to describe my headwear.

Valerie looked at her Rolex watch. "Time for you to get started. I need to get dressed. Today's Standard course in the exterior ring should be all set up. I've got two more Brownie troops getting their badges in...animals or farming or something here today. In exchange, they'll be a mock audience in the stands an hour from now, so you'll move into the barn enclosure then. One of the den leaders will act as the judge and will be timing you."

"So the same deal as last Saturday. Got it."

"Yes, well, hopefully a full second better than last Saturday." She gave me a smile so forced-looking it was more of a grimace.

Per usual, I played with Sophie for twenty minutes. I suppose only dog owners can begin to know that having a dog as a pet allows us to act like kids and just play to our heart's content.

"Are you ready to go to work now?" I asked Sophie. She yipped twice and hopped with all four paws leaving the ground. When training, the better phrasing would be to simply state: "work." But I tended to chatter away at my charges when I was stressed. Jesse talking about Valerie having a "Mr. Hyde" part of her personality had, for some reason, lodged itself into my brain.

Suddenly, a horrible vision of Baxter, lying prone in an agility ring, wormed its way into my brain. I whipped out my cellphone and called his phone.

"Hey," he answered.

I sighed with relief.

"Hi. I just called to say I love you."

He chuckled, and waves of joy and love ran through me at the sound. "Are you going all Stevie Wonder on me?"

"Not quite. His singing voice is better than mine."

"What are you up to?" he asked.

"Training Sophie. And being paranoid that we're walking into a major trap."

"In other words, pretty much par for the course, yes?"

"Pretty much." I looked at my watch. I shouldn't have indulged myself by calling. This was an interruption of Sophie's routine; she expected to be racing around the course like an adorable little banshee. "I've got to go."

"I love you, too. Thanks for the call."

I smiled back at Valerie and called out, "Forty minutes," meaning how long it would be until I wanted her and the girl scout troops in attendance.

Truth be told, I didn't especially like Valerie. I had the utmost respect for her, however. She knew how to train show dogs, and I'd learned a lot from watching her. I glanced again at today's course diagram. Valerie was making Sophie run through the tunnel at three different points in the course. Our surrogate judge would stand to one side of the center of the tunnel. The tunnel was Sophie's weakest element, and frankly, mine as well as far as coaching her. In a competition, handlers weren't allowed to carry food or treats into the ring. As for speeding up Sophie through the tunnels, I'd tried a few things—tossing a ball to chase in the tunnel, calling "go get it" and throwing a treat through it. Those tricks had increased her speed a little. Now that we were following competition rules in our practices, I settled on calling, "Whee!" as I ran and calling "good dog" when she beat me to the tunnel exit. That procedure worked best when the judge was stationed anyplace other than the tunnel. If I had to run around the judge to reach the tunnel exit, Sophie easily outran me without full effort. Hence, Valerie's decision to position the judge in the worst possible place for me.

Self-timing with a stopwatch was not sufficiently accurate, but all four of Sophie's run-through times looked great to me. I put her on leash, and we left the outdoor ring and went into the competition arena. Dozens of girl scouts squealed in delight at the adorable doggie. The prevailing cry was: "Oh, she is so cute!" I literally bit my tongue to stop myself from joking to the crowd, "Thank you, but what about this dog?"

Oddly, Valerie was not in the audience yet; she was always prompt. A fortyish woman walked up to me and we exchanged greetings. She showed me her stop watch and said Valerie had done a thorough job training her to play her role as the judge.

"Have you seen Valerie recently?" I asked.

"No, that was back when we first arrived...a couple of hours ago. Should we go ahead and start?" she asked.

I hesitated. "She likes to be in the audience herself." I didn't want to give Sophie's leash to the stand-in judge; that might confuse her about the role the actual judge would play during the real thing. "I'm going to take Sophie with me and make sure Valerie isn't tied up with something."

As we left, a cumulative groan of disappointment arose from the kids, and I called out, "We'll be right back."

Sophie was in perfect heel position as we crossed the yard and went through the back door. I gasped as I immediately spotted Valerie on the wicker chair that overlooked the barn. Valerie was slumped over, her face resting on one arm, motionless.

I raced over to her and grabbed her arm. "Valerie?" I cried, fearing the worst and cursing inwardly.

She sat up. I sighed with relief.

"Good grief," she muttered. "I fainted just now. The room suddenly went gray, and I couldn't keep my eyes open. I must have blacked out."

She looked pale and a little out of it. I grabbed my cellphone in case she needed medical assistance. "Do you feel all right now? Are you dizzy?"

"No, just groggy."

"Thank goodness. When I saw you slumped over in the chair, I was afraid something serious had happened."

She snorted and said something under her breath that sounded like a string of curse words. "You're probably right to assume the worst. But nobody got that lucky." She glared at her coffee cup on the small table next to her. She dabbed her finger in the last bit of coffee and rubbed it against her thumb, as if testing to see if the liquid was granular. She dried off her hand with a napkin. "It's the coffee. Someone spiked it."

"With alcohol, you mean?"

"No, with some kind of narcotic to make me sleepy. If not *dead*. I always take my coffee black. The only possible explanation is that the coffee itself was spiked."

"Could the coffee have been decaf, when you expected caffeine?"

She stood up with a slight wobble. I promptly dropped the leash and rushed over to help steady her. Within a second or two, she batted my hands and said, "I'm able to walk. Let go of me."

She tottered into the kitchen. "I never drink decaf," she said. "What would be the point in drinking coffee without the pick-me-up?" She reached into the refrigerator, grabbed a full bag of coffee, and held it out to me.

"It's decaf," I said, reading the label.

She yanked the bag from my hand, grabbed her reading glasses, and dropped into a chair at the kitchen table. After studying the labels on both sides, she let out a harrumph. "Somebody loused up. Either the shelf stocker or the cashier. I never buy decaf." She threw the bag into a trashcan.

"Are you awake enough to watch Sophie's arena run-through?"

"Of course." She winced as she rose, and as she took a step, she reeled so badly that I grabbed her and steadied her. A moment later, she waved me off. "Let's just not spread this around, shall we? As far as anybody needs to know, I was tied up in an important phone call. All right?"

"Got it."

Sophie had been trotting along next to Valerie, her leash dragging after her. Valerie bent down to pet her. Using her squeaky voice, she said, "There's my little girl. You're going to win for me and show that mean old Messy Jesse that nobody can mess with us, aren't you?"

"Um...let's not lose track of the fact that I'm going to be trying hard to get Dog Face to win, too. It makes me uncomfortable when you've got a vendetta against the one other dog I'll be handling."

She snorted. "If my little Sophie Sophistica the Third can handle the pressure, so can you."

"Well, but then, *Sophie* doesn't understand what you're saying."

Valerie laughed, or more accurately, cackled. Then her mood darkened. "I'll rephrase. If my enemies get away with their attacks on me and on my business, I won't live to see another Colorado state competition. *You* don't know the first thing about *pressure*, young lady."

Chapter 4

To tell the truth, I loved dog shows. I went to one or two in Colorado every year. Baxter and I never missed watching the Westminster on TV. We'd eat microwaved popcorn and talk about each dog, weighing our own favorites. Even so, the next morning, I was sprawled on the carpet of the living room floor, with our three dogs, feeling gloomy. As Baxter left for work at the crack of dawn, he'd warned me he would be gone at least twelve hours today and every day this week. He had already made some improvements yesterday, while I was off training Jesse's and Valerie's dogs. He'd replaced last year's judge by swapping her categories. She was now the judge of the Working Class category, and the Terrier Class was now being judged by a man named Mark Singer, whom I'd never met, but had excellent credentials.

Meanwhile, I was still checking for falling pieces of sky. Part of my fearfulness was due to a terrible loss I'd endured. Pavlov, my beloved German Shepherd, passed away four months ago from a degenerative spinal disease that Shepherds are especially prone to. I loved my Cocker Spaniel and our two King Charles Cavaliers dearly, but nobody could take Pavlov's place. She was my protector as well as my loyal companion. That made it all the harder to be confident that my days of stumbling into homicide investigations were behind me. One day, I knew, I would get myself another big dog, but not today, and not this month.

My cellphone rang. I smiled at the caller's picture; it was Baxter—a face I totally adored. We greeted each other, and he said, "Sweetie, can you reschedule your noon appointment and come up to Fort Collins Fairgrounds? A presenter has apparently gone missing, and we might need you to fill in. He invited his clients here this afternoon and was going to walk them through a couple of laps in one of the arenas."

I paused, confused. Surely he'd meant for me to fill in as a *handler*. "In agility trials?"

"No, conformation."

"But I haven't shown a dog since I was a teenager."

"I know. But for the time being, I'd just like to be able to say that you can be the guy's backup.

And reassure a couple of worried entrants. Chances are he'll show up tomorrow or so and you won't need to show the dogs in the actual competition. He just hasn't been answering his phone, and nobody's seen him is all."

"By '*he*,' do you mean Cooper Hayes?"

"Oh. That's right. You two are casual friends. Sorry, sweetie. My mind's going in three different directions at once."

"Maybe he's not answering his phone because he felt humiliated at being asked to relinquish has job as the Terrier Class manager."

"Could well be. But he told everyone at the time he still wanted to stay on as a presenter. He undoubtedly feels beholden to the show-dogs' owners. They're the ones that pay him. And he's also willing to be on-call if a presenter gets ill. He told me once he considers himself the dog-show equivalent of a public defender. When newbies don't know who to hire or aren't sure if they're willing to commit to the big bucks, the Fort Collin's Dog Club has been giving his name to anyone who calls in and asks."

I already knew all of that about Cooper, but Baxter was talking too quickly to be interrupted. He got a little agitated when he had too many cups of coffee. "There's only one Terrier that Cooper was supposed to show," he continued. "A Bull Terrier named Waxy."

"*Waxy*? Like candles?" Bull Terriers were short and muscular, with oversized muzzles. Target, the chain store, had a Bull Terrier mascot named *Bullseye*—not a great name, in my opinion, but better than *Waxy*.

"I suppose. Can you fill in?

I agreed, although I asked him to call me if Cooper showed up after all. I got ready slowly, then made the fifty-minute drive, hoping the whole time that my phone would ring to no avail. I truly didn't want to make many pre-show appearances. My taking on two dogs for the agility trials was plenty of work where I was concerned.

There were two or three dozen cars in the parking lot, and I once again felt leery as I entered the larger of the two buildings. My memories of all the acrimony that erupted last year at this venue were fresh in my mind. My heart seemed all too willing both then and now to put me into "fight or flight" mode. My best course of action would be to head straight across the huge space toward Baxter's office, which he'd described as "underwhelming," without looking side to side to increase my chances of running into anyone I knew. With luck and a nice, brisk pace, I could avoid being stopped by someone who wanted to rehash last year's fiasco.

"Hey, Allie," a familiar voice called. I turned. *Not even ten steps inside the door,* I complained to myself. It was Tracy Truitt. She was a friend, not a disparaged member of the dog community, but she was always looking for stories for her newsy radio talk show and/or podcast. She was wearing her typical bold colors, fire-engine red Yoga pants with a purple iris pattern on her draped tunic. She strode toward me, saying, "Aha. As soon as I heard Baxter was running the show, I figured I'd see you here sooner or later."

We exchanged hugs. "He's not really 'running the show'. Just the Terrier Class conformation portion."

"Close enough. But...guess what! I enrolled Bingley in the agility competition!"

I stared into her eyes, assuming she was kidding. Her beagle was thoroughly spoiled and only trainable in spurts. "He's...never done any agility training, has he?"

"No. Which is why I decided to wait here until you arrived. We've got to get started as soon as possible. I'll hire you to train him for however-much free time you've got available between now and the competition."

"But the agility trials take place in just four days! Even if I worked with him twenty-four hours a day, he won't get anywhere close to competition ready! Besides which, you have to register him and get him measured, and all of that takes weeks and weeks!"

"I know someone willing to pull some strings for me. This is just a one-time thing, so it's not going to ruffle anyone's feathers. Or fur, as it were." She grinned. "Hey, that rhymes!"

"But I can't get Bingley anywhere near even attempting to run the agility course."

"I know. It's not like Bingley or I will be crushed when we come in last."

Tracy gave me a long look. We were close friends, and I enjoyed and liked her, even though she was a real character. Yet she often tried to avail herself of my services. She'd convince herself that doing so was good for my business. Sometimes she was right and gave me invaluable publicity. Other times she just plain exhausted me.

"Honestly, Allie, you worry too much."

"Why are you entering him in agility? Why not let him come in last in the Beagle conformation instead? He'll have no idea what his handler wants him to do there either, but at least he's leash trained. Sort of."

"Well, I wasn't going to enter him into *any* competition, but then Baxter said how he was all busy here trying to handle a batch of kerfuffling Terrier Terrors, and I realized I could get several shows' worth of stories out of it."

"Oh, Tracy. Please don't tell me you're going to do a Vlog and podcast and make this an enormous deal! You know what a mess that caused the last time you did it at the Pet Expo in Denver!"

She cocked an eyebrow and tapped her chin with her index finger. "Hmm. Are you talking about the show where you and Baxter met, and he turned out to be 'The One"? she asked, adding air quotes. "You mean *that* disaster?"

"Quit with the selective memory, Tracy. You passed out when your dog was bitten by a parrot, and *you* wound up being accused of murdering Russell's ex-girlfriend." The show had taken place almost two years ago, before Russell and I split up. At the time, I was doing my utmost to convince myself that my feelings for Baxter were merely platonic.

"I remember. I just choose to always put the *happy* memories in the forefront." She grinned and gave me a playful jab in my shoulder. "You should try that sometime."

I couldn't help but smile. We both knew I'd once been advised by the head of the Boulder Police detectives to close my dog-therapy business in order to reduce the murder rate in Boulder.

"Besides, it's not like Bingley has to balance things on his nose and walk a tightrope. I mean, all he'll have to do is follow you around the course, and Bingley has been really good at that. Most of the time, I don't even need a leash, thanks to your training."

"He's a Beagle. He is always going to be a Beagle. He's adorable, but a pill. Secondly, the rules of agility trials dictate that the handler can't lead him over the obstacles. Or even touch them. Or lure the dog with food or toys. Furthermore, the dogs must run through tunnels...those things that look like oversized clothes-drier attachments. They have to jump over walls, panels, double and triple bars...go over a seesaw, which is scary for a dog. Climb over a bridge. The weave posts are utterly counterintuitive for dogs. Sorry to rain on your parade, but the whole idea is a nonstarter, Tracy."

She held up her palms. "Okay, okay. I'll hire you to handle him *and* to train him."

"No, Tracy. That's the exact opposite of what I'm trying to tell you. I already have my hands full with two Terriers. I can't add Bingley to the mix."

"Sure, you can. You can fit him into crazy hours that nobody else would presume you'd be open for business."

"I am not going to work with Bingley at three a.m., Tracy."

"It'll be great for your business. He'll be clickbait. Everyone will want to watch you and Bingley on the obstacle course."

"I know you're going to tell me that all publicity is good publicity. But I am not going to make myself look like the world's worst trainer."

"Nor should you. I'm going to narrate and explain that I only gave you a few days to do this, and you only agreed to do this because we're friends, and because we wanted to publicize the dog show, and...drum up support. We wanted to demonstrate to folks who've never seen agility races just how hard this competition really is." She spread her arms. "I mean, I'm proof of that right there. I thought it would be a breeze."

"No, Tracy."

"Don't make me play my you-owe-me-one card," she said, putting her hands on her hips.

"Arggh." I snatched up my wallet from my dog-trainer travel pouch (otherwise known as a fanny pack, but it was way too pricey to be called that). "Fine. Here's a card of someone who works with newbie agility training. Use her, and I'll try to work with him in addition."

"Awesome. You won't regret this, Allie. I promise your business will expand from all the notoriety you'll get from the funny videos that audience members will post." She started to walk away.

"I didn't agree to show him in the agility trial."

"But you *will*." She turned and stepped closer to me. She studied my eyes, a sadness in her own. "Allie, come on," she said gently. "The lawsuit still hasn't been settled, right?"

I shook my head.

"I know how much you guys must need money. We both know Bingley's antics are going to be hilarious in the video, and the audience will love it. Let me do this one little thing for you."

She had made a good point. Then again, there were so many possible problems. "What if it backfires? And I wind up looking like a complete incompetent?"

"It won't backfire. I won't let it."

I shut my eyes for a moment. "Baxter and I called a moratorium on discussing the stupid lawsuit. It's not like we're desperate. We're just getting a little strapped for cash. That's the real reason he leapt at this assignment."

"And we're going to make lemonade from the lemons. We'll get a YouTube out of it that will make viewers laugh, and you'll look great in it." She gave me a nice hug. She grabbed my shoulders afterward and said, "I'll splice in shots of you working with one of the Terriers as well as my Beagle boy and generate some free publicity. What can go wrong?"

"That's exactly what you said about my business plan with the combination dog kennel/training business."

She shrugged. "We didn't predict a new housing development springing up at your property line. And some crazy cat ladies moving into them. But this time I'm right. Law of averages."

Once again she turned and called, "Toodles" over her shoulder. I watched her walk away. By 'crazy cat ladies,' Tracy was referring to the houses built in the former cornfield that abutted our property line, right next to our barn, which we had converted into a kennel and dog-training facility. Six of the new families owned cats, and two of those families insisted that their cats had a right to be allowed to roam freely; there was no way to keep an outdoor cat within a fence.

The cats quickly discovered that they could tease the dogs enclosed in the kennel by climbing onto the windowsills at night and slipping into the building whenever the doors were open during the day. Unbeknownst to us, one of the free-roaming cats got shut inside of the barn one night.

In the wee hours the next morning, a panicked woman came over and pounded on our door, promptly greeting us with the accusations that our dogs must have eaten her cat. Baxter immediately countered that, because our dogs were in our house or in their kennels in the barn, the cat must have been eaten by coyotes. That was not one of his more sensitive moments. The woman went ballistic. I pointed out that the cats loved to slip inside the building and suggested we try there. We marched over to the barn, Baxter opened the door, and her cat bolted out the door and back to her home. We promised we would thoroughly check the barn for trespassing cats from then on. Even so, a finger-pointing argument ensued.

Baxter and I believed cooler heads would prevail in another day or two. Instead, a few weeks later, we got a visit from a government official for possible land-use violations. They had received a flurry of complaints about our dog-kennel business, along with a petition signed by every resident in the new development. As it turns out, Baxter and I had been granted the right to use my property for training dogs and as a "kennel," but the new homeowners claimed that was not the same as an "animal boarder," and therefore we were operating an illegal "dog ranch."

Tracy sincerely wanted to help us financially by entering a dog that would often not sit or stay into a competition that required the mastery of astonishingly complex tricks. She had a big heart. Meanwhile, all I would need to add to her video was a nice pratfall while I buried my pride. And probably my career.

Chapter 5

Baxter was talking on the phone as I shut his office door behind me. From his end of the conversation, I gathered that the caller was trying to coax Baxter into giving a money-back guarantee for all six of her male dogs, should another dog-in-heat incident occur this year. Demonstrating his annoyance, he rolled his eyes as he negotiated the caller down to returning the admission fee for one dog, should her highest-ranking dog's reputation be tainted somehow. I quietly took a seat, noting the lack of windows or a single spot of color or interest in the space. The metal desk, filing cabinet, and chair frames seemed to be circa 1980s or so. Finally the conversation ended. He smiled at me.

"Hi, sweetheart. Cooper Hayes is still a no-show. Apparently nobody has seen him since his firing-slash-resignation from my current position."

"It doesn't look like you're having all that great of a time in the job," I noted.

"Yeah. It pretty much consists of handling current complaints while trying to prevent future complaints. According to Kiki, they'd downplayed Cooper's release from his salaried position by telling him that they needed him too much as the go-to guy for dog owners who needed to hire a presenter for their dogs. They told him they blamed the lower numbers of registrations on being unable to give their usual spiel about him being for hire at a reasonable price."

"He's certainly better-suited for that role. Cooper stops and chats with me whenever we bump into each other at dog shows. He strikes me as one of the gentlest, least-ambitious men I know. But maybe he was hurt even so and just decided to take a vacation, or something."

"Maybe he's pining away in a cabana on a Mexican beach." He sighed. "So you'll meet Waxy soon. His owner's name is Gregory. There are two other Terrier owners who declined Cooper's offer to bring in their dogs this afternoon. I called and left messages about Cooper not being available today, just so I could stay ahead of things." He handed me a slip of paper. "Here's their names and contact info."

I glanced at the two names under Gregory's. Neither rang any bells. "Did you give them my number as his substitute?"

"I said words to that effect. It'd be great if you could call them and introduce yourself and assure them plus Greg you're ready to fill in for Cooper if he can't show their dogs. You should probably add something like: 'despite our expectations that he will indeed be here.' There's a fourth owner that Kiki said she was speaking to, but she didn't—"

He broke off as Kiki Miller popped her head in the office doorway. "Hi, Allida." She seemed a tad annoyed at my being here. Terrington Leach, looking resplendent in his tailored suit, stepped into the doorway beside her. Terrington was the exact opposite of Cooper. He was a dog hander for the stars, showing at Westminster and other prestigious shows. She grinned at him. "You've met Allie Babcock before, haven't you, Terrington?"

"No, I don't believe I've had the pleasure," he replied, smiling slowly and giving me a head-to-foot visual examination.

"We met at the show in Denver last spring."

"Really?" He stared into my eyes. "I so rarely forget a pretty face." He winked at me.

"I must have been having a bad-face day. That happens sometimes. When I don't get enough sleep."

"*Allida*...did you say your name was?"

Baxter cleared his throat. "Actually that's what *Kiki* said her name was, and it still is."

Baxter was not the jealous type, but his arms were crossed, and though his voice had been amiable, he was clearly annoyed at how Terrington was ogling me.

"Sorry, hon," Baxter told me, "but Kiki and I have a meeting scheduled." He held out his hand to Terrington, saying, "Nice to meet you."

"You, too. As Kiki was likely about to tell you, we'll be seeing a lot of each other. I'm showing a future prize-winner in the Terrier class. Plus one in the Toy, Sporting, and Non-sporting classes. I'm guaranteed to have the Best in Show."

Baxter gave him a nice smile and a nod, but I knew him well enough to be certain he found Terrington's boundless ego galling. Baxter shifted his gaze to me. "Lunch in an hour?"

"Sure thing."

I strode out the door, and Terrington followed, shutting the door behind us. A familiar-looking woman strode toward me. She was attractive, in her forties or so, but her wrinkles were permanent scowl lines. Terrington, meanwhile, put his hand on the small of my back. I whirled around, ready to karate chop his arm.

"Aha!" he said, grinning. "Most people call you Allie, right?"

"My friends do," I replied. I glanced at the woman who'd stopped next to me. She was glowering at Terrington.

"I knew it," Terrington continued. "I *do* remember you. And speaking of lovely women, this is my dear friend, Marsala Podna-something."

"Podnowski," Marsala growled. "That's my ex-husband's name, and I haven't gotten around to changing it. No thanks to *my* dear friend, *Terrington.*"

"No thanks necessary," he said in a rather odd non-sequitur. "Allie here is handling Jesse's and Valerie's Terriers in the agility trials this year. Marsala breeds Bull Terriers." He winked at me. "I've been hoping she'll breed them to Shih Tzu, and make a crossbreed called Bull Shihtz."

He laughed merrily, but I'd heard that joke a dozen times. Marsala clenched her fists as if she wanted to punch his face.

"I remember you and your dog from last year's show. She was judged the best Bull Terrier and was in solid contention for Best Terrier."

"Yes, I have two lines of Bull Terriers with blue ribbons on both sides," she answered. "To be honest, I truly thought Chardonnay was the Best-in-Class last year. With Valerie now competing again this year, I very much doubt there will be impartial judging this time either."

"Oh, come on, Marsala," Terrington said. "You don't seriously believe Valerie's dogs have a chance. I'm not even presenting them this year! Furthermore, the judges all know she led the boycott that was responsible for the low enrollment. That's like entering a beauty pageant with a big black eye."

I wondered if his last statement was true. I honestly didn't know how Valerie's actions to date would affect the judging.

"Oh, Bull Shih Tzu!" Marsala snarled. "The judges are going to be cowed by her, just like always."

"It's Jesse's rookie Airedale, Eeyore, that will be hard to beat," Terrington said. He grinned at me. "I'm handling—"

"Jesse is enrolling a dog in conformation?" I interrupted. "I talked to him just yesterday. He was leaning toward *not* entering at that time."

"He changed his mind this morning. He called me and begged me to show Eeyore." He rolled his eyes. "Just a terrible name for a prized dog. Better than Dog Face, at least. In any case, Eeyore is going to be a very tough dog to beat. Especially since I'm his handler. I wouldn't want to bet against us."

Marsala glared at him with unmasked contempt.

He lifted his palms in response. "I'm just saying."

"You've been 'saying' too much of nothing," Marsala snapped. "I'd like to hear what Allie has to say about the elephant in the room."

Terrington scanned our surroundings. "The St. Bernard?"

She clicked her tongue. "*No*, the conflict between Jesse and Valerie. One of them is lying about what happened, obviously. Allie, you've worked with both of them. Which one do *you* suspect?"

This was precisely the topic I'd been actively trying to avoid. Then again, I'd refused to give my opinion for a year now. Maybe my reticence was why it kept coming up again and again. "Frankly, I'm not convinced that either of them is lying. It could have been an honest mistake on the part of an inexperienced helper, who brought a dog in heat to the show. And it doesn't seem at all unreasonable to conclude that the dogs jiggled their crates closer, or someone other than Jesse pushed the two cages together. Such as someone who wanted to create a feud between two first-rate Terrier breeders."

"To get them both disqualified, you mean?" Marsala asked.

"Yes. That's almost exactly what wound up happening, after all. In any case, I think we'd all be best served to take both of them at their word and let...sleeping dogs lie."

Terrington chuckled. "I doubt *that's* going to happen any time soon. Those two are far more likely to fight tooth and nail than to let go of their bone of contention."

"Maybe so. But the *rest* of us can," I replied.

Terrington merely smirked at me.

"I need to get to work," I said. "I'm supposed to take a dog named Waxy on a stroll around the ring. It was nice meeting both of you."

Marsala's eyes widened. I assumed she'd recognized the name of a Bull Terrier. "I need to have a word in private with you, actually," Marsala said. "It will just take a moment." She crossed her arms and glared at Terrington. "It was nice seeing you again, Terry."

"Yes, it was great seeing you again, my dear." He placed his hand on my upper arm. "Let's have a chat over coffee tomorrow. My treat."

I wasn't eager to spend more time with Terrington than necessary. "I'll have to see how my schedule works out in the morning. I'm awfully busy with preparations for the show. Thanks for the offer, though."

Marsala waited a beat as she watched Terrington leave. "Allie, believe me when I tell you, Terrington is a skirt chaser like nobody's business. The last thing you'll want to do is encourage him by taking him up on his offer of a coffee date."

"Yeah, I picked up on that. Besides, Baxter and I made it clear to him that we are a committed couple."

"Which is precisely *why* Terror Terrington is coming on to you. I'm sure *you* know he broke up my marriage."

I sighed. *No wonder Baxter was feeling less than chipper about this job. Dogs can be trained out of their bad habits!* "Is that what you wanted to discuss with me? To stay away from Terrington?"

"No. I wanted to ask you to alert Baxter to the problems with the judge he hired to take Julie Cameron's place. Mark Singer is about as corrupt a judge as I've ever seen. It was a shock to me that Baxter actually managed to find someone even *less* qualified to judge the Terriers."

"Don't you think it would be better for you to discuss this with Baxter yourself?"

She shook her head. "I'm trying my best to stay away from all men at this damned show. I was going to skip it this year, but, frankly when Jesse and Valerie were out of the picture originally, I thought this would finally be my big chance."

She was making a case for herself *having shoved the two dog crates together.* "So you're seriously not going to talk to Baxter or the male judge, even though you think the judge takes bribes?"

"Right. I'm going to avoid *both* of them. Whereas *you*, Allie, have a reputation of righting wrongs in the Front Range dog-lover community. I think the whole nonsense about Valerie's and Jesse's dogs mating last year was a deliberate distraction. Someone wanted to pull everyone's attention away from the bribes that were being raked in by the crooked judges. Of which Mark Singer was leader of the pack."

"You think all of the bad feeling in the Terrier Class last year was a coverup?"

"Bingo! I don't know how deep it goes...if it's all of the event management or just a couple of rotten-apple judges and dog breeders. But it's a real thing, Allida. A real *criminal* thing. And now that I know how contemptible Terrington Leach is, I'd watch my back around him if I were you."

"Are you suggesting he's in on bribing judges to select the dogs he shows?"

"Oh, I think it's *much* worse than that. I think he gets information to use against everyone. I think he's raking in money hand over fist. He flirts with abandon and thinks nothing of trampling over girlfriends and male buddies, and ruining people's lives and careers."

I had no reply.

She studied my features. "Just think about putting your weight behind the effort to clean up this show. Please." She handed me her business card. "Call me any time." She paused. "And, by the way, Waxy is a dud."

She pivoted and marched toward the exit. I watched her leave, trying to weigh her words. Maybe she was being completely forthright with me. Or maybe she was being vindictive to the people she felt had mistreated her and misjudged her dogs.

"Allie." I jumped at little, even though I recognized Baxter's voice. I turned to face him. "I'm glad I caught you. Something else has just come up."

"What?"

"Kiki has received a petition from a couple of the Terrier breeders—*not* Jesse or Valerie—who want me to replace two of last year's judges. They're basically basing their claims on bias toward particular breeders and handlers in previous shows."

"Which could simply be a matter of personal preferences within AKC standards," I added.

"Exactly. As Kiki already knew, I can't fire a judge unless credible evidence is presented to the AKC, which they haven't done."

"Marsala Podnowski was telling me about Mark Singer. She's convinced he's crooked. She tried to recruit me to tell you that in so many words."

Baxter furrowed his brow. "Marsala is one of the founders of the petitions. I'm going to go ahead and discuss this with Davis Miller. There's no sense in making this decision on my own. It's likely to backfire either way."

Several minutes later, I noticed a man with a Bull Terrier on leash standing near the ring where Cooper had arranged for them to meet. Sure enough, the was Gregory and Waxy—who was a nice, complacent, overweight dog. We went through the rituals of walking around the ring and gaiting the dog—pretending the judge had asked me to have Waxy maintain a steady trot in typical patterns—a diagonal line from the judge's vantage point, an L-shape, and a triangle. We then had him take a fictional turn on the examination table for a close inspection by the judge. I nearly lost my balance lifting him, and I suggested he try feeding Waxy green beans or canned pumpkin with a smaller amount of kibble, so Waxy would feel full but would lose weight. Greg was so pleased with my advice, he left in great spirits and told me he no longer cared if Cooper Hayes showed up or not.

After escorting Greg and Waxy to the exit, I joined Baxter in his meeting with Davis. To neither of our surprise, Davis spent several minutes lecturing us on all the negatives of reassigning a dog-show judge that we already knew. Baxter, in fact, had voiced those very points at the start of the conversation. Nobody is allowed to judge the same category of dogs that they own personally, although judges should have good knowledge about the class they are judging. As Davis stated, "They've all been given their assignments and schedules for weeks. We are giving them a vote of no-confidence before they as much as set foot on the premises."

"Yet that's already what the Terrier owners have given *us*," Baxter said, "a vote of *no confidence*. That's what I was hired to fix."

"Not by insulting two of our most experienced judges," Davis countered. "You'll only be making things all the worse."

"Not necessarily," I interjected. "We can explain to them that changing assignments is merely the best way for us to put last year's trouble behind us. None of us want that to happen again this year, including those judges. We're simply distancing ourselves from all the personnel involved by giving the entries a new slate."

"That's a good point," Davis said to Baxter, even though I'd been the one to say it. Changing judges was merely common sense. It was baffling to me that the management hadn't taken care of this themselves before hiring Baxter.

"Allie and I will meet with the judges individually and find a way to make this work," Baxter said. "Thanks for the advice," he added, rising. I stood up as well.

"You're welcome," Davis replied.

Baxter ushered me out of his office and shut the door behind us. "Sorry I said you'd help me without asking first. I wanted to be sure you got a little credit. You don't actually have to go with me."

"I think I can squeeze it in. I'm not half as busy as you are."

"Great. Thanks. I want to talk to the female judge, and I'd like both of us to talk to the male judge. I know it's sexist, but I just think that will work the best. The guy's been known to show favoritism to the young, pretty handlers."

"Oh, gag me," I grumbled.

"That's why I want to be your wingman, in case he's a real jerk. They both live in Denver. We'll pay them home visits, then meet for lunch."

"In that case, I might as well be your wing-woman with the female judge. We should just take one car."

"Sounds good." He paused. "We can have a picnic at Washington Park, and I'll stop by a grocery store and get the food."

"Your frugality reminds me...I accepted a job, training Bingley. Tracy registered him in the agility trials."

"Are you serious?"

I nodded. "I'll be working with Bingley all week at full salary."

"It's not possible to train a dog, who's never so much as jumped over an obstacle, how to run an agility course."

"She wants to produce some YouTube fodder," I replied. "I suspect she's largely doing it this so she has an excuse to pay me for training her dog."

Baxter grimaced. "I hope this financial hiccup of ours doesn't turn into serious illness."

Chapter 6

I managed to contact the two dog owners who had hired Cooper and to have preemptive phone conversations with them. When I explained that Cooper might have had a mix-up regarding the show dates—which I decided was a white-enough lie that I didn't mind telling it—they were happy to hear that I would meet them and their dogs for no fee and no obligation, but if Cooper was able to straighten up his conflicts, I would quickly step aside.

Baxter and I had a pleasant time venting as we made the hour-plus drive south to Denver. We even snuck in a kiss after we'd parked near the female judge's house. Linda Hastings had been expecting us, and she all but led the conversation. She told us she'd already heard unsubstantiated rumors about bribery charges being leveled over her judging in last year's show. Ms. Hastings was going to take those bogus and slanderous charges to a court of law and directly to the AKC, and she had decided to resign as a judge this year.

Safely out of sight from the former judge's house, we gave each other high fives, then drove to Mark Singer's house. Baxter held my hand as we climbed the somewhat crooked front steps. He rang the doorbell, and we listened to a chorus of at least four dogs. "Collies," I said. Baxter and I enjoyed playing the game of "guess the breed" from the barks.

"Goldens," he said.

Our optimism regarding this second meeting, however, faded the instant Mark opened the door. He was a scruffy-looking man, tall, stooped over, uncombed salt-and-pepper hair and unshaven, in his sixties or so. He was wearing a safari vest. I half expected to see cans of beer in its pockets.

"You wasted your time driving here," he barked at us. "I just got off the phone with Linda Hastings, and I'm not about to let baseless, petty accusations force me to resign. I know full well it's that damned Marsala Podnowski who's behind this. You ask me, *she's* the one that pushed the dogs' crates together and probably convinced Valerie's employee that the damned bitch wasn't in heat. If y'all want to replace me, I'm raising holy hell with the AKC and suing you for defamation of character."

Baxter and I exchanged glances. I put on a smile and held out my hand to shake Mark's. "I don't believe we've met. I'm Allida Babcock."

"Oh, sorry. Didn't mean to forget my manners." He shook my hand. "It's nice to meet you, Miss Babcock."

Baxter was also extending his hand.

"I assume you're the new guy, Baxter Something-or-other, the scab in charge of the Terrier class."

Scab!? I widened my eyes and felt Baxter flinch.

"Baxter McClelland. Nice to meet you." His voice and smile were remarkably complacent.

"Would you all like a drink of water or anything before you head back to Fort Collins?"

"That would be lovely," I said, hoping maybe we'd at least be able to sit down and converse with him and improve our current *person-non-gratis* situation.

"Okay. Wait there. I'll be right back."

He shut the door, leaving us on the front stoop. "Yikes. He really, really doesn't want to talk to us," I told Baxter.

"Maybe his house is too messy for visitors."

"I guess. I thought you said he was a ladies' man. Should I have worn something with a plunging neckline?" I joked.

"That and maybe asked for a martini."

Mark returned. He stepped onto the porch, shut the inner door behind him, and handed me the glass. "Oh, thanks for the ice," I said.

"No problem. Making ice cubes is one of the few things I can do without recipe."

I chuckled. The dog barks were still muffled. Apparently, we weren't going to get a sighting to see if one of us could add a point to our running tally. Just then, I caught sight of the doorknob turning behind Mark's back. The door opened a crack, and an Airedale rushed toward us, followed by two black Labs.

"Conrad! No!" Mark cried, grabbing the Airedale's collar and one of the Lab's. He tried to drag them back inside while pushing the third dog with one foot. "Conrad is not my dog," he said over his shoulder. "I'm just taking care of him for a neighbor. He...knows how to open doors. The Airedale, I mean. Not the, uh, neighbor." He managed to close the storm door behind the dogs, then leaned back against it to bar anymore jail breaks. His face had reddened. "Since he's not mine, I'm not in violation of the rule about not judging the same category as a dog you own."

"Which neighbor?" Baxter asked.

His cheeks reddened further. "He lives a couple of miles from here. Loose definition of a neighbor."

Baxter was eyeing the doorknob of the storm door. "There are teeth marks on the doorknob. So the Airedale opens the door to get *into* your house? And yet you're just dog-sitting him?"

"Um..." He scratched the back of his neck as he looked at the incriminating door knob. "One of my Labs taught him how to do that. Those are Labrador teeth marks you're looking at."

Baxter and I let his statement hang in the air.

His eyes suddenly brightened. "Hey, I got certified in Agility Trials. How 'bout I opt out of the Terriers and judge that? To help you all out of your jam."

"Deal," Baxter said.

I inwardly groaned. I hid my disapproval by taking a couple gulps of water. "Thanks for the water." I handed him the glass. "Let me know if you'd like me to give you some tips on training Conrad not to open doors."

"See you both on Thursday," Mark said as he shut the door behind him. "I'll be preparing my agility ring for competition."

I pivoted and headed toward the car. With a couple of long strides, Baxter was by my side. "Sorry," he said. "I hate to saddle you with him as the judge. Mark's the judge that gave Valerie's Westland Terrier the Best in Class. I had to get him out of the conformation judging. At least that's a timed event and not subjective. The original agility judge is also qualified to judge Terriers."

"I understand that," I said gently. "Still, I would have been much happier without having a judge who's quite possibly partial to Valerie's dog. Not to mention whose integrity is in question. And, besides, Jesse Valadez breeds *Airedales*. If Jesse's Airedale wins best overall in agility, Valerie can make a stink about Mark's bias toward Airedales. We'll be right back where we started. And *I'm* her dog's handler. She'll find out we came to Singer's house today for a private meeting, and she'll be livid about how bad the whole thing looks."

"Yeah, I should have thought of that. Still, *I* was here the whole time you two were talking and can attest to nothing untoward going on during your scandalous *tete-a-tete*."

I laughed. "That's very reassuring." I glanced back at the house. "I do find it awfully hard to believe that he's considered to be a 'ladies' man.'"

"Well, to be fair, the rumor was just that he *was* one, not that he was any good at it."

Once again, Baxter made me laugh, and we were in good spirits as we headed to buy something inexpensive for lunch.

That afternoon, I had some free time to work with Bingley. Tracy was busy with her podcast and radio broadcast by then. She suggested I pick up Bingley, bring him to my house, and have him spend the night. She threw a ridiculously generous sum at me for doing so, and after she told me twice that, yes, she was sure it was not too much money, I accepted the offer.

I worked with Bingley first at the course on our property. A few months ago, when I'd agreed to coach Sophie Sophistica, Baxter had felt that this could eventually be a new source of income to replace our kennel earnings. He constructed all of the apparatuses himself. His were made of wood; colorful plastic pieces would be used on the actual course in Fort Collins.

Bingley and I easily spent an hour on the weave between posts, with very little to show for it. I also set up little ramps to teach him how to jump over the bars. That was somewhat successful, as long as the front ramp was in place so he only had to hop down. No matter how many times I jumped over the bars myself, cried "whee," and coaxed him to the other side with treats, Bingley had the attitude that, unlike me, he had too much dignity to jump over something he could simply run around.

Determined, I moved one of the hurdles into a gate in the fence and tied the swinging gate to the hurdle. I then jumped over the gate myself and held out a piece of bacon to get him to jump over to me. He managed the feat. I made such a big deal about it, you would think he'd rescued a child from a well. I leapt back over the hurdle and called for him, offering another piece of bacon. He peed on the gate, then started rolling on the grass. This was not going to be easy. We were talking about a dog ignoring *bacon* here!

Finally, I did at least have some limited success at getting him to come to me from one obstacle to the next along the path I'd designated in my head. Even at that, I had to strike my desperation-come stance; when an off-leash dog runs away despite a "Come" command, the best enticement you can offer is to go down on one knee and hold out your arms as if you are now signaling the dog that he will be receiving a big hug as he rushes back into your embrace. Bingley broke the record for the most times I had to assume that pose in the least amount of times. My thighs a nice workout, at least.

The following morning, I worked again with Bingley. I could get him to run beside me while on leash, but even though I'd prepared each apparatus by placing a treat at the top of the bridge and seesaw and middle of the tunnel, he leapt off the side or the front of immediately after scarfing up the treat, and fought like the dickens if I tried to pull him along the correct path. Leading horses to water and actually making them drink was a cake walk compared to leading a spoiled Beagle along an agility track.

As embarrassing as it was, I then tried having him chase a remote-controlled toy helicopter dabbed with peanut butter that I steered to fly directly over the course. I finally got him to jump over a hurdle that way, but halfway up the seesaw, I had an operator error and crashed the toy. Bingley promptly chomped the helicopter and grounded it permanently.

Next, I tried tying a slice of salami to a string and attached the other end to a fishing rod. I managed to get him to run the entire course in a little over an hour that way, although he missed every post in the weave. And committed countless foot faults. A decent run is under a minute. He was more than sixty times too slow.

For a moment, my hopes soared when I managed to locate a beginner-agility trainer who said she could check this week's schedule. She asked Bingley's breed. I longed to claim he was a Border Collie. But I told the truth, and the answer came back that she couldn't possibly find enough time for a Beagle. That gave me a silly idea for a possible money-maker in the canine field: creating dog costumes that could make a Beagle look like a Collie, or vice versa. It wouldn't be as lucrative as our kennel, but the neighbors would have a hard time suing us for owning sewing machines.

I was in a bad mood when I arrived at Jesse's house. He and Dog Face were waiting for me on his front porch. Judging from his facial expression, he was in the same state of mind.

He pointed at me with one of his crutches as I climbed his steps. "So you threw me and my dog into the fire, I hear."

I stayed on the top step, waiting until he quit aiming his crutch at me. "I assume you're talking about Mark Singer being switched to judging the agility contest."

"There are all kinds of ways a partial judge can rig a contest, you know." He lowered his crutch. "He can make little noises while he's in the ring with the dog. He can shift his position and block the entrance to an obstacle, take a step at precisely the wrong time, or make a gesture at the dog that confuses him."

"I realize that, Jesse." I cautiously stepped onto the porch. "But I'll be in the ring with both your and Valerie's dogs. If he makes noises or motions or stands in the wrong spot, I'll file a protest. If he does something to distract a dog while my back is turned, the staff and his co-judge will catch it on the replay."

"Mark Singer owns an Airedale, according to rumors. No way he's going to want to give a ribbon to *my* Airedale." He snorted. "Valerie must be thrilled. I wouldn't be surprised if she orchestrated this whole thing herself."

"There's no way she could have. And it's doesn't tilt the competition in her favor to have Mark Singer as the judge."

"Sure it does! She's the one who's been bribing him in past shows! For years now! We just haven't been able to catch them in the act! Furthermore, we were told last year that we'll have all new judges. But yesterday the program online was posted with most of the same judges. We're told it was an oversight. Then we're told that the worst judge of all, who's practically broadcast he's taking graft money from Valerie, is going to judge Valerie's and my Terriers in a direct competition."

This was worse than what I'd imagined he'd be yelling at me about. "I understand why you're upset, Jesse. I would be, too. I *am* upset, even. But we're just going to have to make the best of it."

"Easy for you to say."

"Not really. I want my dogs to perform well almost as much as you do. It's important for my career." I decided against telling him that my business was in such shambles I had considered selling dog-breed costumes to disguise dogs. "But we've got the judge that we've got. If you want to withdraw Dog Face from the competition, I understand."

"That's precisely what Valerie wants me to do! No freakin' way! I'll have Dog Face in that competition even if I drop dead first."

Chapter 7

The following morning, I, along with many counterpart agility handlers and presenters was getting the feel for the rings and the general layout. We wouldn't receive the map of the agility course until Friday morning, the day of the trials. Even so, familiarity on the part of the handlers was integral to exuding the confidence that our charges would sense. I could take educated guesses on where the course itself would logically begin and end. Once I got the actual map, I planned on taking four short runs around the course—two while I was visualizing Sophie, and two while I was visualizing Dog Face.

I spotted Terrington, who grinned and headed toward me. "There you are, Allie. Let's cash in on my offer to have coffee together, shall we?"

"Now isn't a good time. I'm trying to do some advanced visualization of what the agility trial will be like. I'm also going to check out the competition in conformation. Maybe I'll be free in another hour or two."

"Scouting competition is a waste of time. You'd be much better served by taking some tips from me. Over a latte at the Brunswick Café. Afterwards, we can find a private spot where I can show you some of my moves."

I let out a guffaw despite myself. "You can't be serious."

He grimaced. "That didn't come out right. I meant how to hold the leash for the dog's ideal head position and how to pivot effectively."

"That reminds me. Have you heard if Cooper Hayes has been located yet?" Terrington's face was blank, so I added, "The local dog handler for the conformation competition? Your peer?"

Terrington recoiled. "My *peer*?" He's never as much as gotten a dog of his place in an opening round, let alone win a competition."

"Well, that's hardly his fault. The vast majority of dogs he handles are, by design, newbies in the dog show circuit, and their owners are enrolling them strictly to build up experience."

Terrington shook his head. "Cooper is an amateur. Amateur dog handlers get amateur dogs to show. Almost always. Outstanding presenters lift the inexperienced show dogs' performance levels so significantly, they become winners very quickly."

"Oh, I don't agree that it's quite—"

"I won contests my first year of showing with dogs who were also in *their* first year. But then, that's what makes me a Westminster Dog Show regular. I only do these Colorado dog-and-pony shows because I happened to be born here."

How fortunate for Colorado dog breeders, I thought sourly. "That sounds like your results were truly exceptional."

"Yes, they were. Thank you."

"But because your results were the exception and not the norm, doesn't that prove my point? Cooper shouldn't be considered bad at what he does, but rather par for the course. Right?"

Terrington sneered. "True. He's not bad, he's simply mediocre."

"*Or* he's happily willing to teach younger canine students. Whose owners typically choose to advance his charges to highly accredited presenters once they're at a truly competitive level."

"I suppose that's another way to look at him...as a puppy trainer." He looked past my shoulder. "Speak of the devil."

I gasped a little as I turned, happy to see that Cooper was indeed finally on the premises. My smile faded. Cooper's left arm was in a cast and supported by a sling. I had truly not wanted to try to acquire the craft of dog presenting on the fly. Especially not when working with paying clients' dogs.

Cooper was a tall, middle-aged man with a ring of brown hair and an ineffective comb-over. I had a warm spot for him, but in truth, Terrington was right about his being mediocre at handling dogs. He plodded when he walked and looked even less graceful when he trotted beside his canine charges. As he neared me, he appeared to be panting and looked truly out of sorts.

"Cooper," I cried. "What happened?"

"Allie. Hi. You're a sight for sore eyes. I've had the worst couple of days." He tried to smooth his hair on the top of his pate. While he did so, he nodded in greeting to Terrington, who merely raised an eyebrow in acknowledgment. "I was on a hike in Gregory Canyon. I slipped and fell, head over heels."

"Must have been one hell of a fall, by the looks of you," Terrington declared.

"It was. I knocked myself out and broke my arm." He ducked down to show us the large, square bandage on his scalp that his comb-over was partially hiding.

"Lucky for you," Terrington said. "You're already bald and didn't have to have your head shaved."

Cooper and I glared at him. He at least had the decency to look away with embarrassment.

"My dog, Matrix, woke me up, licking my face," Cooper continued, turning a shoulder toward Terrington as if to exclude him from the conversation. "I'd dropped my cellphone. It took forever to find, and it was broken. I had to stay overnight with no provisions."

"That's dreadful," I said.

"It gets worse. By the time Matrix and I finally made it back to the trailhead, my *car* had been stolen. I hitched a ride home, spent the night in the hospital, and had to find a boarder for Matrix. I had to fill out the police reports with my left hand."

"Good grief! What a terrible ordeal!" I said.

"What kind of a dog is Matrix?" Terrington asked.

"Uh, mixed breed," Terrington answered over his shoulder, then continued, "I don't know how the heck I'm going to present dogs when I can't grip a leash in my left hand."

"Maybe Terrington can take on some of your dogs." I faced Terrington, who looked alarmed at that concept. "What do you think?"

"That's not possible. This is my *career*. I charge my clients lots of money to show their dogs so that they can improve their chances of winning. It's not like I can suddenly just...pick up strays and work for free!"

"I charge a hundred dollars, per dog, per showing," Cooper said.

"Like I said, in *my* world, that is free for all intents and purposes." Terrington eyed Cooper from head to foot. "Dear God, man! No wonder you're always able to find dog owners willing to hire you."

Cooper looked ready to throw a punch, despite his broken arm.

"If you want to prove your full worth to new clients, Terrington," I said, "this is a golden opportunity. Think of how impressive it would be to take a neophyte dog from a backyard breeder and earn a ribbon. You can't *buy* the kind of publicity that such a thing would bring."

"I have plenty of clients," he countered, "and I *would* be buying the publicity. I'd be paying with lack of commissions and I'd likely lose a client or two by virtue of not honoring my side of the contract with them. I have a set limit on the number of dogs I will show at the events. It's part of my guarantee of the amount of care and time I'll put in with each dog. I could hardly expect them to pay my lofty fees if I'm showing dogs that are in competition with one another."

Probably due to my own personality flaw, I truly wanted to goad Terrington into demonstrating that the dogs themselves are massively more important than their handlers. "But your clients at this show wouldn't be worried in the least about amateur clients upstaging theirs. They'd be impressed with your willingness to help out a fellow team member."

"Actually, Allie," Cooper interjected, "I heard you were already showing a Bull Terrier. I was going to ask if *you* would take on my two other Terriers. A Scottie and a Wheaton."

"I'm already showing a Wheaton," Terrington said. "And I already have Valerie Franks' permission for her to show her Westie herself if the Wheaton advances to Best in Class. The fact that you've already scheduled three Terriers only goes to show how you always expect to lose."

Once again, Cooper looked furious. "In that case, I'll take both the Wheaton and the Scottie," I quickly interjected. "Will that be okay with your clients, Cooper?"

"I already spoke with the owner of the Scottie. I'll have to let you know about the owner of the Wheaton." His teeth were clenched as he spoke, but I distracted him by exchanging phone numbers, then getting the contact information for the Scottie. I suggested he give me the information for the Wheaton as well, just in case. He shook his head and said, "I'll get back to you this afternoon."

"I'm glad you and Allie could work this out," Terrington said to him. "No offense intended." He held out his right hand to shake, which Cooper merely glared at.

"I can't shake hands, Terrington. My hand is in a cast. That's kind of what I've been trying to get across with my words...for the sake of anyone who isn't blind, deaf, and dumb."

Terrington merely smirked at him, then shifted his focus to me. "Well, Allie, we'll take a raincheck on that coffee."

I nodded, and Terrington strode away. As I watched his confident gait, I felt a horrible pang of guilt. I hadn't stopped to think Terrington would only debase Cooper all the more, due to my efforts to goad Terrington into putting his money where his mouth was. That was never actually going to happen. The man was far too cagey for that.

"I hate that guy," Cooper said. "What a jackass."

"He's quite the egotist. I'm sorry, Cooper. I put you in an awkward position by asking him to cover for you. He'd been bragging, and I wanted to bring him down a peg or two. I should have simply volunteered to take your shifts myself."

"Quite frankly, it's my worst nightmare that the jerk might actually manage a win with one of the dogs I should have been showing. The judges freaking love him."

"I've been hearing some grumbling about the judging. What's your take on the rumors that some of the judges are accepting bribes from some of the breeders?"

He studied my eyes. "That subject warrants a whole conversation. Someplace private. Or at least off-premises." He scanned the immediate vicinity. "Listen, Allie, I have to go inform some dog owners of my current injury status and see if I can help them find a replacement. I think I could handle a miniature Terrier. If you hear of anyone needing a hand...ler, give 'em my name. Okay? After warning them about—" He lifted his casted arm.

"Will do. Maybe we can meet off premises tomorrow."

He nodded. "I'll call you."

I watched him walk away, feeling worse than ever. I hoped he *would* call me. He was a really nice person, not merely the consummate dog-lover, but an appreciator of dog owners. He was the direct opposite of Terrington Leach. Despite how repellant Terrington Leach was, I might get valuable information from him. I was curious about the charges that Marsala Podnowski had made yesterday. Not only could it make Baxter's efforts more effective, I did indeed want to expose whoever was causing the upset in the dog show.

Deciding to take the opportunity to spend some time with Baxter, I headed into the main building. Just as I was a few steps from Baxter's office, I crossed paths with Kiki. "If you're trying to catch Baxter, he's in a powwow with my dad."

"Okay." I stopped, pondering if I should leave him a note.

Kiki let out a little sarcastic chuckle. "You don't have to get all defensive, Allie." She squeezed my upper arm. "Stop being so sensitive."

I opened my mouth to tell her I had no idea what she meant, but decided there was no point. I did my best to disguise a growl of irritation by clearing my throat. "Thanks for the info," I said as we went our separate ways. Not trusting her, I switched directions and stood close to Baxter's door, listening. It did indeed sound like he was in a conversation with Davis.

Maybe I should get my coffee with Terrington off my to-do list, after all. I consulted an email from Fort Collins Dog Club, found his number, and called. He answered with a cheerful, "Allie!"

Simultaneously, I noticed there was a competent-looking woman taking a Schnauzer through his paces in the otherwise deserted ring ahead of me. "Hi, Terrington. I'm back in the main building. Are you here by any chance? We can go get that coffee."

"As a matter of fact, I am indeed still here. I got waylaid by a couple of fans while I was in the parking lot. How 'bout we meet over at the Brunswick Café? It's directly across the street from the front parking lot. I've got a few things to finish up first, but I'll see you there in say...fifteen minutes."

He had spoken with a disturbingly flirtatious tone of voice, yet I really did want to ask him some questions. "Sounds good." I hung up and called the Scottie owner, who told me that she didn't care that I was inexperienced myself; she was only entering 'Scottie' because she'd promised her ten-year-old daughter she'd do so. "He's just a nice family dog, you know? Please don't feel like you need to take your time to get to know him in advance. We aren't even planning on getting to Fort Collins until Friday. We'll get together then." I agreed, grateful now that Terrington hadn't been the one to place this call. He would have rubbed Cooper's face in it relentlessly. I focused my attention on woman practicing her presentation with the Schnauzer.

* * *

I'd been fortunate to watch three different handlers practicing with presenting the dogs. I found myself visualizing myself in their place, with Waxy and Scottie, followed by a Wheaton, as the dogs. Some woman I didn't recognize whatsoever was practicing her presenting skills on a gorgeous sable Collie. He reminded me of Sage, my mom's Collie. I was immediately captivated. The woman smiled at me. I realized then that I'd lost track of the time. I checked my cellphone and stamped my foot in frustration. I was already five minutes late.

I strode out of the building and into the parking lot. Though I was probably just kidding myself, I couldn't help but think I'd have been kept on time by Pavlov, if only she'd been here with me. The line of thought always battered me; I started playing what-ifs with myself—if only I hadn't gone to work that day and had gotten her to the vet sooner, or if I'd sensed her time was coming soon and could have taken a few days off to pamper myself with her presence.

I saw Marsala in tears, running toward her car in the parking lot. She had just crossed the street at the crosswalk I was now heading toward. Oddly, Mark Singer was running after her. He was once again wearing his safari vest. "Marsala! Wait! I already called the police! We're both witnesses!"

"Leave me alone!" she sobbed, turning. She turned my way. So did Mark. They both stopped and looked at me.

"What's wrong? What's happened?" I called out.

"Cooper killed Terrington," Marsala answered, still sobbing.

Chapter 8

"What do you mean? Terrington is dead? How? Why?" I started trotting toward Mark as Marsala got into her car. "You saw Cooper kill him?"

Mark shook his head. I saw spots of blood on his safari vest. "Marsala did. I heard her scream and rushed toward her. Cooper looked like he was about to stab him again. He saw us standing there, dropped the knife, and ran."

This was all so unbelievable. I'd spoken to Terrington around twenty minutes ago. Had the world started spinning double-time? My phone rang. I looked at the screen. Cooper was calling me. "Cooper?" I said into the phone, incredulous. My heart was pounding, and I'd had to struggle to keep my voice even remotely calm.

"Allie. You've got to help me," Cooper cried. "Mark Singer and Marsala just...saw me with.... I was trying to...Terrington's dead. Someone killed him. Stabbed him. His throat. I'm in such a mess. I'll never survive this."

Police sirens were wailing. They were turning into the parking lot of the café where I was expecting to meet Terrington.

"Where are you?"

"I'm in the parking lot. Of the Brunswick Café. The police are on their way. I'm just...I'm going to surrender to the police. But I didn't do it, Allie. You have to tell them I didn't do it."

"Tell the police, you mean? I can't. I can't know that as a fact, one way or the other."

Three police cars with flashing lights had rounded the café across the street. "Mark's here. I was on my way to meet Terrington. Mark says *you* killed him."

"He's wrong. I didn't kill him. I...I found his body is all. And I tried to do mouth-to-mouth and...and to stop the bleeding. But there was nothing I could do. It was too late."

"We've got to go back to the scene, Marsala," Mark shouted.

"He's right, Marsala. You need to return to the restaurant with us," I called to her.

"No. I don't want to. It's too horrid. Mark, tell the police I will wait right here. I can't go back and see all that blood." She, too, appeared to have red spots on her white blouse.

"Allie! Please," I heard Cooper shout over the phone. I returned the phone to my ear. "You know me. You know I'm not a killer."

"You need a lawyer, Cooper," I said.

"I'll get one. But I heard the stories people tell about you...about all the help you've given to the Boulder police, solving murders. That's what I need. Someone I can trust to be my private investigator. You! I trust you! I'll pay you...somehow. You know these same people I do.

The same people Leach knew. People with a real reason to want to see him dead."

"Look, Cooper. Let's— I'll be right there." I hung up. I had been walking during my phone call and now realized that I'd reached the crosswalk. The walk light illuminated. I headed across the street. The police cars were behind the building, out of my periphery.

I rounded the building. A pair of officers were in the process of taping off the crime scene. I could see even at a thirty-feet-or-so distance that Cooper was shaking. His knees and shirt were stained with blood. He was being led by an officer toward the patrol car.

I didn't really know Cooper Hayes all that well. I didn't know if he was capable of murdering someone. He needed more help than I could give him if Mark's story was accurate.

"It's not true," Cooper cried. His eyes were wide with terror and he was sweating profusely. "Terrington Leach. Somebody killed him. Not me."

I couldn't tell if he was talking to me or to the four police officers who'd emerged from the two patrol cars. I walked toward him, not wanting to make the officers edgy and think I was any kind of a danger to them.

"Leach confronted me in the café and told me to meet him outside. He was rolling up his sleeves. I didn't want to fight. It was all too stupid. I waited a couple of minutes, then headed to the men's room. He was leaning against the back door. He...I don't know. Maybe he came in from the kitchen. Or outside. His face was white and his eyes were...blank. He was bleeding. He had a knife in his neck. The door opened from his weight, and he fell backward. I was frozen for a while. I yelled for help and was trying to hold his wound closed. Nobody came. Then Marsala did. Then Mark did."

He looked over at me, his eyes wide. "Ask her. Ask Allie. She'll tell you I wouldn't kill anybody."

"Are you a witness?" an officer asked, blocking my view as the officer's partner started to put handcuffs on Cooper.

"Allie. Listen to me. Somebody *listen*. I was trying to save his life. Just as Marsala rounded the corner." He sobbed. "I didn't like the guy, but I didn't murder him. I barely knew him."

A third officer came toward me and gently pushed me away from Terrington and the other officers. "Miss, we're taking him to the police station to ask him some questions. Are you related to the victim, or to this man?" He indicated Cooper with a slight gesture of his hand.

"No. I'm acquainted with both of them. I was supposed to meet Terrington Leach for coffee. I've watching a dog presenter practice in the main building of the fairgrounds and lost track of time. I was ten or fifteen minutes late."

"Wait inside the restaurant, Miss."

"Should I—" I vaguely gestured at the back door.

"No, go around—" He started to turn, then pointed. "Go wait under that tree. I'll get an officer to talk to you as soon as I can."

Several people dashed toward us along the sidewalk of the café. "Do not go to your cars," a loud, amplified voice reverberated from behind the group. An officer must have been using a bullhorn. "Everybody go back inside the restaurant. You are not in danger. You can leave the restaurant after giving contact information."

I went ahead and crossed the parking lot the short distance to the tree where I could stand in the shade. The officer who'd spoken to me was now arguing with two families. He was trying to block their view of Terrington and herd them back along the sidewalk. I took a couple of slow, calming breaths, then grabbed my phone to call Baxter. I heard footsteps behind me and turned. Mark and Marsala had followed me here. Marsala was weeping.

As Cooper was being helped into the police vehicle, she took a couple of steps toward him. "How could you do something like this?" Marsala screeched at Cooper. She turned toward me. I saw for certain that she, too, had spots of blood on her hands and on her blouse.

An hour or two later, I felt completely drained of energy and numb. Baxter had locked his office door behind me, pulled his two bargain-basement office chairs close together and allowed me to lean against him as he wrapped his arm around me. After a while, I felt like talking and relayed the details of what I'd already told the police during their long, tedious taking of my statement. "Did you find out what Marsala actually saw?" Baxter asked.

"She told me she saw Cooper with the knife in his good hand, and he dropped it when she screamed. She said it looked like he'd been pushing him down with the arm in the cast. I think he claims he was trying to keep compression on the wound after pulling out the knife."

"Where did the knife come from?"

"The café kitchen, apparently. Right after Marsala and Mark got there, a cook came out and cried, 'That's my knife. Someone took it.' So the killer must have snuck into the kitchen. It looks bad for Cooper, but Marsala also had blood on her clothing. She told me she got it from the back door, when she got woozy and was trying to stay upright."

"Did that sound likely to you? To get it on her clothing?"

I nodded. "The door looked pretty gory. And it was on her sleeves. Mark said she'd gotten it on his clothes, too, when he was trying to comfort her." I was starting to feel a little woozy myself.

Baxter kissed the top of my head. "You're caught up in another murder. I'm so sorry, darling." His voice was gentle and soothing.

"Did the police talk to you, too?"

"Not yet. For once, a long conversation with Davis Miller was lucky for me. We both have irrefutable alibis for the other."

"That's a relief."

Someone knocked. Baxter stood up and opened the door. "Come in," he said. Two uniformed officers entered.

"We're investigating an incident that occurred across the street around noon. Are you Baxter McClelland?"

"Yes, I am."

The older-looking officer eyed me. "And you are?"

"Allida Babcock. I spoke to the police earlier at the restaurant."

"We're just trying to get background information. The manager, Davis Miller, directed us to you."

"Should I stay?" I asked.

"No," both officers replied in unison.

"Are Jesse and Valerie still here?" Baxter asked me. "Do you have appointments for working their dogs this afternoon?"

"That's a good question. I'd better talk to them and find out."

He took my hand and helped me to my feet. We squeezed hands in a tacit goodbye. I stayed on the lookout for Jesse and Valerie as I walked the length of the building to the front door. I then headed straight to the second, smaller building and entered the agility show room. The ring was empty, and only one person was in the seats— Marsala Podnowski. She was gazing straight ahead, although there was nothing to see. I climbed the steps to her row. She glanced at me for a moment, then returned to her contemplative stare. She was now wearing a plain gray tee-shirt and a slightly tattered-looking pair of sweat pants. She had probably turned over the clothes she'd been wearing to the police.

"Hi, Marsala. How are you holding up?" I asked.

She exhaled loudly. "I can't stop replaying the scene in my head."

"I know what that's like. Unfortunately."

She stared at me. "So the rumors about you are true? That you've been involved in a couple of murders before this?"

I nodded. "I've been the first person to find a murder victim more than once."

"Terrington and I used to date," she replied, already back to staring at the arena below. "It feels so unreal."

"I'm sure all of this is taking quite a toll on you."

She gave no reply.

"You told me about your relationship with Terrington yesterday."

"That's right. I did, didn't I." Her voice was flat. I couldn't help but wonder if she'd taken a tranquilizer to calm herself. "Mark hated Terrington. If Cooper is telling the truth, I wouldn't be surprised if Mark killed him."

"Really? Weren't you two with each other the whole time?"

"No. Mark said he'd been heading toward the café coincidentally, and that he'd heard some men arguing behind the building. So he claims he happened to hear me scream just before he could arrive at the scene."

"Huh. So you didn't know he was even there until after you'd seen Cooper and Terrington?"

She nodded. "Pretty convenient coincidence," she said, echoing my thoughts.

"Do you think Mark is lying when he claimed you'd transferred blood to his shirt?"

"I don't know, Allida. I wasn't in my real head when the police interviewed me. Nor when Mark was trying to help me calm down."

I nodded and held my tongue. I wondered if fingerprints on the knife could prove who the killer was. But then, the killer could have snatched a pair of latex gloves from the kitchen, along with the knife.

"Mark said something about following me toward the restrooms, but I didn't even know he was in the café. He always seems to be following me around. I'm almost surprised he actually left me alone here like I asked him to."

"You're no longer certain *Cooper* killed Terrington?"

"Not at all." She shook her head. "By the time I talked to the police, I realized I'd panicked and wasn't thinking clearly at first. All I'd seen was Cooper with a knife in his hand. He could have been telling the truth about pulling out the knife and trying to stop the bleeding."

"Well, that's a relief. Cooper called me saying that you saw him at precisely the worst possible moment. I'd like to think he's innocent."

Marsala searched my eyes. "Now that I think back, *Mark's* the one who was insisting to me that I'd caught Cooper in the act. It freaked me out even worse. That's why I ran away. I was scared for my own life."

"Is that still what you think? Could Terrington have been ambushed by someone else...someone who'd grabbed the knife from the kitchen right when Terrington happened to be standing by the back door?"

"I guess it's possible." She studied my features. "I hadn't heard any of their conversation. Then Terrington stood up, saw me, and said to Cooper, 'Meet me out back.' He looked at me again, and he actually *winked* at me. Then he marched out the front door."

"Are you sure he left through the *front* door?"

"Positive. I noticed how odd that was, too."

"Why would he leave by the front door, if he wanted to start a scuffle in the back?"

"*I* can't understand why two men in their forties would want to exchange blows in a parking lot."

"Maybe Terrington just wanted to argue verbally. Maybe he cooled down, decided to drop the whole thing, and came back in through the back door."

"I don't know. I don't understand any of it." She closed her eyes. "That was the last I saw of him." Her voice was choked with emotion.

"I'm sorry," I said.

"Welcome to my world," Marsala grumbled. "My freaking ex-husband made our marriage a nightmare. I should have left him years ago. Instead I was stupid and desperate enough to fall for a serial flirt like Terrington. And, of course, Terrington dropped me as soon as he learned I was now single. I was safe and tantalizing to him just when I was a married woman."

She was hardly painting herself in the best possible light. She had a good motive to have killed Terrington herself. All she had to do was hide herself at the corner of the building until she heard someone else discover Terrington's body, and then rush around the building to make it look like she was there for the first time.

"Meanwhile," she continued, "my ex moves back to Nebraska, marries his high-school sweetheart and is happy as a clam. While I'm having creeps like Mark Singer stalking me."

"He's *stalking* you?"

She sighed. "Sort of. He's always keeping an eye on me. Let's just say I'm really glad he's judging agility, not Terriers, and that I don't have any dogs entered in agility."

"So...that's all he's done, though, so far? Follow you around?"

She grimaced. "So far. He was buzzing around me like a gnat at last year's dog show in Greeley, too. He told me a couple of times that if I was available, I should ditch Terrington and look for a man who would treat me like a king."

"Hmm. His house is hardly a palace," I muttered.

"You can say that again. I'd be 'the queen of nothing at all,' to quote from a song lyric." She shook her head. "I don't know why I'm telling you all of this. It's just...it's been such a miserable day. My former lover was brutally murdered. The police talked to me for hours. Meanwhile, Mark

Singer is bullying me. He kept correcting me when I tried to say what I saw—even though it was the worst thing I've ever seen in my life." She started crying. "I just wanted to get it out of my mind, but he was being a complete jerk. I told him I'd gotten enough of that from my ex-husband."

"You might want to report your conversation with Mark to the police. It could be important to their evidence-gathering."

We sat in silence as she got her emotions under control. "You're right, Allie. I didn't think of that, but he could have been trying to confuse me as a witness, so he could frame Cooper for a crime he himself committed."

"It's at least a possibility," I said. If anything, though, my thoughts were how convenient it was for the killer to have two other suspects. I rose. "I'd better get going. I was looking for Valerie and Jesse to see if my appointments for dog training were still on for late this afternoon."

"*How* late?"

"Four thirty, then five-forty-five."

"I can already tell you that won't work. Mark just finished telling me that Davis was notifying all of the judges, presenters, and staff members that they would have a mandatary meeting at five."

Indeed, at five--quarter after five actually—everyone associated with running the show was called into an emergency meeting in the "conference" room, as it had been termed; it was just a reasonably large room in the very back of the staff-only portion of the building. It had some sort of built-in dais where Kiki and Davis Miller stood with a handheld microphone. Davis started saying, "Testing. One, two—" and Kiki took the microphone out of her father's hand.

"We are all in shock, obviously," she said. "This is a terrible, terrible thing that happened. But we can't let it distract us from the job we're doing. Believe you me, if we were to cancel at this late juncture, we would essentially bankrupt the FCDC (Fort Collins Dog Club.)"

Kiki continued to drive home her point about prevailing in the face of tragedy, until Davis literally yanked the mic from his daughter. "We need to stop any and all rumors. No more talking about the murder, even amongst yourselves." He leveled a sharp gaze at me. "There are already radio reports going out. The story is on the internet. I'm sure it'll be on the evening news. I don't want anyone talking to the press. Or to their friends in the local media." Again, he glared at me. Maybe he knew Tracy Truitt and I were friends. "If the dog owners ask you, any of you, any question, your answer is, 'I heard some drugged-out-of-his-mind lowlife stumbled in through the back door of the Brunswick Café and stabbed the first person he saw.' You will be telling the truth, because you just now heard *me* say it.'"

I raised my hand. Davis grimaced at me, which I decided to take as an acknowledgment. "Mr. Miller, it really isn't a good policy for us to spread fake rumors. There hasn't been an arrest, so if people believe that there's some drugged-up man with a knife on the loose in the immediate area, they'll stay away. We'll lose our audience as well as our attendees. We might as well cancel the show."

"Good point," Davis said. "We need to, er, change that message. Let's tell everyone we heard that the police just arrested a druggie lowlife."

"Let's just tell them that we don't know anything more than what was released by the police in the media," Baxter stated firmly.

"Brilliant idea, Baxter," Kiki declared. She turned to face her father. "Let's do what Baxter says. People *do* get killed, after all. It's not like we're going to be dealing with a stabbing epidemic, or anything."

"Okay. Fine." Davis sighed, handed the microphone to Kiki, and sank his hands deeply into his pant pockets. "Everybody out there okay with that?"

A general smattering of concurrence arose from the fifty or so attendees.

"Well done," Baxter whispered in my ear.

I looked at him, sincerely unsure of myself. "Really? Everything that's happened in the last twenty-four hours feels...loony tunes."

"Someone getting killed is of course way beyond the pale. These pet-show events are always in a state of chaos. Pet shows are the new zoos."

The next morning, I drove in with Baxter to the Fort Collins Fairgrounds. I wanted to stay close to him, afraid for both our sakes that more chaos was to come. The news stations were reporting that Cooper had been designated as a "person of interest."

With Baxter absorbed in answering one phone call after another from worried dog owners and dog lovers, I set out to get a look at as many dogs as I could on the fairgrounds. I loved being at dog shows, seeing the various beautiful animals looking their best. For my money, no human's head of hair could match the luster and hue of a well-groomed Irish Setter. I'd been starting to picture myself with a pet Setter in my future.

Despite Davis's oration yesterday, I was quite certain Terrington's murder would be the constant topic of choice from now on. The show started tomorrow and lasted until Sunday night, when we could all pack up and go home.

The park itself was filling with trailers. This was the preferred method for show-dog owners to travel in style, enabling their entire families and their dogs to make the trip in a portable home. Weather permitting, many of the show rings were outside, so the dogs could merely trot ten or thirty yards from the trailer to the site of their competition. There were already plenty of dogs in the main building. Many of the old-guard dog owners were so used to the benched competitions, they were turning the main hall into a de facto bench competition, with the owners and handlers socializing and bringing dog beds and crates with them.

The groomers had already set themselves up in the designated room and were working on their clients' fur, nails, and teeth. This was a space in which the childish aspect of sense of humor came out; the sight of dogs with curlers and hairpins in their fur always made me chuckle.

As I strolled around, I was pleased to see that there were several families with children here, looking at the dogs. Apparently the horrible news about Terrington wasn't spooking potential attendees.

As I entered the Terrier section, a blonde, overweight woman dressed in all plaid—including her headband—rushed up to me. "Miss, do you work here?"

"Sort of. I'm going to be—"

She grabbed my wrist and pulled me toward a Westie that was fast asleep. "You need to tell us something. Why is Richard Cory out like a light? I can't even wake him!" She lifted him out of his crate and held him in front of her as if she was presenting me with a tray.

"Allie Babcock," someone called. I took a quick look and saw Valerie. She was holding a lovely Westie—not Sophie Sophistica—but I needed to concentrate on Richard Cory. I promptly took note of his slow breathing and gently pried an eyelid open. His eye was black—one large, dilated pupil.

"He's been drugged," I said.

"Somebody must have given him a shot! Who would do something like this?" She cradled her dog to her chest and whirled around. She looked at Valerie to one side and a woman I didn't know to the other. "One of you two did this!"

"No, I didn't," they both cried.

"You can't possibly suspect I would drug one of my dogs from my own stable!" Valerie continued. "I would never hurt a dog."

"Besides, if someone did this to make your dog too sleepy to compete, why would they do it now? The competition doesn't start for another two days," the other woman pointed out.

"Richard Cory!" I shouted, testing his ability to respond. He opened his eyes, gave a little whimper, and went back to sleep. "He's at least coming around a little."

"Thank goodness!" The plaid-dressed woman gently put him back in his crate. "We need to get to the bottom of this. Immediately." She put her hands on her hips and eyed Valerie.

"Don't look at me like that! I was never even *near* your dog." Valerie pointed at the camera in its dome above us. "There are only two security cameras in this entire building, and that's one of them. Hopefully it's up and running right now. Allie, go look at the recordings. The culprit has to have been caught on the camera."

"Right," I said. "I'll get Baxter to give me access to review them." I headed to his office and went inside. To my pleasant surprise he was shutting his computer and slipping it into his desk drawer.

"Hi, hon. I was just about to call you." He rose and locked the desk. "Do you want to head outside with me? Davis asked me to make sure all the trailers are parked within the designated areas."

"That has to wait. We need to look at the recording of the camera in aisle nine—where most of the smaller Terriers are. Someone drugged a Westie."

He gazed at me for a second or two. "Okay. Let's change my question. Would you like to walk *indoors* with me, while we head to the security room? I need to examine a camera recording." He unlocked the desk and grabbed his laptop. "Might as well bring this. I'll want my own copy of the incident, regardless."

Chapter 9

Fifteen minutes later, we had a partial answer to what had happened to Richard Cory. While the plaid lady and Valerie were engaged in conversation, a boy, somewhere around the age of ten, grabbed the dog out of his crate and sat down on the floor with him. When the boy realized his mother was starting to enter the aisle, he pushed the dog off his lap and hopped to his feet. Mother and son continued down the aisle, the son taking one long look back before he left the camera's viewing range. Meanwhile, Plaid Lady grabbed her phone from a pocket in her skirt as if it had just rung. She promptly covered her free ear and strode out of the camera's range without a glance at the empty crate. The third Westie owner arrived, spoke to Valerie, and the two of them walked away. Several minutes later, Kiki appeared, carrying the groggy-looking dog. She looked to both sides, checked his name tag, then put him back in his crate, which had the name "Richard Cory" in large black letters.

"Jeez!" I grumbled. "Look at how Kiki's gawking from side to side. She's hoping nobody sees her."

"Jim?" Baxter said to the security guard. "Copy this section of the recording and send me a video."

"Will do."

"Let's head to my office," Baxter said to me. He grabbed his phone and a few moments later said, "Kiki? Can you come to my office, ASAP?"

With Baxter's long strides, I was taking two steps to his every one. He glanced back at me and said, "She's on her way."

He held the door for me and followed me into his office.

"I think I should sit in the back of the room," I told him, "so that I'll be out of Kiki's direct line of sight during your conversation."

He shut the door behind us and watched me move one of the two chairs. I sat down.

"This is going to be interesting. Even though Kiki was acting guilty, I doubt she did anything intentionally. The dog had been wandering around, unsupervised."

"Yeah, but how could he have been drugged accidentally?" Baxter rounded his desk and sat down, struggling a bit with his creaky metal drawer as he stowed his laptop once again.

"Some dogs love to eat tissues. My top theory is that Richard Cory could have found Kiki's purse and eaten a small tablet she'd folded into a tissue."

"Have you ever seen that happen?"

"Not personally, but I've heard about it."

The door opened with no corresponding knock. "Hello, my dear," Kiki said, entering the room. She spotted me, and her smile faded. "Hi, Allie. Is this about Richard Cory?"

"Yes," Baxter replied.

"Uh oh." She plopped down in the chair, as if fatigued. "I was so hoping nobody heard about that. I tried my best to keep it on the down low. Nobody happened to be looking when the little guy came running up to me, so I slipped him back into his crate. He was exhausted. I know I should have reported it, but with everything already going so terribly with the Terrier class once again, I didn't want anyone to panic and start pointing fingers."

"Somebody appears to have given Cory a sedative," Baxter said.

"Oh, no! I found the little dear in my office, sleeping on the floor."

"You just said he came running up to you," Baxter noted.

She glanced at me, then made an almost comical grimace. "I was trying to glaze over things. He was sound asleep. Is he doing better now?"

"Yes," I said. "He woke up for a moment when I called his name. But it was really obvious that he'd been medicated. That's not the kind of thing his owner could fail to notice." *Way to stay out of the conversation, Allida,* I chastised myself.

She sighed and shifted her gaze to Baxter. "It was my fault. I take Xanax. I don't want that to get around. I swear I didn't give it to the dog, but...my purse was open on the floor by my desk. When I looked through my purse, I realized my tissues had been torn up, and I was missing half of a pill. I was hoping I'd find it someplace on the floor. But no such luck."

Baxter glanced at me. "That's precisely what Allie thought had happened."

She raised her chin as she looked at me. "I wish you'd warned me," Kiki said.

"*Warned* you?" I snapped. "About pills I didn't know you were taking? And brought in a purse I didn't know you'd placed on a floor? In a dog-accessible area I didn't know existed?"

"Well, *somebody's* sure touchy," Kiki grumbled.

Oops. An unplanned outburst, I told myself. But then, nobody could have kept their mouth shut under the circumstances. At least I'd stayed seated and gripped the chair. As opposed to hurling it at her.

"I'm so sorry, Baxter," Kiki said in a babyish voice. "To my credit, I *did* already enter the incident in my log book. In case the owner grew concerned."

Kiki's main job at the dog show was precisely that: she maintained a historical log of all incidents that were reported throughout the event. Technically, the dog show ran from Friday through Sunday, but the FCDC allowed their members and entries to be present today.

"We need to talk to Davis," Baxter said.

"I wanted to keep my father out of this," Kiki said with a groan. "He doesn't even know I take meds for my anxiety."

"Be that as it may, we don't have any choice," Baxter said. "A dog getting drugged by a stranger is way too serious. This leaves us open to all kinds of negligence charges."

Kiki opted to call her father herself and ask if we could get him up to speed with what she called "a minor mishap that involved my purse." Davis would probably assume a dog had chewed up her purse.

Shortly after the three of us arrived at Davis's office, Kiki drew her dad into a conversation about the name "Richard Cory" and its probable origins from the Simon and Garfield song—neglecting to mention its origination in a poem by Edward Arlington Robinson. Baxter interrupted and gave the salient details of the Xanax being ingested, at which point, Kiki grabbed the reins from him and talked at length about how she had left the purse in her office and had taken just a tiny dose because of her stress at hoping she could live up to her dad's expectations despite the death of the state's best-known dog presenter, and how she'd needed to get water from the water fountain across the room, and so on. All told, her description took longer than it would for both Sophie and Dog Face to complete five or six agility courses.

Davis was not an especially easy man to talk to. He always took a defensive stance. This was no exception. After merely staring at us one by one, he said, "Okay, look, Baxter. This is precisely the type of thing I entrusted you to handle."

"What is?" Kiki interrupted. "The Richard Cody incident? Because you've got to admit, Terrington

Leach getting murdered is *way* above Baxter's paygrade. That's a police matter. And one dog accidentally getting drugged is peanut dust in comparison."

Davis grabbed his coffee mug as if he were strangling someone's neck, then said, "I'd like to talk to Baxter in private."

I rose. Kiki stood up, too, and said, "Okee dokee. By the way, Dad, Baxter had nothing to do with either of those things and had no way to prevent them. If you fire him you'll look like you picked on him to protect yourself." She struck an almost childish pose as she waved at him with one hand on her hip and a big smile. "See you later."

Kiki and I gazed at each other as I shut the door behind us. "Why were your pills in a tissue in the first place?" I asked. "Wouldn't it be more sensible and easier if you kept them in the bottle?"

She spread her arms. "I know that *now*. But I don't bring my prescription pill bottle with me. I'm always worried my dad or somebody will see it and think badly of me. If I didn't worry about stuff like that all the time, I wouldn't have to take Xanax in the first place. Now would I?"

"Apparently not," I replied. "But Baxter would have been better off if you'd told him right away what had happened, instead of trying to cover up the whole thing."

"I didn't want him to have to get involved. I had the best of intentions, Allie." Once again, she spread her arms dramatically. "*Someone* has to have his back."

I balled my fists. "Baxter and I have each other's back. Always."

She snorted. "According to Marsala, not to mention Terrington himself, Terrington was bragging that *you* were going to be his next conquest."

"If that's truly what he thought, he was badly mistaken."

"And yet you had a date with him at the Brunswick Café."

"For coffee. I wanted to ask him about the rumors about bribing judges. Some people claim he's been a part of that for several years."

"Which is only partially true," Kiki said. "It really isn't *literally* bribery. It's just…influencing human nature. Playing the game to your advantage." She paused and grinned. "You look so surprised. I've been in this world my whole life…the dog-show circuit. It's how the game is played. Terrington knew the game better than anybody. Cooper didn't stand a chance of showing a winning dog. Not if he'd been handling Rin-Tin-Tin."

Feigning naivety, I said, "I don't understand what you mean by 'playing the game.'"

"It's a bit like the way record labels used to get extra play time for their artists' singles so they'd climb the charts faster. The elite dogs and their top-shelf presenters constantly put themselves in front of the judges' eyes. They buy ads on social media, with the dogs' pictures. And they get a buzz going. They get friends and employees to catch the judges' ears. 'Isn't Rover a perfect specimen? He's heading to Westminster next, you know. Such a treat for us to have Rover here in Fort Collins first. Why, he's positively canine royalty. And so on and so forth. It's not like money changes hands. Well, not counting the ploy of giving to the judges' charities.'"

"Surely most judges know better than to fall for mere gamesmanship, don't they?"

"Most of them probably *think* they do. But in their hearts, they're big dog lovers." Kiki shrugged. "They can't help but develop a fondness for the dogs they see the most often. And, let's face it, it's all so subjective. Also, success breeds success. A judge hears a particular dog won best in show at two previous competitions. He can't help but be impressed."

"You're right," I conceded. "That's part of the reason I'm so fond of agility competitions. They're judged on easily measurable standards."

Kiki gave me no reply, but her knowing smile was just short of a sneer. It seemed to me that there was no point in pressing the issue. Especially considering I would be handling three different dogs in agility. It was best for my peace of mind to believe the competition would be unbiased.

Baxter emerged from Davis's office and strode toward us.

"Dad didn't fire you, did he?" Kiki immediately asked.

"No. We merely talked about security issues. And about our helping owners to reassign the dogs Terrington was going to present." He shifted his focus to me. "Davis is going to talk to Richard Cory's owner himself. He's going to comp the entry fee she paid for him."

"Has he already found substitute handlers for Terrington's clients?" I asked, "as well as Cooper's?"

"Cooper had a light load this year...just five, counting the three Terriers," Kiki said.

"That's odd," I said. "As manager of the Terrier class, he wouldn't have been allowed to show Terriers. I assumed he had mostly non-Terrier clients."

"Clients had been dropping him like flies," Kiki said. "That's probably why he killed Terrington Leach. The guy had been badmouthing Cooper something fierce at last year's show, and he'd doubled down all this year."

"Cooper says he's innocent," I replied.

"Yeah, right," Kiki said, rolling her eyes. "We can take his word on that."

I glanced at Baxter to see if he was finding Kiki as annoying as I was. I couldn't tell from his expression.

"Mark and Marsala disagree on what they saw, too, so it truly isn't an open and shut case," I replied. "That's undoubtedly why the police haven't arrested Cooper."

Kiki put her hands on her hips and glared at me with contempt. "It sounds like you've been talking to Marsala. Yesterday afternoon, Marsala told me Cooper did it. Then at the emergency meeting, she said she was afraid *Mark* was actually the murderer."

I wondered if she'd spoken to Marsala before or after I'd talked with Marsala in the second building. "When did you talk to her the first time?"

"Just after it happened. The murder, I mean. When I came back from lunch. She and Mark were in the parking lot, and she was all freaked out. The police were already there and everything. I waved at you as I drove in, but you were too absorbed in your phone conversation to notice me."

"I was on the phone with Cooper," I explained. "He called me and told me he was innocent and needed help. He was panicking at the thought no one would believe him."

That brought the memory of my crossing the street to the forefront. I had a vague recollection of seeing Kiki, waving, alone in her car. She, too, could have been at the murder site. Considering she was in her car, she had the means to leave the crime scene quickly. Was she cold-hearted enough to wave at me, minutes after committing a murder?

"Well," Kiki said, "one thing my dad got right is that we shouldn't keep our focus on that tragic mess. We all need to put it out of our minds until the show ends on Sunday. Heaven knows Baxter and I have plenty of work to keep us busy from now until then. And I'm going to go add my apology as a follow up to whatever my dad's telling the poor Westie's owner. I'm going to keep my purse zipped tight from now on."

She had her purse on her shoulder. It was unzipped.

"Thanks for letting Allie and me know this was just an accident," Baxter said.

"I know. Right?" Kiki said with a chuckle. "I should know by now that plenty of dogs will eat tissues, so it's not a good idea to wrap pills in them. Catch you guys later."

We both watched her walk away as if she hadn't a care in the world.

"She certainly doesn't seem all that remorseful about accidentally putting a dog's life in jeopardy," I said. "I wonder what's going on in her head. And whether or not she's on Xanax right now." My remark brought yesterday's conversation with Marsala to mind. Maybe Kiki had given her the Xanax she'd told me she'd taken. For that matter, I wondered if Kiki's medication could have allowed her to calmly give me a wave as she fled the scene.

Chapter 10

Baxter and I had planned to have lunch together, but he had to cancel. We promised to have dinner together, even though our schedules were so tight; I'd decided to bring it from home after I'd fed the dogs. Grabbing lunch, however, turned out to be easier; a fast-food counter had opened for business today in the second building. I wandered over there and got myself a vegetarian cheeseburger and fries and entered an adjoining room where a few folding chairs and tables were assembled. Marsala was sitting in the corner, looking almost as unhappy as she did yesterday afternoon.

She lifted her gaze as I neared. Although she didn't smile, she didn't grimace at me either. "May I join you?" I asked.

"Sure. Thanks." She kept her eyes on me as I took my seat. I felt a prickle of alarm from the intensity of her expression; she seemed eager for me to speak to her. Her dark hair was more than a little unkempt, and her eyes were so wide, it was unnerving. She looked a tad unhinged.

"I'm glad you're here," I said, "despite your terrible ordeal yesterday."

"I did think about withdrawing my dogs and staying home. Then I realized that would have been like letting the killer win, you know? Frankly, I felt like I'd put up too valiant a fight to undermine myself like that. I've kept my head held high despite Terrington dumping me. I've finally taken it on myself and stepped forward to protest the favoritism that Valerie and all of Terrington's high-society clients have been getting. I'd discovered that being dumped by that jerk was the best thing that happened to me. Then Mark or Cooper killed him...all but right in front of me. What am I supposed to do now, you know?"

I waited, expecting her to continue, but she merely stared at me. "Did you find an answer to that question?" I prompted.

She shrugged. "To carry on. To do precisely what I had been intending to do. Try to open the eyes of my fellow members of the Fort Collins Dog Club, so that they'll at least *try* to make it a fair competition."

"Good for you," I replied. I had tried to put some gusto in my voice, but she was still giving me the creeps. She continued to strike me as not being all there. Her eyes looked glassy. I should have brought my lunch over to Baxter's empty office. I was in no way confident that Marsala hadn't killed Terrington.

"Do you think Cooper's arm is truly broken?" she asked.

"Yes. His arm is in an authentic looking cast."

"He could easily have gotten someone to put a cast on his arm...asked a favor of a physician apprentice or assistant or whatever. Someone he knew in the medical field."

"Why would he *do* that?"

She leaned forward, put her elbows on the table, and scanned the room as if worried someone could be listening in on us. "Maybe it was part of his plan. Maybe he was planning to kill Terrington and make it look like he was physically incapable, due to his broken arm. So he went ahead and made up this whole lost-in-the-mountains story."

"But if the cast on his arm is fake, he'd get caught in the act immediately. The police will verify his seeing a doctor and getting a cast put on. Plus, the cast didn't throw off any suspicion. You thought he'd done it when you saw him yesterday, and he says his prints are on the knife."

"That's true. Maybe I've just seen too many murder mysteries on TV. And I know he's a criminal. I already know he's a thief."

I'd only just taken a bite of my burger and nearly choked on it. A moment later I said, "Cooper Hayes is a thief?"

She nodded. "Didn't you hear about my accusations last year?"

"No."

"He stole my jewelry out of my locker."

"You're saying that Cooper Hayes stole your jewelry at the dog show last year? Yet he wasn't banned from showing dogs this year?" I knew my tone of voice was making my skepticism obvious, but baseless accusations weren't going to help matters. "How and when did this happen?"

"Cooper is a locksmith of sorts. He can open anyone's locker and take just enough out of wallets or what have you that you're not sure you should bother filing charges. He'll take a twenty and leave a ten. He does it so easily and swiftly it's all but impossible to catch him in the act. So the police didn't find any evidence that he was the one who stole my diamond ring and my wedding band. I had stashed them in a locker each day last year because of, well, my affair with Terrington."

"How do you know it was Cooper?"

"I caught him taking money out of a woman's purse. It turned out to be his ex-wife's purse, which she eventually claimed she had given him permission to take. But he'd been holding some sort of lock pick. So not even five minutes after I caught him stealing cash, I checked my locker. Sure enough, my rings were gone."

"He claimed it was a coincidence?" I asked.

"Right. And I don't think the police really believed me about the rings having been stolen. And it was pretty freaking clear Davis Miller and his cronies didn't believe me. They never would have given him the post as manager of the Terrier Class in the first place. Which he was a disaster at, by the way. It was up to me as a member of the dog club to sound the alarm, although my fellow members all agreed."

"Valerie suggested Baxter take over for him, right?"

She snorted. "And what Valerie says, Valerie gets," Marsala replied. She widened her eyes even more. "But Baxter was a great choice. Don't get me wrong. That's not a knock against Baxter. I just meant...no matter who she chose, they'd get the job. That's how Cooper got the job originally, despite being a lousy choice."

"I'd assumed *Valerie* was the one who insisted on Cooper being *replaced*."

"No, you're wrong. Just ask around. *Dozens* of us were complaining, and I stepped up and spoke with Kiki and Davis about it. So Valerie heard her Terrier-owner disciples complaining, *then* she told the Millers to hire Baxter. Who's a Godsend, by the way." She stood up. "Thanks for listening, Allida. I'm sorry if I talked your ear off. I get a little pent up."

"Don't apologize. I'm surprised, is all. I guess the theft of your rings was overshadowed by the mess with Valerie's and Jesse's dogs."

"Yeah," she grumbled. "Who could've believed Valerie's pregnant dog would get so much attention?"

Later that afternoon, I noticed that a few dozen members of the FCDC were holding some sort of get-together in the middle of what, starting tomorrow, would be the main show ring. There were the pleasant sounds of laughter and happy chatter. I scanned the faces and spotted Marsala chatting with five other women. They were all smiling at whatever she was saying. The sight made me feel better about our lunch conversation. She did have friends within the club, and she might have been completely truthful about Cooper's incident with his now-former wife's purse. Maybe he stole Marsala's rings. Or someone else stole them. Or she'd lost them. Whatever the case proved to be, it was great that there was some kindness in Marsala's life. It was also comforting to see several people who were enjoying one another's company.

I spotted the plaid lady then, who was looking right at me. She smiled and beckoned me. We met on either side of the fence that enclosed the ring. "I just wanted to thank you for your help today," she said. "Richard Cory is good as new. And I accepted Kiki's apology. My little boy does indeed love to eat tissues, but it's not like anyone else would have known to worry about such a thing."

"Right," I said, agreeing that was true enough. "I'm really glad Richard Cory is okay."

"Me, too. He's the light of my life, now that my kids are grown...and haven't given me grandkids yet. And even if he can't top Valerie's line of Westies in a show."

"Well, you never know till you try."

She gave me a knowing smile. "This is his fourth try at this one show alone," she replied. "But maybe his fifth will be a charm."

"Right," I said again.

"I'll be happy regardless. Just as long as nobody else is killed. And nobody else's dog is drugged. And, well, nobody else brings a dog in heat."

"And nobody else's jewelry disappears," I added, testing her reaction despite my better judgment to leave well enough alone.

"Oh, that's right. Marsala's diamond ring. I'd forgotten about that." She glanced over her shoulder where Marsala was still holding court. "That whole thing struck me as odd," she said, lowering her voice. "It happened the last day of the show...when Marsala insisted she'd seen Cooper raiding the locker room and called the cops. The thing is, I'd happened to ask Marsala about her rings on the very first morning of the show, when I spotted her putting them in a locker. I said something like, 'Be sure and remember they're there when you leave.' And she said something like, 'No biggie. It's just a zirconia.' I went ahead and brought that up when she accused Cooper Hayes. She snapped at me that she just fibbed about it being a fake because she hated her husband and didn't like to admit he'd ever given her something so expensive."

"Do you think she was telling you the truth *that* time?" I asked.

"Maybe. Probably. I don't really know Marsala all that well. But I'm sure nobody would go through all of the trouble of calling the police over losing a *fake* diamond ring."

I nodded. She turned around and headed back into the gathering. My mood once again faltered. Marsala was having an affair, so she probably wanted to call her engagement and wedding rings worthless. She also probably wanted to upstage Valerie, considering how vehement she'd been as she claimed the judges were partial to Valerie. And if Cooper had indeed stolen the ring, I had been thinking too highly of the man. There was no simple way to take much solace in this sorry dog show. People were once again not measuring up to their dogs.

Chapter 11

I quickened my pace toward the front exit. I wished I'd planned today's schedule better. When I set up my training sessions, I'd envisioned myself working from home or my office in Boulder. Instead I would be traveling to Tracy's home in Boulder, Valerie's house in the eastern boonies near my house, then to Jesse's home in Longmont—fifteen miles or so closer to Boulder. I'd stop off to feed Doppler, Barker, and Ginger, then return north to Fort Collins. It was not unlike being a contestant in *"Amazing Race,"* with my challenges at each location to train dogs how to improve their times on obstacle courses. Although when it came to Bingley, my challenge was to get him to participate in something resembling a race on a designated course.

Just as I reached the door, I heard Kiki call my name. I stopped and waited as she managed to trot toward me in her high-heel shoes.

Kiki grinned at me, which was a little surprising. We'd had a less-than-chummy day. "I'm glad I caught you before you left for the day."

"I'm coming back later tonight. Baxter and I have dinner plans." By "dinner plans," I hoped she'd assume we were eating out at a romantic restaurant. Her crack about Baxter needing *somebody* to have his back still stung.

She looked at her computer tablet. "Good for you. I have a couple of assignments for you. If you don't mind."

"Okay," I said, cautious but also too curious to instantly decline.

"Cooper hasn't been arrested yet," Kiki began, meeting my gaze. "He now insists he can show dogs, despite his arm in a cast. But, for obvious reasons, it would be best if he stayed away from the dog show completely."

"Does *he* think that would be best?"

"No, and that's where your assignment number one comes in. You'd likely be the best person to tell him to stay home. You two have obviously bonded. Other than his hair, he's quite handsome, don't you think?"

"Not especially, no." I studied her features, hoping to get a read on her. *Was she trying to pique my interest in dating him, or her own?* I decided to be blunt. "Maybe that's just because Baxter and I are in our relationship for the long haul."

She arched an eyebrow. "You two make a cute couple."

Her voice was just a tad short of haughty. No sense in antagonizing her, though. "Thank you."

"So can I count on you to dissuade Cooper from attending the show?"

"You can count on me to suggest strongly that he skip the show, but there's no guarantee that he'll follow my recommendation."

"Okee dokee," she muttered, again glancing at her tablet. "Onto assignment number two. Dad and I have been maintaining contact with all of Terrington's clients. Most of them already had a backup handler in mind. If you can offer to present one more dog in Terrington's place, we'll be all set. The owner is Eleanor McCarthy."

That was the name of the woman who was suing Baxter and me. "Eleanor McCarthy?" I repeated, trying not sound alarmed. "Does she live in Dacona, by any chance?"

Kiki scrolled on her tablet. "Yes. Do you know her?" Before I could answer she said, "Oh. That's right! She's super close to where you live, isn't she?"

I couldn't get a take on Kiki's cheerful expression. She could have orchestrated this deliberately, or she could be totally unaware of Eleanor's and my unpleasant entanglement.

"Yes. Her property backs to ours. I didn't realize she owns a dog, as well as a cat." I was referring to the cat that had trespassed into our barn. And inspired her to write up a petition stopping us from kenneling dogs.

"She owns a Toy Poodle. This will be the dog's first show." She started typing on her phone. "There. I've just texted Eleanor's contact information to you."

My phone made its "text" beep accordingly.

"I'm hoping this will work out okay, since she and her pooch are such neophytes," Kiki continued. "With a newbie like Eleanor, I have no way of knowing if she'll agree to anyone other than

Terrington. Typically, Terrington's clients are absolutely convinced that they have hired the cream of the crop to present their dogs. But if you can just give her a call and offer to present her dog on the show's behalf, that will let the McCarthys know that we did our best."

"I'm flattered. Thanks so much for saying I'm your best!"

She apparently took my words at face value and snorted. She looked again at her notes. "Whoops. I shouldn't have pluralized 'McCarthy.' She's divorced." She furrowed her brow. "Oh, that's right! I need to clue you in on something."

She waited for me to ask: *What*, but this time I could easily ascertain that she was trying to gain the upper hand. I held my tongue.

"There's a rumor that Eleanor McCarthy was dating Terrington Leach. This could be a little awkward."

"Thanks for the heads up."

"You're welcome," she replied,

"What about the Wheaton that Terrington was showing? Has that owner found a handler?"

"A Wheaton?" she asked. She again referred to her tablet. "He was never supposed to present a Wheaton."

"Terrington told me he was. He must have said that as an excuse. I'd asked him to take on a Wheaton that Cooper was originally presenting. Which reminds me. I still have to ask Cooper for *that* Wheaton owner's contact info."

Again, Kiki made a face as if she couldn't believe how misguided I was. "Cooper was never showing a Wheaton, Allida. He was showing the Bull Terrier, Waxy, Scottie the Scottie, and an Airedale named Eeyore. That's it. You have Wheatons on the brain."

She pivoted on her two-inch heel and walked away. At least she'd made it clear that she truly was trying to antagonize me. Which also made it clear that I'd rather not give her the pleasure of getting a rise out of me.

As I rounded Tracy's corner lot in north Boulder, I saw that she had at least gotten the agility apparatuses that she'd borrowed from us placed in her back yard. She heard me drive up and came out to greet me, Bingley tucked under her arm like a rolled-up newspaper.

"Finally!" Tracy grumbled. "I know you have the murder and everything to deal with, but I really thought you'd be spending more time training than this!"

"Have you been doing the training exercises like I asked?"

"Well, yeah, but not happily."

"He needs as much repetition as he can possibly get," I pointed out. "And training a dog more than two hours at a stretch is counterproductive."

"So is having his trainer ignore him. Plus, I thought you were having financial problems. Happiness can't buy money, you know."

"And old tricks can't teach a new dog."

Tracy pursed her lips. "I ran out of stupid sayings. Please just give me a really good two hours. Both of you. I need the grins."

"Rough day at the radio station?"

"Yeah. The Fort Collins police won't talk to me. They say I try to sensationalize every news story I get."

"That's true, isn't it?"

"Well, sure. Nobody in the media searches out *boring* content for their broadcasts." Her eyes lit up. "Which reminds me. Did you hear the latest rumor about Terrington Leach?"

"That he'd been dating my neighbor Eleanor?"

"Is that the lady with the cat?"

"Plus a Toy Poodle she had signed on with Terrington as his handler."

"Oh, goody! Is she a suspect in the murder?"

"I don't think so." An annoying possibility occurred to me. "Were you playing me just now? Tricking me into giving you a tip about the investigation? Or did you actually have a juicy rumor about Terrington to share?"

"Meh. I'd say fifty-fifty. I did hear that Terrington and *Kiki* had been a couple at one time, and it ended badly."

I'd never heard that, although it didn't surprise me. I nodded, determined not to reward her with even more information about Terrington. "I heard that, too," I fibbed.

"They were in the immediate area, weren't they?" Tracy asked. "And either Eleanor or Kiki could have felt so betrayed by him that they had a motive."

"I guess that's always possible." Especially with regard to Kiki, because she was indeed in the immediate vicinity of the murder scene. Definitely not something I would tell Tracy, who would be broadcasting that tidbit with abandon in tomorrow's show. "I can't have a regular conversation about this with you, Tracy. I don't want my opinions about the show to hit the airwaves."

"But I'm not saying anything that's going to take audiences away from the show. My own dog's going to be performing there. I want the show to be a huge success." She set Bingley down and snapped a leash onto his collar. "I'm not about to tell my listeners: 'Hey, guys! Watch out! There's a killer on the loose in the Fort Collins Fairgrounds.'"

"Good to hear." I grabbed Bingley's leash. "Bingley and I are going to get a great two-hour workout on the obstacle course now."

An hour later, I had done a lot more running than the dog. He was better on weaving through the posts than I had any right to expect. That is usually the hardest obstacle because it requires dogs to move in unnatural, counterintuitive ways. I did get him to jump over the rails. He would not enter the tunnel, regardless of what I did. At one point, I got so frustrated I put him in the tunnel then lifted that end and tried to slide him through and dump him out. The material was too flexible for that, so I tried to pull it out from under him like a magician pulling a tablecloth out from under a set of dishes and glasses. He was too good at running along with the moving tunnel. Same story on the bridge and seesaw.

The biggest problem with all of that was that when he was competing, I couldn't touch the dog or the equipment. If he repeated this behavior in the ring, it wasn't going to be entertaining; it was just going to be a few minutes of a dog lying down in an agility course until I carried him off. Desperate times requiring desperate measures, I called Valerie and asked if I could please bring Bingley to her house and let Bingley watch Sophie and follow her around the course once afterward. As I anticipated, she said no to the latter; she didn't want another dog to "teach Sophie bad habits." While she would allow him to *watch* Sophie and use the course by himself afterward, she told me to bring someone to control the Beagle while Sophie and I were occupied with the agility course; she was not about to pay an employee to assume that task, and she had better things to do than watch a Beagle mess up. Baxter was, of course, busy in Fort Collins. The only viable option was to ask Tracy to come with me to watch my final training session with Sophie Sophistica.

During our drive to Valerie's ranch in my Toyota Corolla, I told Tracy that Valerie might respond to flattery on her part, which could perhaps persuade her to grant us the opportunity to have Bingley chase Sophie around the obstacle course. I assured Tracy that such a thing would be immensely helpful with Bingley's learning curve, which, if anything, was upside down.

"Great idea!" Tracy said to me, then spent the trip with her eyes glued to her cellphone. Bingley, meanwhile, spent the trip jumping back and forth over the seatbacks, tunneling under the seats, and doing an amazing military crawl on his elbows, squeezing himself on the shelf behind the back seat and the rear window. I had no doubt that if there were weaving posts attached to a seesaw on my floorboards, he would also be weaving while teetertottering with breathtaking ease.

We arrived at Valerie's home, and she answered the door. Sophie was sitting beside her in the doorway, her tail wagging furiously. Tracy was holding Bingley in her arms, in order to delay Valerie discovering how poorly trained he was on leash.

"I'm Tracy Truitt," she said before I'd had the chance to make introductions. "It's such an honor to meet you. I've got two friends who bought puppies from you. I don't think I've ever seen such perfection on four paws before."

Valerie beamed. "How nice of you to say so. What are the dogs' and owners' names?"

"Aaron and Susan Fleischer, with the esteemed little Barron Chastwick. Also Deborah and George Bering, the proud owners of Melrose Esther."

"Two of my champions! The Fleischers live in Denver, and the Berings live in Grand Junction. How did you meet them?"

"Through my job as a talk show radio host. That's how I met Allie and developed such a deep affection for dogs myself. She's has such an uncanny expertise on dog behavior. As do you. It's no wonder you were smart enough to hire her."

Valerie glanced at me, then beamed at Tracy. "This was actually my first occasion to need a trainer's assistance since I was a teenager. My knee has slowed me down too much to handle the agility trial work."

"Ugh. I know just what you're going through. I had to have surgery on my knee not too long ago. A softball injury. Forgive me if I'm being too forward, but can you possibly join us while Allie works with Sophie Sophistica, and Bingley and I watch? I'd love to hear any insight you can give me."

"Of course. We'll meet you at the back door. Allie can lead the way." She glanced behind her, still grinning. "Let me just get Sophie's leash." She slapped her thigh, and Sophie obeyed and trotted alongside her.

Tracy winked at me as she set Bingley down. The dog tried to race away, but the leash thwarted him. I then led the way to the red-slate path to the back yard. "You were reading up on Valerie as we drove out here, I see."

"I know how to do research, girl. Furthermore, 'Obsequious' is my middle name."

"Really? I would have thought it would be 'Assertive'," I teased.

"It *should* have been, but then some jerk at City Hall would have shortened that particular name to 'Ass.'"

"Well, then. Wise compromise, Ms. Tracy Obsequious Truitt. I'll just call you 'Tot' from now on."

A minute or two later, Tracy and Valerie were chattering away like the best of friends, and the dogs scoped each other out as we made our way inside the barn and surveyed her arena. Valerie had brought her stopwatch. Midway through our hour-long session, she acted as a proxy for the judge—standing in front of one of the obstacles' entry point. After two more practice runs, Valerie invited Tracy and Bingley down from their seats in the stands to watch Sophie from inside the ring. Tracy sat on the ground with Bingley in front of her, gripping Sophie's collar with both hands. He started whining, trying to join Sophie, which was an excellent sign.

Sophie flew through the course. As we crossed the finish line and turned to face them, Valerie did a doubletake at her watch.

"Great run, eh?" I asked Valerie.

"Quite nice, yes." She slipped the watch back into her pocket. "You know, I feel fine with letting Bingley follow Sophie in some just-for-grins runs. I'm now reasonably confident that doing so won't throw her off her game. It might be fun for her, too."

"That's wonderful, Valerie," I said, truly happy about this. Allowing an experienced dog to help teach an inexperienced dog was an excellent training technique. "Thank you so much."

"You're welcome. Don't forget our appointment tomorrow morning, when Kiki Miller sends all of the agility competitors a map of the course layout."

"Eight o'clock, right?"

"Better make it seven. Unless that's going to conflict with your meeting with Jesse."

"No, I'm meeting Jesse later. He'll be staying onsite in his trailer starting tonight."

Valerie snorted. "As if being holed up in a trailer for three days is better than making a forty-minute drive from home. And he was so eager to get a good space, he had to pay for the lot starting on Tuesday, when he isn't even *using* his trailer. It's absolutely inane, if you ask me."

I held my tongue, thinking what a strange figure of speech "if you ask me" was; it was only appropriate to say when you *hadn't* asked, which logically means you don't *want* the speaker's opinion.

Tracy strode up to Valerie. "Thanks a million! Bingley entering the agility competition is merely a publicity stunt. I twisted Allie's arm into doing it. I think it will really help the attendance by publicizing my attempts to get Bingley working an agility course at the show. I have contacts with the local TV news shows."

"I don't know if I agree that it will increase attendance. But I suppose we truly could use a good story on the Fort Collins Dog Show. Considering it's now all about Terrington Leach's murder."

"Right. Time to shift the focus away from the search for the killer."

Valerie snorted. "Oh, I heard from the police chief's wife that he's already convinced Cooper Hayes is guilty. They just need to keep making a good show that they're still investigating other leads." Her brow was furrowed. She'd returned to her typical prickly mood. "Let's just get this over with, shall we?" She looked at her wrist watch. "I've got things to do. You have free run of the course and my little future champion for thirty minutes. Then bring her back to the house."

"Thanks again," Tracy said, her smile now less confident.

"Don't mention it. Nice meeting you."

"You, too," Tracy replied.

We watched her walk away. "I said way too much, didn't I?" Tracy whispered.

"She's always moody. Let's just make the most of our time." I removed Bingley's collar. "You guys ready to play?" I asked, petting first Sophie, then Bingley; it's always important to maintain dogs' pecking orders, and we all needed Sophie to be the leader.

I took off on my run through the course pointing at the apparatus and giving verbal commands as well: Jump, up, down, under, over, around etcetera. Bingley was naturally competitive and was mimicking many of the feats that Sophie was doing. Other times, he was simply running around the obstacles. Sometimes he tried to lure Sophie into chasing him instead of following my instructions. But all four of us truly had fun. Predictably, as soon as I had Tracy pick up Sophie so that Bingley had to follow my commands on his own, he lost interest in our game. I could tell, though, that he knew what I was telling him to do; he just didn't want to follow my instructions.

"Dang it," Tracy said. "He was doing so well."

"He's a Beagle," I said with a shrug. "Obstinance is their middle name."

Chapter 12

I dropped off Tracy and Bingley at their house, then drove out to Jesse's, now kicking myself for once again having muddied up my schedule. Jesse's home was much closer to Fort Collins than my house was, and I had yet to call my neighbor.

As soon as I'd pulled into the driveway, Jesse opened the door and stepped onto the front porch. "Look at me, Allie!" he cried, a huge grin on his face. He turned and walked in a tight circle. "Ta-dah! I feel like myself again! I got a walking cast."

It was impossible not to share in his glee. My brightened mood continued. He joined me in Dog Face's training, and we had a wonderful training session. For the first time, I thoroughly enjoyed his company. Furthermore, the dog's performance was excellent. At the end of our session we gave each other a high five, and then another high five to Dog Face.

As we headed back toward his house, a male dog came out through the dog door and joined us.

"This must be the dog you're enrolling in the conformation competition. He's stunning."

"Thanks! This is Eeyore."

I positioned myself to be sideways with Eeyore—the least threatening position from the dog's perspective. I stroked his curly fur and told him how handsome he was. Dog Face trotted toward the back door, and Eeyore followed, his gait flawless. The dogs turned and sat down next to the door to await us.

"Wow," I said. Jesse smiled with unmasked pride for his dogs.

Jesse resumed his slow but even pace, saying, "Come over to my trailer sometime tomorrow morning, so we can go over the map of the agility course."

His statement brought Valerie's snipe to mind, and I suddenly realized its significance. With Jesse having access to a private trailer at the F fairgrounds for the last two days, he, too, could have been in the vicinity yesterday when Cooper was murdered. He slid open the door, and the dogs entered, wagging their tails.

I stayed put on the concrete pad. "Valerie mentioned you had booked a lot for the trailer starting on Tuesday. Is it already in place?"

"Yep. I booked the space for five days back when I thought my leg would make it impossible for me to drive, and I'd be on crutches the whole time. But it turned out my neighbor works in Fort Collins and has been happy to give me and my dogs rides for the past couple of days. So I'm not moving in until tomorrow morning. And my doc agreed to put me in this cast this morning. Anyway, my trailer is a metallic purple JetStream. It's right by the road at the intersection."

"Across the street by the Brunswick Café?" I asked, my heart racing.

Jesse's stared at me. "I had no beefs with Terrington Leach, if that's what you're thinking. I'd hired him to show Eeyore, Dog Face's brother, after I'd broken my leg. Furthermore, I was still immobilized by my big cast when he was murdered."

"I realize that. I wasn't thinking you were a suspect, or anything," I lied.

"When Kiki called and told me Terrington had died and asked if I needed to find a handler for Dog Face's brother, I explained someone had already volunteered...back when Cooper was trying to unload his dogs, because of his broken arm."

"*What* volunteer? The only volunteer handler I know of for Terriers is *me*."

"Precisely." He grinned.

"But...I'd only agreed to take on a Scottie and a Wheaton. And the Wheaton turned out to be a mistake."

He gestured for me to go inside, then slid the door shut behind us, two females—judging by their small size—joined Dog Face and Eeyore in his messy kitchen. "Not exactly. Cooper called me a couple of months ago, when he was the Terrier-class manager. He said that he was pushing to get the FCDC to reverse their decision to block Valerie's and my dogs and asked if he could save a spot for Eeyore. I said no, but he said he was having a hard time meeting his quota of entrees, so he'd give a slot to a fictional Wheaton so no one would give me any grief about registering one of my Airedales when I'd been banned. He also put himself down as the presenter, which was a bit odd, but he claimed that, since he wasn't allowed to show Terriers, it wouldn't matter to anyone, but it would help him keep Davis off his back."

"That's really convoluted," I said.

"It is," he replied, watching Eeyore who was now sitting at my feet, "but it boils down to the fact that you're showing this handsome guy in the Terrier class on Saturday."

I hesitated. "I'd be honored," I said honestly, giving the inarguably handsome Eeyore a pat on his shoulders.

My mood sank as I left his house. Our conversation had reminded me that I still hadn't performed the first task Kiki had given me—I hadn't discouraged Cooper from attending the show. I drove a block or two, then pulled over and dialed Cooper's number.

"Hi, Allie," Cooper said as he answered his phone.

"Hi. Kiki said she spoke with you earlier today."

"Yes indeed. My doctor gave me a less-cumbersome cast that allows me to move my fingers. I'm able to show dogs after all."

"Are you sure you want to do that? I would think presenting dogs with a less-secure cast would really pose a risk to the bone break. Did you tell your doctor about the leader you'd be using? And that you'll be handling big Terriers?"

"Yes. He said it isn't a problem."

Drat. I wasn't going to get anywhere by sidestepping the matter of his being a murder suspect. "Have you hired a lawyer, I hope?"

He hesitated. "They're so expensive! I can't begin to pay the upfront money!"

"But the money is irrelevant when you look at what's at stake."

"I know. I know. But I'm innocent. If they can just find the culprit, I'll be exonerated, and I won't *have* to hire a criminal attorney. But that's also why I need to get as much cash together as I can, as fast as I can. I have to pick up as many canine clients to present as possible."

Whoops. So much for my talking him out of going to the show. "Shouldn't your bottom line be to stay out of the lime-light?"

"I wish I could. But, again, I've got to earn money. In fact, that's something I need to talk to you about. It's a long story, but the Wheaton you were going to show is actually Jesse Valadez's Airedale."

"Jesse just now explained that mix-up to me, and he—"

"Would you mind terribly if we switched that back? Let me be the presenter?"

I rolled my eyes. This wasn't going well at all. I stared out the windshield at a cottonwood tree being buffeted by the wind. "Gee, I don't know, Cooper. I mean, my loyalties are first and foremost with Baxter. He's managing the Terrier Class, as you know. I want to do whatever will let that group go smoothly."

"Of course, but I think—"

"Cooper, the thing is, people at the show are going to be suspicious of you until your name is cleared." I felt like a heel, but I continued. "You'll be working with a tender arm that could break a second time. Is the few hundred dollars you'll make showing some dogs really worth the risk?"

"Yes, Allie. Yes, it is. I am innocent." He cursed. "I had nothing to do with the murder. I tried to save his life, for crying out loud! I can't control the rumor mill or what people think about me. I've never had a single unsatisfied customer, or problems in a dog show. Now all of a sudden I'm Son of Satan. By trying to save a man's life."

"I'm sure that's incredibly difficult for you." A pickup truck sped past me.

"It is. But if you're set on the idea of presenting Eeyore yourself, I'll be fine. It's just that he's a magnificent dog...and I want the honors." He paused. "I have so much more experience than you do. And I think Eeyore is going to be Best in Show. I need those kinds of credits on my resume."

"Plus, *I'm* going to look almost comically small leading him around the ring. But Jesse seemed pretty happy about my showing Eeyore. Maybe that's the visual Jesse wants the judge to see, and it's ultimately his decision."

"True." He sighed. "You and I bring different skills to the table. In fact, I've been thinking. Once this murder gets solved and the murderer is in jail, maybe you and I can team up professionally. Put together a multi-purpose dog-care business."

Team up professionally? Where on earth did he get *that* idea? "That's pretty much what Baxter and I are already doing, Cooper."

"I didn't realize that. I thought you were a dog therapist and Baxter was an event manager...and also built customized dog houses."

"We also run a kennel with a dog-training option. Though that's on hold for the time being."

"I don't suppose you'd be interested in getting another business partner then."

"I'm afraid not." I was a little put off by the turn our conversation had taken. Here he was short on cash, and Marsala was claiming he'd stolen her diamond ring. My stomach was in knots, and I hated myself for what I felt like I needed to say next. "I heard something about you having some trouble last year, too. With Marsala."

There was a long pause. Though I now felt a touch of guilt over my cowardice in bringing this up on the phone, I was glad we weren't face-to-face.

"Allie," he said, his voice flat. "I did not steal her diamond ring. I had told my then-wife that I'd forgotten my credit card and needed to buy enough gas to get home. She said to get it from her wallet in the locker room. She gave me the key. She didn't remember the number, just that it was in the second row from the top, so I was checking each locker with her key when Marsala arrived. She saw me go from one locker to my wife's locker and take money. I didn't even know she was there until she finally spoke up."

"Didn't your ex-wife back you up on that?"

"Eventually," he growled. "At first, though, she lied and said I'd taken the key from her without her knowledge and had stolen money from her purse. Let's just say the ending of our marriage wasn't easy or kindhearted for either of us. We got to the bottom of it, eventually, but I allowed the police to search me and my car and anything else they could think of. They didn't find it because I didn't take it."

"That's got to be hard for you to swallow."

"Tell me about it. Allie. I need this job. I need to prove to myself that things can be normal again. That I haven't wasted my life. That I'm still a good person."

I battled a lump in my throat. I didn't know for certain who was telling the truth, but it was clear Cooper was in emotional pain. "I need to talk this over with Jesse." *Not to mention Baxter.* "The Terrier-class competition doesn't begin until Saturday. I'll call you tomorrow morning. Okay, Cooper?"

"Sure, Allie. Talk to you then. Goodbye."

"Wait, Cooper. We should discuss this with Jesse together." He gave no answer. I glanced at the screen. Cooper had ended the call. His voice had been calm and pleasant. Yet I couldn't shake my certainty that he had been struggling to tamp down very real desperation.

Chapter 13

I drove home and stayed in my car in our driveway while I screwed up my courage to call Eleanor. Considering the status of our communication to date, I wouldn't be surprised if she had blocked me. The fact that she was a dog owner herself had truly thrown me. Raising a show dog was a venture that took enormous amounts of time and energy, as well as not-insignificant amounts of money. If nothing else, becoming part of the dog-show circuit truly required being a dog lover. Maybe Eleanor was so singularly devoted to her own pets that she wanted the world to adore her dog only when it was in a showring. She certainly thought nothing of preventing a neighbor from housing other people's dogs. If so, she really should have thought twice before buying a brand-new house with a back yard that shared our pre-existing fence. I dialed, then crossed my fingers—even though I wasn't sure what to wish for.

"Allida?" she answered, sounding as if she was stunned at my calling her.

"Yes. Hi, Eleanor. I'm calling on behalf of the Fort Collins Dog Show." My voice sounded squeaky too me, thanks to my nerves; I expected her to curse at me, which was what happened the last time I'd called. "I assume you already heard the terrible news about Terrington Leach."

"Of course I did. He was supposed to show Minnie Pepper Cocoa."

I paused to squelch a nervous chuckle at the dog's name. It sounded like a menu item at Starbucks. "Right. Are you still planning on showing...Minnie Pepper Cocoa this weekend? If so, have you found another handler?"

"Yes to the first question, no to the second. You aren't volunteering for the job, are you? I thought you were just a dog trainer. Do you *do* that sort of thing?"

"It's not my forte, but I know the basics. I'm showing two dogs in the Terrier division. I'm also handling two other Terriers at the agility trials."

"Oh."

There was a pause.

"I didn't realize you owned a dog in addition to your cat."

"Yes, well, Minnie doesn't go into our back yard, or anything. He considers our enclosed patio to be his domain, though. I keep him separated from the cat so they don't get into fights and risk his getting scratched. And I give him exercise every morning at his breeder's exercise pen. Its Astro-Turf is well-maintained. Minnie is pure white. His feet get stained easily."

"I see." I'd been imagining that he was black or brown from his name. Not to mention a female.

Again, there was silence. I decided to wait her out. "Are you offering because you think it will make me withdraw my complaint about your dog-kennel business?"

"No. I was asked by the show's administration to help out. I was specifically given your name by Kiki Miller. I can assure you that I will do my absolute best when I'm in the ring with Minnie, er, Pepper Cocoa."

"Huh."

Another lengthy pause.

"I'm home right now, but I'll be heading back to Fort Collins in another hour or so," I told her. "Would you like to bring Minnie over to meet me? We can discuss whether or not you'd consider my offer to be his presenter."

Another pause. "I'd prefer you to come to my house."

She was probably afraid of getting dust and whatnot on MPC's pristine coat at my home. "Okay. I can come over there in half an hour. Would that work?"

"I can make it work."

"Great. I'll see you then." I hung up and tried to assess the situation. This was a woman who'd brought a lawsuit against Baxter and me that was literally destroying our finances. Surely my having a conversation about handling her dog in the ring couldn't make things any worse. Establishing even a slim connection between us would have to lead to a modicum of respect, if not camaraderie. Or maybe Eleanor would be able to find a more experienced conformation handler than I, despite the massively short notice.

I had a whole twenty minutes to relax with my own dogs—while I chatted on the phone with my mom. She had called me to see if I was okay, after hearing about the Fort Collins Dog Show and Terrington's murder. Mom owned a Collie named Sage, and her husband of less than two years had brought a Golden into the family. She seemed happier than she'd been in years. So was I, come to think of it. And yet, an instant after I'd had that thought, I felt the stab of missing my darling Shepherd, Pavlov.

By the time I got off the phone, I only had a minute to give the dogs a hug and walk over to my neighbor's home. I took a moment to shore myself up, then knocked on Eleanor's door. She opened the door, and my focus instantly went to the white, meticulously groomed Toy Poodle she was holding against her chest. The little guy was flat-out adorable, with those dark eyes and cute little pink nose. Truth be told, I detest the classic Poodle cut and its pom-pom balls of fur, but there's no point in enrolling a Poodle in an AKC competition with any other cut. The cut itself was considered part of the standard to which the dog had to conform.

"This must be Minnie Cocoa Pepper," I said with a big smile.

"Minnie Pepper Cocoa," she swiftly corrected.

"Oh, right. I'm sorry."

She stepped aside, and I entered her small foyer as the glass door swung shut behind me.

"Do you want to hold him?" Eleanor asked.

"Of course I do," I answered honestly.

She passed him to me with the tenderness of handling an infant. "Hi, Minnie Pepper Cocoa," I said lovingly. "I'm so sorry I got your name wrong." I decided I'd call him "Pepper" in my head, simply because that was my favorite of the three names.

He immediately gave me one lick on my chin and settled into my arms.

Eleanor stamped her foot. "Oh, crap. I was afraid of that. He likes you."

"Um, sorry about that. I'm a dog person."

"I realize that," she snapped. "It's just that I honestly and truly don't want every Tom, Dick, and Harry's mutts running around spreading germs and things from the other side of our fence! Furthermore, the AKC doesn't allow anyone to show neutered or spayed dogs, and I don't want to worry about Minnie Pepper tunneling under our fence whenever one of your kenneled dogs goes into heat. Plus, there really *is* a chance that one of the dogs would attack and kill my cat. That's precisely what happened to Purrball two years ago. It broke my heart! That's one of the reasons my husband and I decided to move here." She paused. "That is, up until things got so awful, and we divorced. I moved here by myself. I couldn't stand being in that house, passing by the cat-killer police dog every time I left the house." She started to cry. "There you were. You and your German Shepherd. And my poor little kitty going onto your property all the time."

I was thrown by her unexpected soliloquy. Not to mention her tears. "Actually, Eleanor, Pavlov died, six months ago. She had a spinal disease that Shepherds are prone to. She was only nine years old."

"Your dog died when he was only nine years old?" Eleanor said, staring at me with soft, tearful eyes.

"Yes. It broke my heart."

"Of course it did! Just like my heart broke, when Purrball died."

"That was probably even *harder* for you to handle. At least *my* pet died of natural causes." To my dismay, I started crying myself. She handed me a tissue, and a minute or two later, we chuckled in embarrassment at our sudden outburst of raw emotions. It was one thing to mourn with one's friends; quite another to mourn with someone who'd become something of a foe.

Eleanor heaved a sigh as she wiped away the last of her tears. "Oh, Allida. I've been such an idiot. Harboring anger at you because of *my* personal history. Let's just...start with you being Minnie's handler this weekend, and afterward, I'll host a gathering with our neighbors and hash out what we can do to make us all happy with your kennel and your dog clients."

"That would be wonderful," I gushed. I didn't know what to even think about her worries of airborne germs, considering she allowed her cats to roam the neighborhood. But Baxter and I could dig a deep trough under the fence and install eighteen-inch wide chicken wire. "I do have to tell you honestly that I don't have much personal experience in the ring at conformation competitions. As a teenager, I used to show my dogs at the annual fair in Longmont. I've done similar event a couple of time since then, and I'm filling in to show a couple of Terriers, like I said, but that's about it."

"You're taking over other dogs from Terrington's schedule?"

"Yes, plus a second dog-handler broke his arm."

"Really? How awful. It sounds like the show is a bit...cursed."

"It kind of does."

She grinned at me. "Where are my manners? Come in and sit down, Allida. I'll get us something to drink and some snacks. We can chat for a while. Okay?"

"Sounds great." I looked down at Pepper, who gave me another quick doggie kiss.

Eleanor excused herself to get us some decaf and cookies in the kitchen. It was all I could do not to jump for joy. Regaining our kennel business was a huge deal for our finances. So was knowing that we were able to return to peace and harmony in the burgeoning neighborhood. By the grace of God, a path had suddenly appeared to achieve precisely the two things that had been cratering our lives of late.

All we needed now was for Eleanor McCarthy to have nothing whatsoever to do with Terrington's murder. Surely *that* wasn't too much to ask.

Chapter 14

Early the next morning, one of Valerie's assistants was leaving just as I was climbing her porch steps. We greeted each other, and she held the door. "Valerie is in the grooming station in the basement," she said. "She's expecting you. Just go on down. The second door on the right."

I went down the steps. Constantine, Valerie's Best-of-Show Westie, came trotting up to me. Valerie was standing with her back to me, dabbing something onto Sophie's fur. "Is that Milk of Magnesia?" I asked.

Valerie jumped at my voice. She turned to face me with her hand on her heart. "Allida! I didn't hear you come in! Are you trying to give me a heart attack?"

"No, sorry. Ann let me in."

I looked at the label on the bottle. It was indeed Milk of Magnesia. She followed my gaze.

"Yes. Dabbing this on my Westies' fur hides their facial stains...the tear-duct markings and dark fur around their mouths."

"Almost as good as White Out," I replied.

"And not poisonous or permanent," she retorted. She seemed less than thrilled to have me witness her little tricks.

I read the label of the spray can on the table next to her: Fur So White. "Does this paint your dogs white?"

"No, it doesn't *paint* them. It's just a nontoxic powder that you work into their fur. It's no worse than sprinkling talcum powder." She put her hands on her hips. "Everybody does this, you know. It's not cheating any more than how Miss America contestants wear makeup. It's expected. It's what one *does* when one wants to *win*."

I held up my palms. "I'm just curious. I'm not judging." Well, I was a tad judgmental. It wasn't as if the dogs themselves were applying makeup. A better analogy would be a car salesman touching up rust spots with paint.

I tried to keep my mouth shut and leave it at that, but I still had a burning question. "It's just that...Sophie isn't even enrolled in the conformation competition. Her appearance doesn't factor into an agility contest."

Valerie snorted. "Surely you're savvy enough to realize that most of us professionals enter dog shows to get new customers for our upcoming crops of puppies. Those are the people who care enormously about the state of a dog's coat. Thanks to Jesse causing last year's travesty, my back orders dwindled. Typically customers must wait two years. Now it's a year and a half. This agility contest has to garner as much positive attention as possible."

"I understand."

She gave me a skeptical look, but then said, "You'll see these same products being used in the grooming room throughout the competition. If you care to look for yourself, that is. Just don't creep up on anyone there, like you did to me just now. They might be holding a sharp pair of scissors."

"Will do. Thanks for the safety tip." I tried to smile, but her attitude was getting on my nerves. "I brought the agility-course layout, as requested."

"I don't know what I was thinking yesterday. The course maps are sent at six a.m., not seven. I have much too much to do this morning. I already dictated my suggestions to Ann, who was supposed to email them to you. You must have missed my email while you were driving here."

I swept up my phone and checked. "No emails. Did you give her the correct address?"

"Of course. Although I might have forgotten to tell her to send them right away."

I told myself to count to ten to avoid snapping at her, but only managed to count to two. "Did you ever find out how the coffee turned out to be decaf?" I asked.

She straightened and glared at me. "I suppose you think I'm just a doddery old woman."

"No, I don't. It's just that last night I didn't get much sleep. I'm worried about Cooper. He has a slimmer cast now and wants to maintain his dog-show clients."

"They should have given him the boot last year. Malavia, or whatever her name is, claimed that—"

"Marsala," I corrected.

"Claimed that Cooper had stolen her diamond ring from her locker. The rumor was he had something on the Miller family...Davis and his daughter, Kiki."

"You think Cooper was blackmailing the Millers?" I asked. My skepticism was already apparent in my tone of voice. It was too late to try to hide it now. "If that was true, surely they would have stuck it out with him."

"No, that simply goes to show my ploy of having everyone who knew me boycott the show was even worse than whatever damage Cooper could inflict on them."

"I suppose so. But what could Cooper threaten them with?"

"Breaking AKC rules, of course. Bribing judges, etcetera." She took a step back from Sophie to study her. "There we are." She grinned at me. "Sheer perfection, wouldn't you say?"

"Absolutely. Sophie is a perfect Westie. And an amazingly good agility competitor."

"She's my little champion," Valerie said, removing her gloves and apron. She looked at me from head to foot. For a moment, I was afraid she was going to suggest I let her spruce up my wardrobe and groom my hair. "So, you're here, thanks to my negligence. Let's take a load off and chat for a while, shall we?"

"Sure."

"I'm paying for this unnecessary visit of yours. I might as well get something out of it. Besides, the nonsense with Richard Cory, not to mention Terrington's tragic death, has poisoned us all. Sophie included. We need to detox."

Valerie ushered us upstairs and into the kitchen nook, with Sophie's adorable clicking foot falls keeping up with us. "Aren't you beautiful, Sophie," I cooed to her. She was circling my legs, one of the few methods of expressing her pleasure at seeing me that Valerie permitted. She'd been well taught not to jump up on me unless invited. By all appearances, she was her normal happy self. I took a seat at the table, patted my lap, and she sprang onto it.

Without asking what I wanted, Valerie placed a cup of minty-scented tea in front of me, telling me that it was very hot and needed to steep for a minute or two. She then poured coffee for herself and caught me sneaking a glance at the bag of coffee on her kitchen counter. "Yes, Allida. This is caffeinated. I realize I'd overreacted at my having purchased decaf by mistake. I checked my receipt, and there it was in black and white: decaffeinated." She took a seat directly across from me. "My mind must have been wandering. I'd also bought a bag of brown sugar when I wanted to buy brown rice."

"That would be a much worse mix-up than getting decaf coffee. Hardly anyone wants a side of brown sugar with their salmon fillets."

She laughed. "Not to mention brown-rice kernels in their cookies." She took a sip of her coffee, then leaned forward on her elbows and peered into my eyes, all signs of good humor having vanished. "I've been meaning to ask...is Kiki covering something up? Do you have any recordings of Richard Cory entering her office? Or going from point A to point B?"

"No. There aren't any cameras by the office doors. But we really don't have much reason to doubt her story about the dog accidentally ingesting one of her pills. I can't see what motive there would be to drug the dog intentionally. And if the boy hadn't taken Richard Cory out of his crate and then pushed him away, it wouldn't have happened."

"No, I suppose not. That's logical." She grimaced. "This is what I mean about needing to detox. For the last two nights now, I've been thinking Jesse Valadez was behind it. That he'd seen an opportunity to scare me and leapt on it."

"Was Jesse even around at the time?"

"I didn't happen to see him. I saw him on the grounds yesterday, though. He was on the path from his trailer. Got to say, he's got that walking cast working so well, you'd never even know he's got a broken leg. The man can practically sprint. I just hope the police didn't take it for granted that he couldn't overpower Terrington and pull off the murder, due to his injury."

Once again, that was an opinion I hadn't especially wanted to hear. I covered for my uneasiness by taking several sips of my tea. It was delicious and soothing, until my thoughts wandered to today's agility competitions.

"For once, I'm glad to be a little old lady," Valerie said. "No way on earth I could have stabbed that man in the neck, unless I'd used a step ladder to get up that high." She gave me a quick appraising look. "That lets you off the hook, too."

"Here's to being petite," I declared, lifting my cup as if to clink mine with hers. I took another sip of tea, but had lost my taste for it. "I should get going to Fort Collins."

She pursed her lips. "You're off to meet with Jesse first thing, I presume. At least it's probably safer for you to be alone with him in his trailer, than at his house. Just in case it turns out the he's a murderer, I mean."

"Thanks for the pleasant parting words," I muttered.

Chapter 15

Jesse showed me around his rented trailer, which took very little time. It had one bedroom and Murphy-bed-style fold-down tables and padded benches. He had brought Dog Face, Eeyore, and Lulu—a rambunctious puppy—with him. Unlike Valerie, Jesse was not only happy to see me but eagerly contributed to our discussion of the obstacle courses his dog would be running. There would be at least two separate courses: the Standard course, which has a pause table in which the dog must jump onto the platform and maintain contact with all four paws for five seconds, and the Jumps with Weaves course, which adds the weave poles and subtracts the table. A third course would be a Jump with Weaves course for finalists only.

Jesse and I had an easy interaction, both agreeing that the trouble areas for Dog Face could be: losing his focus as he exited the seesaw while running toward the audience, having to make a one-eighty turn toward the tunnel—his least favorite obstacle—and his having to weave through the posts so early in the course.

As I stood up at the end of our discussion, Jesse asked if he could get me anything—coffee, cold water, apple slices. He searched my eyes and seemed to be intentionally stalling. He reminded me of how my dogs often tried to engage me in something, anything, to distract me into not leaving the house without them.

"Is there something else on your mind, Jesse?" I asked.

"Not really. I was just wondering how Sophie Sophistica was doing."

"During our practice sessions?"

"Yeah. I just...." He let his voice fade.

"It would be an enormous upset if she doesn't win for the eight-inch-and-under category. As for overall, frankly, it's just so hard for her to beat dogs in the twenty-inch jumps category, like Dog Face. That said, she always keeps her focus, and she always jumps clean. She's going to be hard to beat. So will Dog Face."

He gazed out the small window by the booth-style kitchen table where he remained sitting. "You know, Allie, I've been chewing on this same gritty, sour-tasting bone for a full year now. Changed my dog's name. All because I had nothing whatsoever to do with him mating with Valerie's Airedale. Lately I've realized it's lucky I don't happen to have any kids. I'd hate to be trying to teach them about how to be a goodhearted, responsible adult...focused on what really matters."

He shifted his vision to me, and I gave him a sympathetic nod. Inwardly, I forced myself not to smile with gratitude. *Thank goodness one of them was finally taking the highroad.*

"I've been letting it get to me...lost all of my perspective. I did stupid things like trying to race over my dog's teetertotter." He gestured at his injured leg. "Meanwhile, maybe all that motivated Terrington's killer was the same type of petty nonsense, which they magnified into a battle over their own self-image, or something."

"I agree, Jesse. As my mom is forever telling me: *choose your battles.*"

"Yeah. That's probably what makes her a good parent. That said, I'm glad Dog Face has the edge as the typical-winner size. I still hope my big dog crushes her little dog."

I doubt my effort to hide my unhappy surprise at his non sequitur was successful. "Well, we'll see how the first rounds go for both dogs today."

"At least you don't have to tell me to 'break a leg.'"

"Such an excellent silver lining for us all," I said with forced gaiety.

He laughed. "See you later," he called as I left the trailer.

As I headed toward the main building, I saw Tracy Truitt standing in front of her car, which was pulled up to the curb in the no-parking zone. Bingley, meanwhile, was barking at her in the backseat window. The moment she spotted me, she waved and came toward me. "Let's squeeze a last practice in with Bingley."

"There isn't enough time. The trials start in two hours. We're not allowed to practice on the actual course. It'll take us almost two hours roundtrip to Boulder and back."

"I found a practice course that's only ten minutes away. I got a guy who knows a guy here with a course in his backyard. He gave us permission to use it today."

"Is this *guy*-of-yours-once-removed entering a dog in today's trials?"

"No, his dog just didn't get the hang of it, but the apparatuses turned out to be the hit of the neighborhood with his kids and their friends. He decided he didn't want to tip the scales by letting some competitors use his nearby course and not others. But we're wasting time. Let's go."

I got into the car. Bingley promptly leapt into my lap. "I feel like I'm playing hooky...cutting my classes."

She pulled away from the curb while we both were buckling up. "That's because you're out of your natural environment."

Surprised at her statement, I looked at her. "You think I don't fit in at a place where I'm surrounded by dogs?"

"It's not the *dogs*, Allie. It's the people and the competition. You're surrounded by people who want the other dogs to fail so their dogs can be victorious. That's nothing like you."

"But—" I hesitated. I'd been about to say that the vast majority of people were here for their love of all dogs. Something had gone massively wrong at this show. Something hateful and ruthless had come into play. "You're right. It's got to stop. This particular dog show isn't operating in the right spirit."

"That's all I'm saying. But you and I are going to interject some good old-fashioned belly laughs into the competition. Thanks to my thick-headed Beagle." She gave me a friendly jab on the shoulder. "Good for us!"

"Rah," I said. I gave Bingley a hug. Bingley wasn't thick-headed, of course. He was just resistant to having his trainer demand his attention.

As promised, we arrived at the "guy's" house and were met by the friendly owner and his wife, who escorted us through the gate and into their quarter-acre yard. Their mixed breed and Bingley had a barking-fest that was cut short as the owners dragged their dog into the house and shut the back door. Tracy and I rearranged the apparatuses so that they approximated the course Bingley would face that afternoon in the Jumps with Weaves Novice trial.

Predictably, Bingley was all over the map during our session. He had, at least, gotten the gist of what was expected of him. He knew he was supposed to run with me the instant the judge—in this case Tracy—called, "Go," and, in his best run, he completed about five of the jumps, although he lifted his leg on the tunnel, and popped out of every pole weave except the first and last.

Tracy drove up to the main building and let me out, explaining that she had some business to handle—which probably meant setting up logistics for her cameraman to record Bingley's adventures in agility. Then again, Bingley was not entered in the Standard competition, and would be the first contestant in the Novice category, which, oddly, was scheduled to take place right before the Masters Finals. She also had to prepare for her talk show, which I think was going to be at one p.m. Or maybe at two. Either way, the subject matter was undoubtedly going to be the dog show and its murder investigation.

The moment I stepped inside the building, I spotted Cooper. He appeared to have been pacing back and forth near the front door. He gave me a big grin.

"There you are," he said. "At long last, a friendly face."

"I'm sorry to hear that's taken you awhile to find."

He matched my stride and we walked shoulder to shoulder toward Baxter's office in the back. "It's hardly a surprise. Almost everyone here probably wants me to be arrested, to get rid of any rumors about there being a dangerous killer in the area."

I spotted Baxter up ahead and waved happily, then felt a pang of guilt for having left Cooper's plaint unacknowledged. "I'm sure we all want the killer in jail."

Baxter was heading toward us and greeted us, asking Cooper how he was doing.

"I'm too depressed to stay home by myself. My ex has my only companion...my dog."

Baxter's phone rang. "It's Davis," he said, looking at his screen. "Sorry. I've got to get this," he said to me. He gave Cooper a sympathetic look. "Hope things improve." He then strode away as he answered his phone.

I gave Cooper my full attention. Although he was wearing a nice blazer, his comb-over was unruly and he had dark circles under his eyes. "You look like you haven't been sleeping."

"Because I haven't been. I just...I can't believe this whole nightmare is really happening. You can't prepare yourself for something like this. It's like you're in your living room for the hundred-thousandth time, and the entire ceiling suddenly drops on your head. I fell and broke my arm on a hike I've taken a dozen times. My car is stolen. Then I'm framed for a murder!"

"You think someone deliberately framed you?" I asked.

"Either that, or the Fates are using me as the bull's eye in their dart game."

"Cooper, are you absolutely certain you still want to handle some of the dogs in the conformation competitions?"

"Yes. One-hundred percent."

"Do you remember the Bull Terrier, Waxy, you were going to handle? I think he'll be happy for you to be his handler. And the owner of Scottie the Scottie has only spoken with me on the phone. You can definitely show him."

Cooper smiled and grabbed his phone from his pocket. "Great. I'll call Waxy's owner right now and see. Hang on a moment, in case he needs to speak to you."

He made the arrangements with ease, saying at the start he was standing next to me. Kiki would be less than delighted with me for surrendering two dogs to him, but then, she was never delighted with me, and the feeling was mutual. Furthermore, in my heart of hearts, I just couldn't believe Cooper was guilty of murder. Or of stealing a diamond ring last year. He deserved a helping hand.

Cooper returned his phone to his pocket. "Do you have a few minutes, Allie? Can we stroll the grounds for a few minutes? I'd like people to see that I'm not a pariah to everyone."

I glanced at my watch. My first formal task today would be to handle Dog Face. I still had well over an hour until we'd agreed to meet. "Sure. There's a Labrador competition in the eastern outdoor ring. I'd like to get a look at them. I have to get my presentation get-up out of the car afterward."

"Your 'get-up'? What's wrong with what you're wearing now?"

"This is for my agility handling." I was wearing a white silk blouse and nice-looking light-brown slacks—specifically chosen to hide dog fur better than most—and athletic shoes." Valerie told me explicitly how I should dress for the conformation presentations."

He grinned. "She did? Are you even showing any of her dogs?"

"No, she felt I could use her guidance, though. I'm showing a Poodle in the Toy category. Well, provided he wins the Toy Poodle division."

He furrowed his brow. "Is this one of the dogs Terrington was going to handle?"

"Yeah." I didn't want him to ask if he could take my place. "My neighbor owns her. I want to improve our relationship."

He held the door for me. We rounded the building wordlessly and headed toward the ring. The competition itself wasn't for another couple of hours, but especially for outdoor presentations, breeders and owners of contestants tended to bring their own dogs to the general vicinity of the ring well in advance of the event.

"Are you thinking of getting another puppy?" Cooper asked.

"Not really. One of these days I'm going to be up for getting another dog. But when I do, I'll get a rescue dog from a specific breed volunteer group or the Humane Shelter. I miss having Pavlov by my side. Much as love my little dogs."

"A dog strong enough to defend you," Cooper said with a nod. "After what I've been through, I think that's wise."

"You have a Huskie-mix, right?"

"Part-time. Ex and I trade off every two weeks. That's why I was alone on the trail. My dog was with her." He sighed. "I wish I could shake the feeling that things are going to get even worse for me." He gave me a quick glance. "Valerie has me worried. We spotted each other several minutes ago. She gave me a haughty smile. As if she was triumphant."

"We haven't crossed paths here yet. You don't think *she* was the one who framed you for the murder, do you?"

"I wouldn't put it past her. She saw me and Terrington arguing in the café."

Surprised, I stopped walking and looked at him. "I didn't know Valerie was in the café, too."

"She was getting a to-go order."

I'd become familiar with the setup of the Brunswick Café during my police interview. Its counter was at the front of the restaurant, with a half wall partially separating it from the restaurant tables. It was possible Valerie could have overheard an argument at one of the front tables. The swinging doors to the kitchen were in the back hallway opposite the restrooms and adjacent to the back door.

"Valerie's short, in her mid-sixties, and has bad knees," I said. "I can't picture her stabbing a six-foot tall, athletic man in the neck."

"Neither can I. But it's not impossible that she snuck into the kitchen and through the back door before I finally decided to try and resolve things peacefully with Terrington. In any case, she's more than happy to poison everyone's minds against me...before and after the murder."

"Maybe, but, frankly, she'd much rather blame anything and everything on Jesse Valadez."

"Except Jesse wasn't *in* the restaurant. And the guy's on crutches."

The subject matter still begged the question: *Was Jesse still using the crutches at noon on Wednesday, like he'd said?* Unwilling to mention that concern to Cooper, I said, "They probably have security cameras by the back door of the restaurant."

"You'd have thought so," Cooper said. "But if they had security cameras on us, the police would have cleared me right away. They'd have seen that I hadn't stabbed him. That I'd grabbed the knife just to try to stop the bleeding."

"And they'd have seen the stabbing itself."

Just then, I saw a woman walking a six-month-or-so Lab puppy. "Oh, look! There's—"

Cooper grabbed my upper arm gently. "Allie, I know you're a good person. I know that you've helped the police a couple of times. There was that feature article in the *Daily Camera* about your being the best combination sleuth and dog whisperer around."

"That was a silly story," I said. "It was a slow news day."

"I have the feeling you can help me. I...need a rock. Or a sounding board. Something stable in my life." He studied my features, once again looking desperate. "If things start going south for me...if the police arrest me, could you be my character reference?"

"I can tell the police that you've always struck me as a solid, dependable guy who cares about dogs and is gentle and helpful."

"Thank you." He smiled at me. "Could you *also* help me keep an eye on Mark and Marsala? I don't want to make any wild accusations, but they're the ones who were in the right place at the right time. They heard the argument between Terrington and me. I can't help but think one or both of them realized I was the perfect patsy."

Chapter 16

My heart felt like it was racing as Dog Face's time to compete approached. To advance into the finals, the dogs run two different types of courses in the preliminaries: the Jumps With Weave (JWW), followed by the Standard, the latter of which used the pause table. Barring disqualification in the first race, we would return to race on the Standard course in the afternoon. Both Sophie and DF needed to run a clean course, meaning no knocking a rail down, no foot faults. Foot faults added a full second to the dog's time. Major faults like refusing to perform on an obstacle added five seconds. Their scores were determined by an average of their two race times—to the hundredth of a second.

The four-inch high bars for the Dachsund that went before us were adorable. With an Airedale's much longer legs, the bars would be set at twenty inches. Dog Face's start time was ahead of Sophie's by a considerable amount. The audience was about to be treated to nearly opposite sizes of contestants.

I played around with Jesse's dog in the staging area, which was extremely important; he needed to be in a playful, happy mood to run the course most efficiently. I, however, was struggling to mask my stress. My mouth was dry, and my heart was pounding. Knowing that Dog Face could probably detect my nervousness was only stressing me all the more. I had huge butterflies in my stomach as Dog Face and I entered the ring. I took a calming breath. I was a good trainer. I was also a good handler. I was also pretty good at motivating a dog to keep his focus on me. Those were the three parts of being successful at agility competitions. But the fact remained that this was my very first agility competition. I'd specifically told Baxter not to make any attempt to watch the trial if he had anything else he should be doing. I'm sure he understood that I was really saying: *Try hard to be there for me.*

As Dog Face accompanied me in perfect heel position and sat beside me, I grinned at him. This was his race to run, and he would enjoy it and was well-prepared. I was going to treat this as just another of the twenty-plus practice rounds I'd given him since our recent partnership. I spotted Mark in the ring. He was wearing his safari vest. The sight gave me a flashback to the murder scene, when I'd seen blood on his vest. I wondered if he was wearing that very vest.

"Hooray for, Dog Face," I heard Jesse cry. There was considerable laughter from the audience, thanks to the dog's silly name. Although I tried to stop myself, I looked out at the audience and saw Valerie in the side aisle, halfway up the stands, watching me. With her arms crossed against her chest and her shoulders stooped, her knee-length brown skirt suit making her pale legs look thin, she resembled a barn owl, peering at her prey.

"Start," Mark Singer said. Off we went. The almost eerie combination of adrenaline, rote, and familiarity kicked in. If I had one unique skill over other handlers, it was that I could run backward so quickly, and I used it to full advantage when we had to cross paths and on Dog Face's weak spots—the sharp turn off the seesaw and exiting the tunnel. I could instantly get his focus on me instead of succumbing to distraction or disorientation. I cried "wham" on the seesaw and the bridge at precisely the right time. It all felt fluid and fun.

Dog Face was nothing short of astounding as he went through the weave. I heard a collective gasp from the audience, most of whom were probably so well versed in agility trials that they know how much harder the weave is for a big dog than for smaller ones.

We entered the final line of obstacles. He had to jump over the first gate, then avoid Mark Singer and dip down to enter the tunnel. The jump, then dip was a challenge. Just as Dog Face passed him, Mark made a strange noise—a stifled sneeze perhaps. Dog Face showed no hesitation. He came through the tunnel and sailed over the last gate. No fouls. If he wasn't in first place at the end of this course, I'd be shocked. Ironically, though, this was bad news for me when it came to Sophie Sophistica the Third.

Jesse was literally hopping up and down, though all of his weight was on his right leg. "Outstanding!" he called. "Outstanding job, Allie!"

I gave a slight curtsy and waved, then patted Dog Face as the audience applauded. "You are such a good, good dog!" I told him. I felt exhilarated as I left the ring with Dog Face. I snapped his lead into place. He was likely to be even better in the Standard course. He never broke early off the *paws pause*, as I called the table pause obstacle.

We went up to Jesse, who somewhat to my surprise, hugged me first and Dog Face second. I gave him the leash handle.

"Halfway through qualifying for the finals! Thank you for trusting me with your dog."

"Thank you for bringing out the best in him. I honestly don't think I could have done as well with him as you did."

"Hopefully we'll keep it up on the Standard course."

"I'm pretty confident." He glanced at Mark Singer. "What was going on with the judge?" he asked me, lowering his voice. "Did he sneeze or something?"

"I guess so."

"Good thing it didn't hurt Dog Face's time."

Valerie was approaching us down the aisle. She snorted a little, clearly having overheard Jesse's remark. "Congratulations, Jesse. Your dog was flawless."

"Thanks," he said, his eyes widening in his surprise.

Someone in the stands called, "Hey, Jesse!"

He grinned and waved. Dog and owner started climbing up the aisle.

Valerie watched him leave with pursed lips. She leaned toward me. "If Mark does that again—makes that noise again—you're turning him in. Make no mistake."

"Well, but...it would be balanced out. It's like in any sport. As long as the judge calls the game the same way for both teams, it's fair and above board."

"No. No it isn't, Allida. If he sneezes when he shouldn't, he's tilting the results. It doesn't matter if one dog reacts and another doesn't. We aren't judging dogs' reactions to noises. We're judging how fast and correctly they run through an agility course."

"I see your point."

"Of course you do. Because I'm right and you're wrong."

"Okay. Well, we've got that all straight now. So thank you."

"You're welcome. You did a *great* job with Dog Face. You're looking like the next Terrington Leach of Colorado."

"That doesn't sound especially appealing, give his severely shortened life."

"True. I certainly don't want you to get yourself killed anytime soon. Especially not before today's competitions are finished."

"Thanks. You have a knack for blunt compliments."

She laughed, then glanced at her watch. "Sophie's Jumps With Weaves trial will start in twenty minutes." She glowered at my athletic shoes. "Come to think of it, I got way ahead of myself. If you trip on those shoe laces of yours with Sophie Sophistica, you'll be the most overrated competitor imaginable."

I had no response to that remark. It brought Jesse's "Dr. Jekyll" remark to mind when he and I had first met.

"You might as well wait here," Valerie said over her shoulder, "I'll go get her."

Baxter walked up to us and gave me a hug. "Congratulations, hon. I knew you could do it."

"One down and three to go, assuming both of my charges make it to the finals," I said. *And not counting Bingley's upcoming agility shenanigans.*

"Is Valerie getting any easier to deal with?" he asked in a half whisper.

"Not really. It's a lot easier to handle her dogs than to handle her."

Jesse and Dog Face trotted back down the stands to join us. "I still wish you were the one showing Eeyore, instead of Cooper. Any chance you'll change your mind?"

I stared at him in surprise, feeling myself tense. "I haven't made up my mind about that in the first place. Did *Cooper* tell you I had decided to bow out?"

"Yes. You're *not*?"

"No. Like I told him, I planned to talk it over with you and Baxter. I wanted to wait until after the agility trials to discuss the matter."

Jesse patted my shoulder. "In *that* case, screw him. *You're* presenting Eeyore."

"Excellent!" Baxter said. He grinned down at me, and I smiled back. I was so lucky to have this wonderful man in my life. My mind flashed to Davis and Kiki visiting our house to ask Baxter if he would manage the Terrier class. Now here I was, threatening to present another of Jesse's Airedales in conformation, when Valerie would be presenting one of her Westies. With the exception of Baxter and, for the time being at least, Jesse, I was surrounded by people who wanted me to fail. Maybe Tracy had been right. Maybe I didn't belong at dog shows.

"Wait, Jesse. On second thought, I think it's best for everyone if I keep myself on the sidelines after the agility trials. I'm going to just handle the one Toy Poodle I already promised the owner to present."

"So...you're not presenting one of Valerie's Terriers, either?" he said as if relieved.

"No. The Toy Poodle is in his very first competition. One of Terrington's former canine clients."

"Gotcha. No problem. Eeyore and I will go with Cooper, and we'll hope for the best." Jesse seemed to be truly disappointed in my decision, and so did Baxter. Cooper, however, wanted this more than I did and would be happy. It was a small sacrifice. Originally, I'd never envisioned showing dogs in the conformation competition.

I spotted Valerie standing in the doorway, staring at us. The instant our eyes met, she pivoted and walked away.

Chapter 17

To my utter delight, Sophie's JWW went equally well as Dog Face's. She had a clean run, and she managed to trim four-tenths of a second off her championship time from last year's event. Valerie was ecstatic and gave both Sophie and me big hugs. She was two-tenths behind Dog Face, but that was remarkably good, all things considered. Both dogs would have a clean slate in the finals, so assuming nothing catastrophic happened in the Standard rounds, my dogs were in a great shape. The second half of the competition would begin at one p.m. With both dogs at the top in their divisions, they would be among the last competitors in the Standard run.

I now had to switch into a lower gear. My next duty was to present Pepper in his Toy Poodle competition. I needed to clear my head from agility trials and replace it with the pomp and circumstance of the conformation presentations. I decided to spend my every available minute in the other building, until after my job with Pepper was complete.

As I wandered through the enormous open space in the main hall, I missed the benches of previous years and the ability to look up close at the lovely dogs that were competing. Old habits dying hard, however, the enrollees had set up defacto sections all on their own. The majority of Terriers were in the same quadrant they'd inhabited in previous years at this venue.

I stopped at one crate, hoping I was simply being paranoid. The dog's tongue was out as he slept, which was not something I'd ever seen a drug-free dog do. I jostled the cage, then groaned. A second Terrier had been drugged, this time a Yorkshire. I glanced to either side of me. "Does anybody know whose Yorkie this is?" I called out. Meanwhile, I opened the door and gently removed the little dog.

A man rushed over to me. "Aw, cripes," he said. "Tallyho looks like he's been doped."

"Is he yours?" I asked.

He shook his head. "He's Marsala's."

A volunteer in the standard forest-green apron dashed toward us. "Send the vet here. We need to have a blood test done. Then see if you can find Marsala."

She scampered off.

I cradled Tallyho against my chest with one arm and called Baxter. The instant he said, "Hi," I told him, "A Yorkie has been sedated." I looked up at the sign hanging from the ceiling. "In aisle twelve."

After a momentary pause, he said, "Be right there."

I shoved my phone into my pocket. "What is going on with these dogs!"

The vet arrived, with Davis and Baxter a couple of steps behind him. Davis pulled Baxter aside. Marsala came running. She gasped at the sight of the limp dog in my arms. "My baby!" she cried. She grabbed her head with both hands, making little noises as if she was struggling to breathe. She stamped her foot and studied my face as if she was too upset to even recognize me. "What have you done to my dog!"

"Nothing. I found him this way." Marsala's whole body was shaking. "We're going to test for sedatives. He seems to be responsive." She was no longer meeting my gaze. I wasn't even certain my words had even registered.

The vet inserted a needle into the dog's thigh and was filling the syringe.

Just then someone came up from behind me. It was Tracy. "Allie! What's all the commotion..." Her face paled. Tracy always fainted at the sight of blood.

"Look away!" I said and held my hand up in front of her eyes. I was too late. She was starting to reel.

I grabbed her arm and tried to support her weight. "Baxter! Help!"

Baxter raced toward us, leaving Davis in the middle of a diatribe. Tracy fainted, with Baxter arriving in the nick of time to ease her onto the floor without injury.

"This is the final straw!" Davis said. "I won't stand for watching my dog show get turned into a circus!"

Tracy moaned and opened her eyes. Marsala whisked her dog away and accompanied the vet toward his station without another word.

"Ew. I don't feel so good," Tracy said. She managed to sit up.

"Stay down until your head's clear," I said.

Davis was pacing in a small arc from one side of the aisle to the other. We locked gazes. His face was red and he looked set to explode. "Baxter, Allida, my office. Now."

I made the decision to ignore the "now" in Davis's order. "Are you okay, Tracy?" I asked, bending toward her.

"Fine. Go ahead. I just want to study the floor patterns for another minute, then I'll be right as rain."

Baxter and I followed Davis into his office. It felt as though we were being led into the vice principal's office in school. Just as Baxter was about to close the door behind us, Marsala marched through into the room and brushed past me.

"This is her fault," Marsala said to Davis, pointing at me.

"What?!" I shrieked. "Are you kidding me? I found your dog fast asleep. I got help for him immediately."

"All I know is you're right there on the scene whenever something terrible happens. When Terrington was murdered. When a dog is drugged. So you're either causing the problems, or you're inspiring them to occur because you're *cursed*."

"Cursed? That's inane. I'm on the scene because I'm alert!"

Davis raised his meaty hands and pushed the air in placating gestures. "Marsala, I hear what you're saying, and I am taking action. He pivoted and pointed at Baxter. "You're fired."

"I'm *fired*? Why?" he asked.

My heart leapt to my throat.

"They're in this together! You need to fire both of them," Marsala said, now pointing at me.

Kiki opened the door and squeezed into her father's office with us. "What's going on? Did you just say something about firing someone?"

Marsala shifted her angry gaze to the floor. Davis ignored Kiki and continued to glare at Baxter. "Those of us on the board did not hire you to make this year's event even worse than last year's. We've had a murder, two drugged dogs, and a woman fainting."

"How dare you, Daddy," Kiki said. "This is as much your and *my* fault as it is Baxter's. You know it. You're trying to make him take the fall for us."

"Somebody has to take the fall, Kiki! Otherwise the show will be canceled for good. Our names will be smeared for all eternity. I'm at the end of my career. I deserve better than to be known as the incompetent person in charge of this...this mudpuddle."

All eternity was quite the exaggeration. I doubted future generations were going to be destined to share the story of the Fort Collins Annual Dog Show.

"Fine. *I* will be the goat," Kiki said. "I'm supposed to be the secretary and noting all of these incidents. I'm supposed to be your righthand do-it-all, and I've been slacking off. I am hereby tendering my resignation."

"Nobody is quitting," Davis declared in a booming voice. He closed his eyes and took a deep breath. "Nobody's getting fired, either," he said on a sigh. "We just all have to make it to Sunday afternoon. That's less than fifty-six hours from now. I will then step down as president of the dog club. I should have done that last year. I just didn't want to have retired as the CEO of a company with almost three-hundred employees, only to fall on my face at running a three-day-long dog show."

"Sorry, Dad," Kiki said gently. "I guess running a dog show is harder than it looked."

"I love dogs," he muttered, staring at the floor. "It's just the blasted people who own them that make all the mayhem."

"I suspect we can all agree with you there," I said.

Someone knocked on the door then opened it. The veterinarian popped his head in and said, "Tallyho's blood registered positive for a benzodiazepine drug. It must have been a truly tiny dose. He's coming around."

"Oh, thank goodness," Marsala said. She put a hand on the wall to steady herself.

I grabbed Baxter's hand and gave it a squeeze. He seemed to be avoiding my gaze. Undoubtedly, he was deeply angered by Davis's baseless decision to fire him. We let go of each other's hand.

"Any idea how it happened?" Davis asked. "Can you tell if it was a shot or if he ate it?"

"No. Most likely he had a trace amount in a treat, or mixed into his food or water."

"Can I come get him?" Marsala asked.

"Of course." The vet gave a nod, then left, leaving the door ajar.

"I'm sorry I flew off the handle, Davis," Marsala said. "We'll do the best we can to keep things running as smoothly as possible." She turned and faced me. "I am so sorry I leapt at accusing you, Allida. I totally lost it when I saw Tallyho motionless. I thought he was dead. All I could think was I needed to get revenge. I just...I don't know how this happened."

"Maybe another child took Tallyho out of his cage, and he was sniffing around in someone's purse," I said.

"Hey!" Kiki objected. "I've been keeping my purse zipped." She reached back and zipped her purse as she spoke. "Whenever it's deserted, or I've set it down at dog level, that is. And I got rid of all my tissues."

"That aisle is out of range of the cameras," Baxter said. "I'm going to look at the recordings from the three cameras anyway. Maybe something will show up." Baxter turned toward the door once again.

"Wait." Kiki strode toward him. "I'll come with you to look at the recording. I have to write up the incident report." The two of them left.

"Maybe the Richard Cory drugging gave someone the idea," I said. "It seems there's a deliberate effort to sabotage the show. Maybe the murder wasn't enough to stop it from taking place."

"Again, I'm sorry," Marsala said to me. She, too, started to leave.

"It's okay," I told her. "I'm sorry you'll miss the Toy competition. He'll probably be fine by tomorrow's Terrier competitions."

"I might withdraw him from the Terrier competition tomorrow," she said. "I'll still have Chardonnay, my Bull Terrier to show. I continue to think his time has come." She left quickly, her footfalls fading as she headed in the direction of the veterinarian station.

Davis and I were now alone in his office. Too appalled by Baxter's close call at getting fired so that Davis could have "a fall guy," I decided to leave in silence.

"Allie, you don't think Baxter still thinks he's been fired, do you?" Davis asked.

"I doubt he's checking the camera recordings for his own amusement," I retorted.

"Good point. But someone is trying to destroy the show to get back at me. Probably Cooper is grinding his axe. He's the only person I can think of who would want to see me humiliated."

I didn't know how to respond. "I have to get ready to show a Poodle," I muttered as I walked away.

My stomach was in knots. Marsala's wild accusations made more sense to me than Davis's firing Baxter with no justification. Davis may have been right about one thing: someone did seem to be determined to destroy the event. With Davis on the top rung of our shoddy ladder, he would get the bulk of the blame, whether or not he fired anyone. Contestants were already certain that the fix was in. It might not be a contestant committing the dirty deeds, though. Kiki's efforts to glom onto Baxter might have been designed to keep everyone distracted while she wrecked the show. All of this sabotage could be the work of a massively disgruntled daughter.

My phone rang. It was Baxter. "Hi, sweetie," I said.

"Are you still in Davis's office?" he asked.

"No, why?"

"Turns out the camera in the sponsors' aisle shows Marsala picking up a dog treat or two from a bowl at the booth of the folks selling high-price-point leashes. The treats are in an open bowl, on a table right next to the entrance to their kiosk."

"Oh, no," I cried. "If those were laced with powdered sleeping pills or something, we could be having dogs drop off to sleep, left and right!" *Was this the act of the murderer?* I wondered. If so, what a horrid person to not only kill someone, but risk hurting—if not killing—innocent dogs.

"They'd set out the bowl of dog biscuits less than two hours ago. I sent the security guy out to grab the bowl. We're now going back through the recording and will try to track down everyone who reached into the bowl."

That sounded all but impossible. "Can't someone make an announcement over the public address system?"

"Kiki's going to talk to Davis about that possibility right now. She thinks it would cause too much of a panic. The vet said, judging by Tallyho, it was unlikely that any dog other than a toy will be affected."

"But what about the agility trials?" I said, trying to stay calm. "If any of the agility contestants take even a speck of Xanax or whatever, they're at an unfair disadvantage!"

"I hadn't thought of that," Baxter said, his voice low with discouragement. "I'll...get back to you."

Chapter 18

I had been pacing as I spoke and heard raised voices. They seemed to be coming from the grooming room. I pocketed my cellphone and headed into the room. "Ohmigod, ohmigod, ohmigod," a woman was saying. Judging by the light-blue smock she wore over her clothing, she was a groomer. As I drew closer, I realized it was a white Poodle that had a neon-pink splotch on its fur. An instant later, I spotted Eleanor staring at the Poodle.

"No-o-o-o," she wailed, all but driven to her knees at the sight. "Minnie Pepper Cocoa!"

I ran to the grooming station. "How did this happen?" I cried.

A moment later I saw the groomer set down a spray can she'd been examining. The label pictured a white Standard Poodle. Someone had disguised the can, so the groomer had sprayed hot pink permanent paint on Pepper's coat.

"I'll kill you for this!" Eleanor yelled in the poor groomer's face.

She raised her hands and pleaded, "I had no way to know it was pink paint. Somebody swapped my spray can of powder with paint."

Eleanor started crying. She saw me standing there, a couple of feet away, and her jaw dropped. "You did this, didn't you?"

"*Me?* Of course not!"

"Then your boyfriend did it. I thought you were nice! I thought I'd been wrong about you two. But you're horrible people."

"What's happened?" Baxter said, rushing into the room.

"You did this to my dog!" Eleanor cried.

"No, I didn't. Why would I want to ruin a dog's coat?"

"You and your girlfriend are the only ones with any motive to try and punish me like this! You're determined to get back at me for the lawsuit on your stupid dog-boarding business!"

A crowd was forming around us, and someone in the back shoved forward. It was Valerie, and she looked fit to be tied. She marched up to Eleanor. "Miss whoever-you-are," Valerie said in a harrowing low voice, "you're frightening all the dogs. I assure you, this paint was intended for my Westie, not your poodle."

"What?" Eleanor asked.

Valerie walked over to the grooming station and grabbed a clipboard holding a spreadsheet. "Look at the schedule." She held out the spreadsheet and pointed at one of the rectangular cells. "This slot here was supposed to go to my Westland Terrier. It's been crossed out, and your Minnie...something or other is written in its place. You see?"

Eleanor had stopped crying, but her eyes looked fierce. "I see that. I got the slot instead. So?"

"*So,* I withdrew my dog just this morning and allowed the slot to go to your little dog, out of the kindness of my heart. I assure you, *you* were not the target. *I* was. Because, you're right. This was a targeted, hateful crime for the white dog in this time slot. Ask around. Nobody knows you or your dog. But *everyone* knows me and my championship lines of terriers. Everybody."

It took a moment or two for Eleanor to react. Then she grimaced and turned to face Baxter and me. "I...don't know what to say."

"In a million years, Baxter and I would never have pulled a stunt like this."

"Which begs the question...who did this?" Valerie asked.

I looked at the crowd and had to stop myself from groaning when I spotted Jesse. Sure enough, Valerie glowered at him. "You're the logical suspect!"

Jesse held up his palms. "Obviously *I* didn't do this. We've been arguing the entire time I've been in this room."

"You could have planted the paint can there at any time before then." She balled her fists. "You've had it out for me since I accused you of intentionally conspiring to breed our dogs."

"Which I had nothing to do with and was entirely your responsibility for bringing a dog in heat!" he said.

"And maybe you're right. Maybe somebody else paid off my former employee just to clear the way for winning this year. But you've made my life miserable ever since. Once again, it backfired. Once again someone got hurt! This time you've painted an innocent little Poodle bright pink!"

"My Minnie Pepper Cocoa will be pink for months!"

"Where did you get such a weird name?" Valerie asked. "Did you ask this guy for name suggestions?" She pointed over her shoulder disdainfully with her thumb at Jesse.

"My daughter," Eleanor answered quietly, her voice choked with emotion. "We got the dog for her. Before she died. Leukemia."

"Your child died, too?" I asked, unable to even conceive of that much grief doled out to the same person in less than three years. And now she was divorced. Living in a newly built house by herself.

Valerie and Jesse looked at each other. Their anger instantly dissipated. "Do you have any specialized dog shampoo here?" Jesse asked Valerie.

"No, I—"

"I've got some in my trailer. It's first rate. From France. So, it's probably even made specifically for French Poodles."

"Right. Let's get on this, people!" Valerie snapped her fingers at the groomer, still standing by her table in shock. "You there. Go with Jesse to his trailer and get back here immediately. I'll get the dog's fur wetted down. The longer it's on his fur, the longer it can sink in."

Valerie and Eleanor stared at the dog as if in shock as Valerie grabbed Minnie Pepper Cocoa and started gently shampooing her. The groomer, too, gradually regained her color. "It's coming out," she said. "Maybe it isn't permanent paint after all. There's still going to be a tinge of pink today,"

"Nothing that a dab of whitener and Milk of Magnesia can't cure," Valerie said.

"I assume you left your station unattended for lunch, right?" Baxter asked the groomer.

"Well, yeah, but I thought I had everything locked up. And it was unlocked when I got back. I just...I thought I must have forgotten to lock up my station, is all."

Jesse tired of waiting for the groomer and did his best to rush despite his cast. Baxter peered at the padlock. "The lock's been tampered with," Baxter said. "The catch has been filled in with some sort of clear acrylic. It won't actually lock when you push it shut. I'd better talk to security. Maybe someone saw it."

I looked at a second groomer station that was still locked up. I pulled on its brass padlock. It remained locked tight. I glanced at a third station. They all had the same brass padlocks with keys that the groomers could take with them when they were on a break. Someone could have doctored a lock at home, then swapped locks at some point before the key had been removed.

I walked up to Valerie. "Can I help?"

"You can fill another bin with warm water."

I nodded. As I was readying Pepper's bath water, I heard two sets of frantic and furious growls and a shriek of pain. A dog fight had broken out. I grabbed the square bucket out of the sink and headed toward the ruckus.

"Get him away!" one woman was yelling.

Two Cocker Spaniels were going at it. The dogs had no collars on and were snapping at each other. Although the owners were trying to pull them apart, their actions were futile.

"Oh my God! Separate them! Stop this!" the other, older woman yelled.

"Gwenie!"

"Apple!"

"Get back!" I cried. The owners let go of the dogs and straightened. I dowsed the tussling dogs, which both yelped in surprise. I grabbed the closest one, quickly pivoting so the other one could only see my back.

"Let me take her," the sixtyish woman demanded.

I relinquished my hold, and she swept the dog into her arms. The front of my blouse was now soaked. This dog had a white and brown coat, and there were some red stains on the white fur around her mouth. It didn't seem like the dog was bleeding, though.

"Apple!" the other woman cried, gathering up the buff-colored dog. "Are you okay?" She gasped. "There's blood on the floor! Her paw is bleeding!"

Apple was clambering to escape from her owner's grasp. There was a torn-up plastic sandwich bag on the floor, which had red liquid in it along with what looked like chunks of raw hamburger.

"My Gwenie has blood on her, too. Get your dog out of here!"

"No, you get *your* dog out of here!" Apple's owner shouted.

Meanwhile, I snatched up the little plastic bag. "The dogs were fighting over ground beef that someone must have dropped. And it's just the red juice that forms with red meat."

"Meaning blood!"

"No, the red liquid in ground beef isn't blood. It's water mixed with a protein that turns the water red. Look it up on your smartphone if you don't believe me."

Kiki arrived, her tablet in hand, no doubt having learned about the paint-on-Pepper incident. "What's going on here?"

"A pair of Cockers got into a fight. I stopped it by pouring lukewarm water on them."

I saw that Baxter was heading toward us, as well. I gave him an "Okay" sign, but he continued on his path.

"Someone must have dropped a baggie with hamburger in it, and the two dogs each tried to fend the other off."

"Right," the elderly woman said. "That was my Gwenie's treat. I have her on a raw-food diet. She was simply defending what was hers. So this—"

she flicked her wrist in the buff-colored Cocker's direction "—Apple dog was in the wrong for trying to steal her food."

"Wow!" Apple's owner said, stamping her foot and causing some of the pooling water to splash up. "That's as biased a reaction as you can get! Obviously, *you* are at fault for dropping your damned hamburger on the floor!"

"But you're the one who couldn't control—"

"Stop arguing!" Kiki shouted. "I'll have Allida here dump another bucket of water on you!"

Both women stared at her, stunned.

"I'll have the vet examine both dogs," Kiki declared, "and you'll split the fees down the middle. If either or both of you want to withdraw, it's too late for you to get a refund. But that is up to you."

Baxter arrived and stood by my side. "I have a call into Maintenance for a cleanup. Is everything okay?"

"I think so," I answered.

"Gwenie doesn't need a vet," her owner said to Kiki over Baxter's and my brief exchange. "She just needs another grooming. Now that her chin has...red liquid on it."

"Apple just needs her paws cleaned. It's not fair, but I'll handle that cost myself."

"Plus, both dogs need to be blow-dried."

Kiki was clicking her fingers at a man with a mop and bucket. She pointed at the puddle.

"Did these dogs get paint on their fur, too?" Baxter asked.

"And that's another thing!" Gwenie's owner eyed Baxter's name badge. "Your employee could have seriously injured both dogs by dumping water on them like that."

"You're lucky she knew how to end a dog fight without either dog injuring the other," Baxter said.

"He's right," Kiki added. "Have either of you thought to thank her for doing that?"

"Well. That's true. She did bring the fight to an abrupt stop." She looked over at the maintenance man who was making short work of soaking up the water. "But still, somebody could have slipped in the puddle of water she left."

Jesse arrived, panting with effort as he put the shampoo on the groomer's counter.

"Did these dogs get paint on their fur, too?" Baxter asked me.

"Paint?" Apple's owner repeated. "You're not talking about paint on a dog's fur, are you?"

"She sure is," Gwenie's owner interjected. "Some poor woman's Poodle got spray painted hot pink."

"You're kidding!"

"No, I'm not. That's what had me so distracted that I forgot all about my little Gwenie not having her collar on while I was brushing out her coat. I was afraid there was some kind of a graffiti artist gone bonkers in here...spray painting light-colored dogs."

"I can only imagine. I'd have been distracted, too." She gave Apple a hug, continuing to hold her. "I was doing a little off-leash practicing with Apple. Her fur is practically white. Then this man here goes running past me with another man limping after him. That's what set my Apple off. She saw your precious Gwenie, and I think they were both so unsettled, they misbehaved."

"You're probably right. It was the staff's fault. They shouldn't have been running, and they shouldn't have allowed anyone in here with spray paint."

Kiki groaned. "Look. I'm writing all of these incidents up. But I saw for myself that Baxter was not running, he was simply walking briskly. And both of you were at fault for not minding your dogs and for having them both off-leash."

"That is most unfair of you, young lady," Gwenie's owner said, lifting her chin. "None of this would have happened if it hadn't been for all the chaos caused by the staff."

"Right," Apple's owner declared. "We Cocker Spaniel owners need to stick together. Our dogs' popularity is waning because they're getting such a bad and unfair reputation."

"I agree," I said. "I have a Cocker Spaniel. I love the breed. And Baxter and I own two King Charles Cavaliers, as well."

The women's eyes widened. "You do?" Apple Owner said. "That's so good to hear."

"Well, then. We *all* need to stick together." She held out her hand. "My name's Theodora."

We shook hands. "I'm Allie. My Cocker's name is Doppler."

"I'm Ashleigh," Apple's owner said. "This was all just a big misunderstanding," she said to Kiki. "You don't have to write up anything on our accounts. Not if it's going to get a Cocker owner in trouble."

"Or contribute to the inane belief that Cockers are feisty and nippy and barky," Theodora added.

"Absolutely. It's not the dogs themselves that tainted their reputations."

"No. It's the irresponsible Cocker owners."

"Because they're just so darned cute, they aren't properly trained."

For one moment, I considered passing them my card to see if they wanted my services. The next moment, I came to my senses. "I'm going to change my clothes."

"My office is unlocked," Baxter suggested. "I'm going to talk to the groomer and Eleanor. See if I can do some damage control."

"Speaking of which, did you find out anything more about the drugging?"

"'Fraid not," he answered. "A security officer and I watched the video three times We can't come close to identifying or ruling out suspects. That kiosk had a snarl of foot traffic for several minutes while it was raining. The camera angle made it impossible to see the bowl over the attendees' heads and shoulders. Then Kiki watched it and says she's making the executive decision that, since only Toy dogs would be affected, only those owners and their handlers are going to be notified. Plus that judge."

Baxter started to turn toward the grooming station.

"Maybe I should come with you as you talk with Eleanor."

"I almost forgot," Kiki suddenly chimed in, suddenly standing right behind me. I was startled. I hadn't realized she was listening in on us. "My dad said he wants to talk to Allida for a minute."

"He does?" I said, surprised and annoyed that she'd addressed Baxter instead of me. "Why?"

"Something about the Toy competition," Kiki replied.

"All right. I guess I'll go speak to Davis, then."

"Yeah, thanks. Sorry I forgot about that. With all the histrionics."

"I appreciated how you ended the women's bickering," I told her honestly.

"At one point in my career, I was a kindergarten teacher. Comes in handy sometimes."

Chapter 19

Davis was not in his office. By talking to various staff members and volunteers I finally tracked him down, nearly half an hour later. I greeted him by saying, "Kiki said you wanted to speak to me."

"About what?" he asked.

"She just said it was about the Toys competition."

He stared at me blankly. "She must have gotten something mixed up. I'd told her I wanted to speak to Baxter again. Just to make sure we were still on the same page. And that's all cleared up. So, I'm fine if you're fine."

"I'm fine."

"Good. Carry on." He walked away. I took a couple of minutes to cool down. Kiki had deliberately sent me on a wild-goose chase so she could hang around with Baxter. I didn't want to let her get under my skin. I needed to focus on the adorable little Pepper now with positive energy.

Eleanor was sitting in a seat of a currently unoccupied ring not far from the grooming room, looking at what appeared to be the schedule of events. Perched in her lap, Pepper spotted me and started hopping as if all four legs were springs. I sat down next to Eleanor, and Pepper darted into my lap and gave me a quick doggie kiss. She mustered a smile and said, "I checked out the three other Toy Poodles. I think we've got this one in the bag."

"Great! There's nothing like an impartial rating to build one's confidence."

"Exactly. In any case, he'll come in no lower than fourth." We smiled genuinely at each other. Truth be told, I was starting to really like Eleanor, despite her eccentricities about Pepper never being allowed in her back yard and overly pampering him. Not to mention her brief barrage of accusations. She was wearing a floral dress with a flowing pleated skirt that reached to her calves and sandals with a lattice-like pattern. Her ginger hair was once again starting to come loose from a crooked barrette.

"Pepper's fur looks as white as the driven snow. And I *am* impartial." I held the sleeve of my silk blouse against his shoulder. Fortunately, the blouse had dried on its own with no traces of red. I didn't have a second blouse with me. "See, see, see?"

She chuckled. A moment later, she shook her head. "I'm a little embarrassed. I can't believe how badly I freaked out."

"Anybody would have in your position...seeing their dog get spray-painted."

"Maybe, but then, this is hardly my first freak-out where you're concerned."

I gestured with a toss of my wrist, in a tacit: *That's all in the past.* "Well, if it's any consolation, you're not even in the top five as far as people here getting upset."

"Really?" She furrowed her brow. "Is this...normal for a dog show?"

"No. Not even close."

"That's good to hear. I don't think I have the stomach for the show circuit if this was typical. It's like Terrington's ghost is creating mayhem. Or someone put a hex on the place."

"Davis Miller is probably deeply regretting his decision not to cancel the entire event after Terrington was murdered. But maybe that would have bankrupted the Fort Collins Dog Club, which is hosting it. I have no idea of what kind of insurance policies they carry."

"You aren't a member, are you?" Eleanor asked.

I shook my head.

"Terrington told me I should join them instead of Denver, where we're registered now. He said it would help Minnie Pepper Cocoa's chances in the dog-show circuit and raise his profile. I'm glad I waited. I think I'll stick with Denver."

Not knowing anything about kennel clubs myself, I had no input. Pepper hopped back onto his owner's lap, and I got to my feet. "I brought a skirt-suit and a pair of pumps, so I'm going to change."

While we were speaking, a couple of volunteers entered the ring in front of us. This ring was going to be used to select the top Pomeranian for the Toy bracket.

"There's some open space next in the southwest corner," I told Eleanor. "It's right near ring number five. We can walk him around on the leash there before we start."

"Yeah. Valerie was nice enough to tell me about that. I already brought his crate over there."

"Great. I'll meet you there in ten minutes or so. This will be fun."

Or so I hoped, I thought as I headed to Baxter's office; I'd left my suit and shoes on top of the unused filing cabinet. Eleanor's talking about kennel membership had made me nervous. I truly was a neophyte, despite my life-long devotion to dogs. I had no credentials whatsoever and wasn't even an AKC registered handler. There were only four Toy Poodles enrolled. If Pepper won that round, he'd compete in the big round to determine the Best in the Toy division an hour later. During the break between the two rounds, I could discuss the idea of Eleanor switching to Cooper.

The Terrier Class competitions were all scheduled for tomorrow—Saturday. That would be another time that I would be heavily involved in the goings-on. Sunday would be the Best in Show competitions, which ended by noon. If all went according to plan, Cooper would be showing my conformation dogs tomorrow, and I would be able to kick back and watch the proceedings. Then I would probably help Baxter with whatever closing duties he'd acquired, and we'd go home with our every-little-bit-helps earnings for enduring our week of mayhem and murder. The memory of my horror at learning Terrington had been killed caused me to shiver.

I locked the office door behind me and changed into my brown skirt suit, then realized my shoes were missing. I called Baxter and asked him about my missing shoes.

"Maybe you left them in the car," he said.

"No, I put them next to the cabinet."

Baxter said, "Did you check inside the cabinet?"

"No, I didn't check the cabinet. Why would I? They can't have leapt inside a drawer!" As I spoke, I opened the top drawer. I stared at its contents. "Holy crumb. They're in the top drawer."

"You must have put them in there while you were distracted."

"No, I didn't. I am one-hundred percent certain I put them on the floor."

"Well, I sure didn't put them in there," Baxter retorted.

I dropped both shoes on the floor. "Maybe *you* were distracted."

"Allie, I've been running around so much I—"

"Got it. You didn't hide my shoes. Someone is obviously trying to mess with my head." I jammed my right foot into my shoe and felt a hideous pain in my big toe that seemed to surge all through my body. I screamed and dropped my phone. I yanked my shoe off, cursing, and hopping on my left foot. I heard Baxter yell over my phone, "Allie! I'm on my way!"

"Someone put a tack or nail in my shoe," I wailed at my phone.

I'd locked the door. I limped on the heel of my injured right foot over to the door and opened it. This being a puncture wound, my toe wasn't bleeding badly, but big red drops kept forming. I hopped toward the desk, grabbed a tissue, and squished it into a cap-like shape around my toe. I plopped down on a chair and grabbed the boobytrapped shoe.

Marsala rushed in, asking, "What happened?"

"Somebody boobytrapped my shoe."

She snatched the shoe out of my grasp. "You're bleeding," she said, which was not an especially keen observation.

Baxter charged through the door. He glanced at me, then Marsala, as she reached inside of my shoe gingerly. "It's a tack, or a brad." She pulled it out, and it was indeed a tack with a flat head. There was a pink-colored strand hanging from the head of the tack. "Looks like it was fastened with a wad of chewing gum."

"Jeez," Baxter said. He strode over to me and knelt beside me. "Are you okay? Have you had a tetanus shot?"

"Yes, and yes."

I sat on the floor, pressing against the wound to stop the bleeding.

"I'll get you a Band-aid," Marsala said. "There's a First-Aid kit in the employees' locker room."

Valerie appeared at the doorway. "I've got Band-aids right here," she said, unzipping the pouch on her belt. "What on earth just happened?"

Marsala held the tack up so Valerie could see it. "This was in her shoe." Marsala also held out her hand to take the Band-aid, but Valerie brushed past her as she extracted the Band-aid from its packaging.

"This is just going to keep happening, until the killer's caught," Valery grumbled. She removed my toe's tissue-cap, opened a tiny bottle, and dampened the tissue with the sharp-smelling astringent, and swabbed my tiny injury. She made a new cap for my toe by wrapping a second Band-aid around it. "Was your door locked, Baxter?"

"Not today," Baxter said. "I've just been locking my laptop in my desk, so that Allie and I can come and go."

"Well, that was a highly unfortunate decision," Valerie snapped.

"Did you do this, Valerie?" Marsala asked.

"Of course not! Why would I?" She swept up my left shoe. For a moment, I thought she was going to throw it at Marsala, but she merely checked it with her hand.

"To clear out the competition in the Toy class!" Marsala shouted at her. "Kiki told me that someone had spiked dog treats that were out in the open."

"That makes you as big of a suspect as I am!" Valerie fired back.

"My Yorkshire Terrier isn't even competing today! I withdrew both him and my Westie! After Richard Cory nearly died!"

"Oh, for heaven's sake," Valerie growled. "Try to get your shoes on, Allie." She struggled to her feet despite wincing at her bad knee, then glared up at Marsala, who was much taller. "These incidents...a dog's fur being painted, dog druggings, Allie's injury...are the ripples stemming from the murder. For whatever reason, the killer is continuing to sabotage the show." She gestured at me. "But it doesn't take a genius to realize I'd be the last person on the planet who would injure Allida intentionally. She's handling Sophie Sophistica in two hours!"

I slid my foot as carefully as I could into the shoe, but it was instant agony. This particular pair of pumps was just too tight of a fit. I moaned a little and pulled off the shoe. I met Baxter's gaze. "I need my sneakers," I said. He was already opening the laces as far as they would g and handed it to me.

"Have you seen Cooper?" I asked.

"He left to get lunch," Kiki said. Surprised at her arrival, I looked up. She was standing in the doorway. "Someone told me they heard a scream from this office." She held up her iPad. "Another log-in for the 'Incident List,'" she said with a sigh.

I finished tying my right sneaker and quickly put on my left. I walked in the tiny patch of unoccupied floor space. I could see by Baxter's facial expression that he was cringing on my behalf. The pain was manageable after a few steps.

"I've got to wear my sneakers. I can at least get them on. And I'm going to have to work like hell to keep from limping."

Just then Eleanor came in. "Someone wearing a plaid outfit just came up to me and told me you were in here and had hurt yourself."

"I don't know how this stuff gets around so fast," Kiki said.

"Look. I'm getting my sneakers on so tight that I won't be hitting my toe. I'll be fine to walk."

"She'll be fine for your Poodle," Valerie said snidely. "But once again, this will impact *me*. You won't be able to run, Allie. There's no way you're going to be able to compete with Sophie Sophistica now."

"I'll ice my toe. And I'll see the vet and see what he has to say. I'll make it work."

"I'm filing a violation," Valerie said, shaking her head.

"Fine," Kiki replied. "Just wait until after Sophie competes in the prelims. If Allie thinks she can do it, *let* her. And she'll have another couple of hours until the finals. It's just a puncture wound! It's not like anyone cut off her foot!"

"Thanks so much for the sympathy, Kiki," I snarled.

"It's not like I'm exaggerating," she retorted.

"This is nuts!" Eleanor cried. "Someone painted my Poodle pink! Now I've got a walking-wounded presenter...who's subbing from a *murdered* one. How can this possibly be happening? It's just a local event! And I'm a first-time entry!"

"Once again, my dear," Valerie said, "it's not about you. It's about me. I am quite possibly the best-known dog breeder in the state. Now that our biggest star, Terrington Leach, is dead, some lunatic murderer wants to take the biggest breeder out of the competition."

"Who *are* you?" Eleanor said. "I don't even know you. How big can you possibly be?"

"Big enough to knock you out of this competition!"

Meanwhile, Baxter's phone rang. I gestured at him to go, and he did so.

"Valerie, Eleanor. Stop!" In the back of my mind I realized I was using my mother's voice. That was an eerie feeling, but my tone had worked. "Look at me." I started jogging in place, which hurt, but I didn't care. "I can walk. It's not a big deal. If it turns out to be a big deal as the day unfolds, you can take the chewing gum to the police and pay them hundreds of dollars to see if they can get the DNA on who chewed it before sticking it into my shoe."

Eleanor and Valerie both stopped talking.

"I'm not in favor of that idea," Marsala said. "I don't know how much DNA was left in the wad by the time I pulled it out and got my fingers on it. I don't want it to pick up on my DNA."

"Or is that because it's *your* chewing gum," Valerie said.

"Okay. Enough. Eleanor. Let's get going."

She walked out with me. The throbbing in my toe was still appreciable, but I'd worked through much more painful foot injuries in college on my team. I could manage it.

"Your sneakers look pretty dorky," Eleanor said.

So much for my liking her. "Can you get Pepper on his leash and meet me in ring five?" I asked.

"Of course. He's in his crate in the corner, like you asked."

She sped up her pace and headed toward the corner of the building without another word. I reached the ring. The other three Toy Poodles were already lined up. A volunteer brought me my number, wrapped it around my arm, and pinned it in place. Remarkably, she didn't jab me with the pin even once. I tried to take deep calming breaths. I closed my eyes and visualized myself with Pepper stepping with him trotting beside me as we circled the ring. As I opened my eyes, Eleanor ran over to me, carrying Pepper. She put him down beside me and handed me his leash. Neither of us spoke.

We entered the ring and took our position—third in the row. Each dog in turn would have to be placed on their own table and submit to a full-body inspection—teeth, legs, fur, and stand in the correct position, sometimes with judges lifting their tails and touching their spines and chests to judge how well the animals lined up with the AKA's standards of excellence. The dog would then be returned to the ground and would circle the judge, then go to the far end of the ring and back, and finally stand in perfect position, facing the handler so the judge could examine the dog in profile.

The first Poodle completed his careful examination and his circuit. Like me, the judge was wearing a brown skirt-suit, although hers was a lighter shade and a larger size. She had long, kinky black hair, with a sizable portion of white mixed in. It was fastened in a tight bun in the back. She had a no-nonsense countenance about her. She reminded me of my fifth-grade teacher, whom I liked a lot. That gave me a surge of confidence and optimism, deservedly or not. The second Poodle trotted toward the table. She had an uneven gate. The first Poodle was directly in my line of vision now. His tail was tilting to one side. I glanced back at the fourth Poodle. Imperfect front legs. Eleanor was right. We had this in the bag!

I looked down at Pepper and gasped a little in surprise. White pawprints! They went from the entrance of the ring to where Pepper was standing. The groomer must have gotten overly zealous with the talcum whitening powder. Now the judge was going to notice. There was no way Minnie Pepper Cocoa was going to avoid a penalty.

Eleanor, meanwhile, was so proud and excited, I could hear her chattering behind me. "He looks so regal! My little man could be a pet of the Queen of England."

If he was a Welsh Corgi, I said to myself. *And if he wasn't leaving powder trails with his every step.*

I would have seen the powder if not for my shoe having been sabotaged. If it weren't for the thumbtack, I would have rehearsed our presentation gait before entering the ring. We would have seen this anomaly and circumvented it. My toe was now throbbing.

I caught Eleanor's eye and looked at the white footprints and back up at her. She came closer, grimacing at the trail that led to her regal little man. Her face fell.

Chapter 20

The judge gestured for me to bring Pepper to the table. She then immediately examined the white dog prints extending from the ring entrance to Pepper's position. She wore a grimace as she met us at the table. That was the same expression my fifth-grade teacher wore when she'd seen that Billy Hawthorne had been staring at my test and copying my answers. Pepper's paws were the first thing she examined.

"So, these are nice and white, I see," she snarled.

"He was the victim of a cruel prank in the grooming room an hour ago," I said. "Kiki Miller wrote up the incident. Someone swapped a can of pink spray paint with his—" the correct term had slipped my mind "—fur freshener."

My teacher-doppelganger's expression instantly softened. "That's awful. I'll try to..." She paused. "I wish you'd caught this sooner. Just don't ever let this or any other dog you're presenting leave footprints in a show ring again."

"I won't," I replied.

She took an extended period of time studying little Pepper, who was far too squirmy in the examination, but for a first-timer, that was par for the course.

"Okay, let's get a look at his gait," she said, making a little circling gestured. I put Pepper's leash on and Pepper immediately trotted in a perfect circle around the judge as if he was an old hand at this. "Out and back," she then said with a smile. We did so. Pepper was easy to lead and truly had a wonderful gait—all of his little steps even and his countenance proud and confident.

As the last Poodle made his out-and-back trot and returned to his assigned position, the judge walked the length of the line as she looked at each dog in quick successive comparison to the others. As she made a return trip, she called out the black Poodle with the tilted tail, next the Poodle behind us, then Pepper. She made a circular gesture and had the three of us trot around the ring in quick succession. As we returned from our lap, she pointed at the black Poodle and announced, "Three." The Poodle with the slightly off legs was second. She pointed at Minnie Pepper Cocoa and called, "One!"

I breathed a sigh of relief and happy surprise and walked him toward the others. Pepper had clinched a spot in the Best of Toy division.

"Yippee," Eleanor cried. "Minnie Pepper Cocoa won!"

As was traditional, the three other handlers came over and congratulated me. Eleanor, too, dashed into the ring, and we posed for pictures with Pepper and the blue ribbon that was bigger than he was.

My toe was throbbing badly as we left the ring. I'd be fine, though. I gestured with my chin for her to follow me to a quiet spot. I headed to an empty corner.

"That's good, right? Winning, even though there were only three others? In his first-ever competition?" Eleanor asked.

"Yes, it's really good. And I'm sure you'll feel confident at showing him yourself at the next dog show."

"Yeah. I think so. Maybe. You two looked really great together, though. I'd hate to break up a successful team. You were both so cute and perky."

"Thanks," I said. Those were two of my most frequently cited descriptions of me. I'd prefer beautiful and sultry. But it was better than plain and crabby. "Just a word to the wise, there are a lot of regulars at every show who believe in a certain decorum. No raised voices that might distract the dogs from behaving in the ring. No verbal reaction to the judge's choices."

She winced. "Oh, of course. I wish you'd told me earlier."

"I *would* have if it weren't for my shoe mishap getting me out of sorts."

"Right. I'm sorry that I forgot all about that, even. It was just so exciting for me to see my little man present himself so beautifully." She looked at my injured foot. "Is it feeling okay?"

"It's sore, but at least I don't have to put much weight on the front of my toe when I walk. But...how did Pepper get all of that talcum powder or chalk on his paws?"

"Beats me. He wasn't leaving any footprints when we left the groomers. I didn't notice the prints on my slacks until you pointed at his tracks."

She was wearing light, beige pants. I, however, had a vague recollection of brushing off my slacks when I'd changed out of them without a second thought. Those little spots I'd barely noticed were from Pepper's paws. "Did you put him in his crate between leaving the groomers and having him on your lap?"

"Yes, when I was moving his crate. But—" She broke off. "Someone sabotaged me twice! That terrible Terrier breeder was wrong. Nobody was after her dog. Minnie Pepper Cocoa *was* the target! It's over there."

She pointed at a spot behind me. As I followed her line of sight, I was distracted by seeing Kiki. She had been scanning her surroundings and held up a palm when she spotted me. "The Poodle judge just spoke with me about the incident report."

"I'm not surprised. I'm sure she wanted to verify its veracity."

"Hard to believe the dog's been running around for a full hour and still has powder coming off his feet."

"That's what we're checking right now...to see if his crate is okay."

As Eleanor led us to the crate, I said to Kiki, "By the way, Davis said he didn't need to talk to me."

"Oh, right." She hit her forehead with the heel of her hand, far too gently for my liking. "He'd said he wanted to talk to *Baxter*. Sorry about that."

Pepper climbed to the top of Eleanor's shoulder as she opened the crate. He looked so cute and happy. I reached inside the medium-sized crate and ran my hand over the simulated sheepskin that functioned as soft, thick carpeting. A big white puff of powder arose. When I extracted my hand, my palm and fingers were covered in white.

"This is outrageous," Eleanor said. "Someone has boobytrapped my little boy's crate!"

Kiki swiped at the rug with her index finger and sniffed it. "It's chalk dust." With her other hand, she patted the top of Pepper's poufy head. "This could have been so much worse. Right?" She looked from Eleanor to me and back. Neither of us reacted.

"At least it isn't powdered *drugs*, right?" Kiki said. "He would be dead by now."

Eleanor paled. "I think I'm going to be sick," she said. Holding Pepper tight in her arms, she pivoted and headed toward the women's room.

"Ew," Kiki said under her breath. "Wish I hadn't said that. I didn't realize she was hypersensitive."

Baxter and I finally got together to sit down and have a cup of decaf coffee in his office. My ability to relax was limited by the frigid sensations of Baxter's makeshift icepack on my foot. He'd wrapped a self-sticking bandage around my foot to keep it in place, which was working a little too well. I was mulling the notion of drizzling my coffee on it.

"This is the first time I've gotten to sit down and breathe," he said. "Just four more hours until we've made it through Day One of three."

I pulled at the ice, my hand nicely warmed by the mug. "I have to head over to the agility trials in twenty minutes or so." I'd already changed out of my skirt suit and back into my active-wear. "To tell you the truth, I'm still wondering what else can go wrong."

"I know. Me, too. I'm assuming Davis will fire me again. If so, my plan is to say, 'Fine. Pay me the amount in my contract, and blame everything on me.' Then I'll hand him the keys and walk out.'"

That would be disastrous for his resume. I said nothing and started unwrapping my foot.

"How's that feeling?"

"It's not hurting all that bad. I'm a little worried about how well it will hold up on the agility course, but as long as I don't push down on it, I'm fine. No ballet dancing, and no stubbing my toe."

"Fingers crossed. Then you've got the Bull Terrier and the Scottie to present tomorrow, right?"

"No, I don't. I forgot to tell you. Cooper wants to do that after all. I gave him both dogs. In addition to Jesse's Airedale."

Kiki opened Baxter's door, calling "Yoo hoo."

He grimaced, then said, "Come on in."

"Hi, Baxter! Allie. Am I interrupting anything?"

"No, just chatting about what to expect tomorrow," I said, trying to ease my foot back into its sneaker.

"Expect a hectic eight-hours," Kiki said. "Especially you, Baxter. Expect *me* to hold my breath that we get through the day unscathed in the Terrier competitions."

"Right," Baxter said.

"That's why I stopped by. I just want to see if there's anything I can do for you, Baxter," Kiki said. She shifted her gaze to me. "Oh, and I certainly hope you're keeping your promise to take over Cooper's dogs, at least in the Terrier class."

"I didn't promise that," I said. "And I agreed to let him show Eeyore. As well as the Scottie and Bull Terrier tomorrow."

She gaped at me as if horrified. "You're actually going to give him back the duties? Earlier this morning, I talked to Jesse and he told me he was hoping you were presenting Eeyore. I thought you'd go with the owner's wishes, for heaven's sake!"

Hearing that Jesse was indeed happier to have me instead of Cooper gave me a pang of regret. "I...thought it would be better for the Terrier competition if I withdrew. I didn't want owners to claim judging bias because the manager and I are a couple."

"And how would that be worse than asking the judges to ignore the fact that one of the handlers is the prime suspect in the murderer of a renowned handler? Allie. Think this through! The majority of people producing the show, entering the show, and watching the show believe he has murdered our one and only celebrity. How would it look if we allow him to compete?"

"It will look like we think he's innocent until proven guilty."

"He would unfairly be missing out on walking a couple of dogs. So? Cry me a river!"

"But he needs the money to pay for his defense."

"Fine. I'll hire him to manage the cleanup crew on Sunday. I'll pay him more than he'd have earned in the ring. *Then* will you promise to present the dogs yourself?"

"I doubt he'll be happy. But I guess so. Provided *you* tell him about this compromise and how he'll earn the money back."

"Deal. I'll track him down and tell him that right now." She looked at my foot. "You up on your tetanus shots?"

"Yes."

She gave me a perfunctory nod, then beamed at Baxter. "Keep up the good work, Bax. After tomorrow, it's all downhill."

"As long as it's down a hill and not off a cliff."

Kiki laughed. "You're so witty!" She shook her head and chuckled as she left.

I wiggled my eyebrows at him. "You're witty *and* pretty," I teased.

"Yeah? You should see my better half." We rose and shared a quick kiss. "Back to the mad, mad dog-show world." He grinned at as he held the door for me. "One lucky thing has happened. The skies cleared after the brief rain shower this morning." He locked the door, and we headed into the main space. "Otherwise, we'd have had to move all of the Working Class competitions indoors."

"That is lucky. This way we can probably stay on schedule when you don't need to rearrange—"

Just then, an alarm sounded. An instant later, the sprinkler heads in the ceiling went off.

Chapter 21

The noise from the alarm combined with the screaming and shouting of hundreds of people was earsplitting. This in turn set off hundreds of dogs barking. "There's no smoke," Baxter shouted at me. "Got to be a malfunction. I'm switching off the water main." He sprinted toward a staff-only doorway.

I, like everyone else in the immediate area, tried to move to a relatively dry spot within the sprinkler system. Some people were heading for the exits. Others were more concerned with preventing their dogs' fur from getting wet and were on all fours trying to keep their dogs below their torsos.

In less than a minute, the sprinklers stopped pouring water on us. A minute or so after that, the alarm was shut off. The volume of noise only dropped a little, and a distinct smell of wet dog was prevalent, pleasantly scented with shampoo.

A crackling sound came from the public-address system along the ceiling. I looked up and saw the amplifier near me was above the emergency sprinkler heads. "Remain calm, everybody."

It took me a moment to place that this was Kiki Miller speaking.

"Everyone, please quiet down," Kiki said again. "Stop whatever you're doing and take a deep breath."

"I'm soaking wet!" some man yelled. "I need a *towel*, not a deep breath!"

"The fire-alarm system has malfunctioned. The firemen are on their way, in order to reset and restore the system. Please calm yourselves and your dogs. We will be taking an hour recess in our programming. Afterward, all ongoing competitions will either restart from the beginning or from the point of the interruption, at the judges' discretion."

The PA system clicked off audibly, then back on. "Oh, and thank you for your patience and understanding."

"Tell that to my drycleaners!" a woman shouted. "My designer's suit is ruined!" With this second statement, I recognized Valerie's voice. She was going to be in quite the mood for the Standard trial.

I scanned the main aisle. There was a quarter-inch or so of water on the linoleum floor. The staff and volunteers would have quite a mopping challenge. Clothing and dogs would need to be dried. I glanced at my watch. If a mere hour delay was sufficient, I had ninety minutes before Sophie and I would be in the ring in the second building. Most likely, that building had stayed dry. I would bet my house that the fire investigator was going to discover that someone had tampered with the fire-prevention system by holding a cigarette lighter up to a sensor.

    I headed through the staff-only door, thinking that they considered me staff enough to include me in the meeting last night. I spotted Baxter at the far corner of the large room. His arms were crossed as he stood among a group of seven or eight people listening to Davis Miller pontificate. Davis was red-faced and shaking his fists—sometimes pounding one fist against his palm. He was flanked on either side by a pair of armed security guards. I wasn't sure when they had arrived. Perhaps they'd been here all along, watching in one of these off-limit rooms. Neither of them appeared to have gotten wet in the unexpected indoor shower. Davis, like his audience, wore wet clothing. His suit was now splotched in a darker shade of brown. I slowly crossed the room, deliberately keeping my gaze fixed on Baxter, as if that could prevent Davis from choosing to turn his anger on either of us.

"—not going to get sued for this! Anything suspicious. Anyone standing where they shouldn't be or absent from where they should have been. Tell the security men everything. Let them decide if it's meaningful or not." He paused. "Does anybody know where Cooper Hayes is?"

"Right here," Cooper called from behind me. I turned. He was just ten feet or so away. He must have followed me here. "Why?"

"I...want to know if you...if everybody has an alibi for who they were with when the sprinklers went off."

"In case you haven't noticed, I got just as drenched as everyone else. I was talking to a couple and their young daughter who were thinking of entering their Golden in next year's show. We were near the main entrance, and they left. I don't know if they came back in, though. The little girl's name was Emily."

"Allida Babcock," Davis said, glaring at me. "Do you have an alibi?"

"Yes, Baxter and I were together and had just left his office. A minute or two after talking to Kiki."

"Why didn't you report that someone had taken your shoes and put a tack in one of them?" Davis asked accusingly.

"I *did* report it. To Kiki, who's serving as the secretary and is in charge of the incidents book."

"When and where did this happen?"

"A couple of hours ago in Baxter's office."

Davis merely stared at me.

Nobody spoke or raised their hand.

Cooper was now standing beside me. He bent toward me and whispered, "I wish I'd listened to you and stayed away. They're going to accuse me of setting off the fire alarm."

"Maybe your alibi family reentered, and they can prove you didn't do it."

"Maybe. But my luck would have to change. I'm hoping the security guards caught something on a recording."

"I hope so, too. And maybe they can identify whoever boobytrapped my shoe." Cooper's story came to mind about his using his ex-wife's key to open her locker, and Valerie reading evil intentions into that action.

Meanwhile, Davis was quietly conferring with the two security guards and a couple of men in suits who had rather officious bearings. Baxter joined Cooper and me.

"Hey, pretty lady," he said.

"Hi. Glad you got the water turned off so quickly."

"Me, too. I'm sure nobody's happy with their dowsing, even so. Those are city officials that Davis is talking to. They're probably concerned about lawsuits if someone slips. At least the water damage itself looks pretty minimal. One of the building maintenance guys already found a heat sensor with some black-soot marks around it."

"Hmm," Cooper said. "It wasn't near the front door, was it? Where I was when the sprinklers went off?"

"I don't know," Baxter answered. "I didn't—"

Davis clapped his hands twice to regain everyone's attention. "Raise your hands if you *don't* have an alibi."

"Excuse me?" someone called.

"What constitutes an alibi?" a middle-aged woman asked. "I was walking down an aisle when the water went off. "There were a dozen or so people in the general area. But I wasn't memorizing their appearances or getting their names."

"If you don't know the identities of anyone next to you at the time, that does *not* constitute an alibi," Davis said, annoyed.

"I was standing in line for coffee," a man said. "I could pick out two of the people in the line with me, if I could get them in a lineup."

"We aren't doing a lineup, so that isn't an alibi, either."

Nobody was raising their hands.

"You two should both have your hands up," Davis snarled, pointing at the two people who'd questioned him. Several people raised their hands, all of them glaring at Davis. Cooper had his arms crossed.

"Your headcount is annoying, Mr. Miller," Mark Singer said. "This was probably just a prank. For the record, I left the other building to have a smoke. I heard a big commotion and came in to see what was going on. Nobody was with me outside. So I can take you out to show you the cigarette butt I ground out before I ran over here. Are you going to ask the three or four hundred people that are in the general area if they have an alibi?"

Davis looked enraged. "No. I just want alibis from the people hired to work for me. If anyone has a problem with that, raise your hand."

This time, we all raised our hands. For me, it came down to the principle. I wanted the sabotager to be identified, removed, and subjected to whatever legal penalties were dealt for menacing on a large scale. Especially because the murderer and the prankster could be one and the same. But Davis taking a public rollcall of the paid staff members struck me as demeaning and a time waster.

I looked over at Cooper. He pivoted and left the room.

Chapter 22

The second building had indeed escaped the chaos of the activated ceiling e sprinklers. Neither the cafeteria nor the agility arena was in any way affected. Next up was the Standard trial. This was designed as more of an obedience style of a race. The dogs had to cool their jets in the middle of their race. That was an interesting who's-the-boss challenge. The dog needed to run, jump, climb, as fast as he can, then jump onto a square block and stay there on all four paws for five seconds, then go run, jump, and climb again as fast as he could.

This time we were going from shortest to tallest divisions. That was good for me, in a way. Sophie was a pro at standard agility races. She liked the waiting game. Where she was concerned, it was the chance to show off her speed twice.

As Valerie, Sophie, and I entered the main room, I paused. It was packed. Every seat was taken, and many people were sitting on the floor or in camping-style chairs they'd brought themselves.

"Wow," I said. "I guess the audience members fleeing from the main building during the sprinklers malfunction has helped our turnout."

Valerie snorted. "It's always like this, Allie. If anything, it's less crowded than last year. Sophie Sophistica has a large fan base. Most attendees work, so they can't get here until late afternoon."

I was more than a little skeptical, yet she pointed with her chin, and I spotted a banner that indeed read: "Sophie Sophistica 3rd Fan Club." There were forty or fifty people wearing T-shirts with a picture of Sophie jumping over a gate with the same verbiage as the banner. Their motto wasn't especially creative. They should have gone with "SST" and shown her on a rocket. Or used an emoji of an electric fan in the place of the word.

We both turned our attention to the electronic board, giving us the order or dogs competing. Sophie would be called soon. I needed to go play with her for a bit. "It's going to be up to you to see that she hasn't lost her edge by being forced to compete an hour later than anticipated," Valerie told me.

"Well, *Sophie* doesn't know that she's been delayed by an hour."

She put her hands on her hips and gave me a stare-down "You disappoint me, Allie. You know how dogs absorb their persons' moods and energies. She's been getting anticipatory jitters for an extra hour."

"True. Sorry."

She handed me her leash. "Don't lose."

I led Sophie to the practice jump and unhooked her leash. She looked at me as if surprised I'd deigned to take her for a practice jump, but she did fine. I played a game of patty paws with her and gave her a tummy rub. I decided to forgo hooking on her leash to lead her to the start line and left it on the designated table. This time I could see neither Valerie, nor Jesse from my position at the starting line. I was certain they were both in attendance. The lighting had changed somewhat since the morning round.

The residual tenderness in my toe was only noticeable now when I thought about it. I felt a surge of adrenaline. I looked down at Sophie, and she was looking up at me, awaiting my signal. From this angle, she looked like she was smiling. I could tell she felt it, too. We were ready to fly through this course.

"On your mark," I told her, the command Valerie always used that meant to stand right behind the starting line. Meanwhile, I took several steps in front of her toward the first obstacle—a two-pole jump.

The starter said "go," and we were off. Once again I was grateful for having played competitive college basketball. I slipped into my steely concentration mode. It felt like Sophie and I were on the identical wavelength.

Sophie was at her best. Regardless of what type of enterprise it is, beauty is on display when someone performs as if they were so in tune with their every motion that not a single movement is wasted. There was not even an instant of hesitation or distraction. I was superfluous in the ring; she had memorized the course from the moment she'd seen it. She leapt onto the paws-pause podium.

I eyed the automatic clock and counted along with it: "One. Two. Three. Four. Off!" I cried instead of five.

She tore around Mark as if he was inconsequential. This time, he remained motionless and silent. I, however, had put too much weight on my injured toe and took an awkward step. Yet Sophie did her thing and flew through the tire jump that served as the finish line.

On an impulse, I held out my arms, and she leapt into them with ease. The crowd let out a collective "Aww!" With the added five seconds for the pause table, she came in at 35.55 seconds, which was excellent for a preliminary eight-inch Standard competition. That was within six seconds of her time in the first round and was precisely what Valerie and I wanted to see from her.

There were two other eight-inch class jumpers yet to compete, but Sophie was in first place and would definitely have a top-three seed in her division. Again, her fan club was cheering wildly. I helped her to wave at them, even though I knew Valerie wouldn't approve of my playfulness. To my surprise, when she met me at the exit gate, she put her hand on my shoulder and said, "Well done, Allida. Well done." The lines in *Babe*, a movie about a pig that competes in a dog-herding competition, popped into my brain. Babe's owner says to him, "*That'll do, Pig. That'll do.*" I grinned at the thought but kept it to myself. It wasn't all that flattering to be compared to a pig.

I bided my time while awaiting my Standard-course run with Dog Face. He was the last competitor in the twenty-inch class. I was nervous. He wasn't always disciplined at the pause table. Leaving early was a five-second penalty times the number of second-fractions in which he jumped the gun. Maybe it was bad karma. Maybe it was my anxiousness. Maybe the noise we both heard. In any case, Dog Face did indeed jump the gun. It was a five-second penalty. Everything else was clean and precise. His finishing time was 29.67 seconds, 34.67 with the penalty. He finished in second place in the twenty-inch jumps division. Sophie, too, had bested him in this second round, which I'm sure elated Valerie.

Jesse hugged me as I sagged a little in relief. "He made the finals! Easily!" he said. Border Collies rocked at agility training. They were pretty much born with these kinds of skills. Even so, both Sophie and Dog Face were in wonderful shape to win their respective divisions.

"No pause table in the finals," I said, happily.

Baxter headed toward me. "You nailed it," he said, giving me and then Jesse a high-five. "What's up next for you?"

"Best in Toy," Valerie answered for me as she approached.

Baxter and I merely looked at Valerie, surprise by her interruption.

"The doors here will reopen at seven tonight," she continued, "and we can walk the Finals course. Meanwhile, we need to get going for the Best Toy Dog competition."

"*We* do? Did one of your Yorkies qualify for Best in Toy division?" I asked.

"Yes. I'm surprised you didn't hear Marsala trying to insult me on that very issue. She herself had chickened out and removed Tallyho from competing. Remember?"

"Oh, right." Valerie was getting on my nerves again, and I struggled to keep the annoyance out of my voice. "At the time, I was occupied with having driven a half-inch tack into my toe. How self-centered of me."

She clicked her tongue. "I'll see you in the ring. Good luck."

"You're handling your Yorkie yourself?"

"Yes. Hence my comment about seeing you in the ring." She hesitated. "Do you want to walk over there with me?"

"No, I have to force Bingley the Beagle to race around the novice agility course first," I said. I glanced over at the ring, where the crew was already removing two of the obstacles and simplifying the course.

"They're doing that now? I assumed they did that first thing this morning, per usual."

"I think they want to establish a relaxed mood and lower audience expectations from the Masters competitions. In any case, Bingley is up first."

"I can see how that might be a good idea." She grinned. "In fact, I'm sticking around to watch this, too."

Chapter 23

A few minutes later, the cameraman had gotten set up along with a second crew member who was probably in charge of the lighting. Tracy and I were struggling to help get Bingley measured. He kept turning in circles and growling, barely willing to allow the official to measure his height. Not that it mattered. Tracy and I knew he was going to be disqualified for "failure to perform." Judging by the grins on all of the volunteers' faces, someone had either conspired with Tracy to let him compete, or she'd clued Mark in that this was all for fun. It already felt as if I should be dressed in a clown costume.

Tracy and the cameraman were allowed to be in the ring with us; they just weren't allowed within the vicinity of the obstacle course itself. Mark patiently waited for the cameraman to give him the thumbs up.

Bingley was obeying my "sit" command behind the start line right next to me. There was no reason to get a head start on him. I could outrun him on the course, and if he chose to instead head for the hills, it didn't matter if he outraced me. He'd simply be disqualified sooner rather than later.

Mark gave the "go" command. To my delight, Bingley leapt over the first jump, then the second. Next up, he ran up the dog walk—also called a bridge—and stopped dead at the top.

I tried everything I could think of that was within the no-touching-no-luring rules to get him to come down. He simply sat down with his front paws dangling off the side and looked at me. The audience was laughing and clapping. Finally, I sprawled out on the floor by the foot of the dog walk, and he finally deigned to come down and licked my face. I sprang to my feet and got him to navigate the next jump by racing up to them, making him think I was joining him, but dodging it and running backward beside him instead.

He jumped over the wall. He stopped in front of the seesaw. I did a ridiculous duck walk alongside of him, increasing my height as he slowly walked up to the fulcrum. When it flipped down, I got almost teary-eyed I was so thrilled that he was actually crossing the seesaw correctly. Then, however, he decided to ignore the bottom half of the seesaw and jumped down right in front in front of me. That was a five-point penalty, adding five seconds to his time.

At the start of the tunnel, Bingley lay on his back and begged for a tummy rub. With creativity born from desperation, I straddled the entrance to the tunnel and bent down and looked through my legs at him. That got Bingley to enter the tunnel. I ran to the exit and called his name. When he didn't emerge. I dropped onto my hands and knees to look into the tunnel. He was lying down a few feet away. I kept repeatedly calling his name, told him to come, and patted the floor. He finally trotted out, licking my nose yet again.

Bingley sat down when I gave him the "weave" signal at the entrance to the series of six posts he was supposed to weave through. I tried to click my fingers to get him to peek through at least the first and second posts. He finally did so, but ignored me as I clicked my fingers at the opposite side of the second post. There was zero chance that he would qualify, so I turned and started to walk to the broad jump, his next apparatus. He weaved through the second and third posts perfectly and followed me in a heel position. He squeezed under the next jump, then wove around its supports to return to the entry point. Once again, the crowd roared with laughter.

Mark Singer was still standing in front of the tunnel, and he grinned at me. "You're sure making all the other dogs look good," he said, even though talking to a contestant or vice versa was strictly prohibited.

"Yep. This is an exercise in patience. And/or futility."

"Thanks for being a good sport about it," he replied.

"You, too."

Bingley was supposed to go through the tunnel again, but I wasn't that good of a sport as to make him reenter it and risk his falling asleep inside. For one thing, he'd already surpassed the maximum time limit, so he had already been disqualified.

I made half-hearted efforts at commanding him to jump over the final hurdles. He rounded them with me instead and started walking on his back paws for no discernable reason, unless in his mind he wanted to demonstrate to the audience how agile and yet disobedient he was. The finish line was the tire jump, which he raced in full circles around twice. Time to call an end to this.

After curtsying to the video camera, on a whim, I made a fist in front of Bingley's face, lowered my fist to the ground, and said, "Bow," instead of "Lie down." That particular technique teaches a dog to lie down, because the dog seeks to eat the treat in the trainer's fist. To my and the crowd's delight, Bingley did indeed bow for the audience—more commonly called "downward dog" in Yoga class. We left the ring, with the audience giving us a standing ovation.

Tracy yelled, "Cut" at her cameraman, then swept up her dog and gave me a big hug.

"See? What did I tell you! That's going to be the hit videotape of the entire event. You'll get tons of business, and next year, they'll have a big crowd watching at the agility trials. It's a win-win."

I chose not to mention that we already had a standing-room only crowd. "Can I ask a big favor, Tracy?"

"Sure," she immediately replied.

"Could you ask your crew to splice the previous recording of me with Sophie with this tape of Bingley? They could add captions that read: How to Do This Trick, and then: How *Not* to Do This Trick."

"That's not a bad idea," Tracy said. "Sure. I'll get those out next week. After I post this one on Youtube."

"Great. We can double the mileage, because then it can be presented as a training video. And you can also post it as it is on social media sites."

"Love it," Tracy declared. "At the end of the training video, I'll post your online contact info, with a blurb about how you help troubled dogs all around the Boulder-Denver area."

"Not to mention in the booming town of Dacona."

Valerie was approaching. Her facial expression was inscrutable. "Nothing like a little mockery to spice up a competition, eh girls?"

"Hello, Valerie. Good to see you again," Tracy said. "Not all of your lessons from Sophie Sophistic took hold in Bingley's little brain. But it wasn't for lack of trying."

"No, just for lack of serious practicing," Valerie replied. "But I suppose a little humor is a good thing." She patted Bingley. "He's actually got some potential, you know. If you were willing to hire our Allie for an hour or two, three days a week, he could be competing for real in another six months."

"Or another six years," I added. There are, of course, some excellent agility Beagles. I just couldn't imagine any dog belonging to Tracy Truitt becoming one of them. I would be spending at least half of my time undoing his current behavior.

"Sounds like that idea isn't making either of us jump for joy," Tracy said. "Hey, I guess I missed the fireworks at the main building. Or I should say, the waterworks. What was all of that about?" Tracy asked.

"The rumor is it was someone with an axe to grind that's working behind the scenes," Valerie said. "Probably someone whose dogs were overlooked. Or whose handling skills were overlooked." Valerie picked up Sophie. "I'm heading over there now to get ready for the individual Toy breeds." She nodded at me. "See you for the Finals walk-through."

"Congrats on your rounds with the two dogs," Tracy said as soon as Valerie was out of earshot. "I heard Dog Face kicked ass."

I grinned. "He turned in an under-thirty-seconds first run. The taller dogs are always faster than the little ones. And the way the course distance is determined and divided by a time-per-yard calculation, both according to the size of the dog's jumps, it almost always works out such that the twenty-inch dogs like Dog Face winning the Overall Best in Agility. Knowing Valerie as well as I do, it's hard to fathom why she's needling Jesse about Sophie being able to beat Dog Face. She's set herself up for a big disappointment."

"Which she'll take out on you, I suppose."

"Probably. But for now, I have to get a Toy Poodle ready for his first show competition."

"You do?"

"Yep. I'm presenting my neighbor's dog."

Tracy raised her eyebrows. "This isn't the neighbor suing to force you to shutter your kenneling service, is it?"

"Eleanor. Yes."

"What if she's playing games with you, Allie? She could be sucking up to you, while all along she's still trying to destroy you."

"I'm just going to ignore that possibility." I glanced at the agility course. "It's too big of an obstacle to overcome." Right now, I had a cute little Poodle to show off in the main building.

Chapter 24

I had a few minutes to chat with Baxter as he unlocked his office for me. He had missed Sophie's Standard race, but said he'd try his best to catch us in the finals. I quickly donned my suit jacket and skirt. I also took another ibuprofen to dull the pain in my toe.

On a hunch, I checked the stands of the ring where the Best in Toy division would be taking place. This was one of the two largest rings. Indeed, I spotted Eleanor pacing in the aisle between the rows. I headed over to her.

"I wish I could calm down," Eleanor said by way of a greeting.

"Pepper won a blue ribbon for his breed. Whatever happens in the best of his entire division is just the cherry on top of the amazing sundae."

"Well, sure, I know that rationally, but the thing is...I *really* enjoy desserts. Do you think he can win?"

I took a moment to ponder the question. "I think he'll place."

She looked at me blankly. "Place?"

"Be in the top three."

She clasped her hands together. "You do? Really?"

"Yes, but don't put too much weight on that. Baxter and I make the Westminster Dog Show our Superbowl. We get popcorn and pizza, and we bet on the winners. He's beaten me all three times."

"I should get *his* opinion then."

Baxter, I was certain, had returned to putting out fictitious fires with all-too-real sprinklers. I didn't expect to see him at this competition at all.

Eleanor and I endured the thirty-minute wait until show time. We gave Pepper all kinds of attention, which he ate up. As I said to Eleanor, hers was a dog who knew he was special. It reinforced my belief that Minnie Pepper Cocoa was a winner. If not today, in his second or third show.

Once again, I felt a frisson of guilt that Cooper wasn't the one standing in my place.

Valerie and her little Yorkshire Terrier entered the ring. Valerie, I noted, was trotting around the ring as if both knees were in perfect shape. On the other hand, I could certainly see why she didn't want to be the handler at agility trials; I was winded, and I was much younger and a former athlete.

As we entered the ring and I got a good look at the other fourteen adorable little competitors, I felt sorely tempted to break form and go make a personal visit with each and every one of them. I envied the judge—once again, my fifth-grade teacher's double—who was paid to do precisely that. Yet as I looked at the Bichon Friese, Brussels Griffon, Chihuahua, Papillon, Pinscher, Pekingese, Pomeranian, Pug, Shih Tsu, and miniature Terriers, I was worried about my prediction that Pepper would get a ribbon. So many dogs! So few ribbons!

The competition proceeded without a hitch. If I didn't know better, I would never have believed that so much chaos had reigned around this event. When Minnie Pepper Cocoa's time to put her best paw forward came, she was a pro. At the inspection table, the judge made a show of examining her paws, which made me laugh. "Nice manicure," she told me with a grin.

A few minutes later, to my delight, Pepper was called forward for a final prance around the ring. The winners were then announced. The Bichon Frise came in first. Pepper came in second. Valerie's Yorkie came in third. I was delighted. I felt vindicated, even, to know that I'd shown a dog that had beaten Valerie's. My thought pattern was probably immature. At least I didn't stick my tongue out at her or shout, "Nanny boo."

To my delight, I spotted Baxter near the entrance to the ring. He had a huge smile on his face and raised his fists in the air and shook them triumphantly. It made me so happy, my eyes misted. He rounded the ring and asked if he could treat me to a quick dinner to celebrate.

The burger place in the Fairgrounds kitchen was swamped, and neither of us had the time, energy, or creative brain-power to think of any better place, so we walked to the Brunswick Café.

They didn't offer dinner, and all they had on the menu at this hour was sandwiches and salads. Baxter got a Denver sandwich. I got a Caesar salad.

    I couldn't stop staring at the hallway to the back door, where Terrington had been brutally murdered. I told Baxter I needed to use the restroom. I stood outside the women's room and stared at the kitchen door. Although I wasn't tall enough to see the counter space where the killer could have spied a knife, a tall person could have. Just then, a waiter pushed through one of the two swinging doors. As I peered through the doorway after him, I saw a knife, just two or three strides away. A chill ran down my spine.

    My walk-thru and conversations with both Valerie and Jesse for the Finals course were unexceptional. Valerie was a tad snide; Jesse was gracious. We'd already seen the diagrams, of course, so the purpose of walking the course was purely a matter of my visualization skills. They both left me alone with my thoughts and took reserved seats in the front row.

    Once again, I had a bad case of the jitters. I was pacing in the waiting area. When I glanced over, Jesse gave me a reassuring thumbs up and mouthed the words: "You got this." I then spotted Tracy Truitt leaning against the wall in the aisle. She made a megaphone with her hands. "Allie Babcock rocks!" she called.

    "Attention, everyone," Mark said into a microphone. "We now have the top three finishers of their respective size categories in the Masters Agility competitions. One of the five division winners will be named our Best-in-Agility, as determined by an exhaustive and infallible computer program that works to level out a size advantage." He looked over at Tracy. "I'm sorry to say, Bingley Beagle did not qualify." The audience groaned. Continuing to play for the crowd, Mark nodded and held up his hands. "I know. He was my favorite, too. Better luck next year." There were a few whoops and a smattering of claps.

"In a first for this competition, two of the finalists will compete with the same handler...the human representative of a Toy category, little Allie Babcock."

"Ugh," I murmured.

"We're going from small to large," Mark continued, "so we're all set to begin."

My thoughts were in a jumble as I watched the three adorable little dogs make joyful four-inch leaps and run so fast their little legs were not unlike the circular blurs of speeding animated cartoon characters.

When the jumps, seesaw, and bridge were all realigned for the eight-inch heights, I turned my back to the first two competitors and spent my time playing with Sophie. I didn't want to know their times and get that playing in my head while we were competing. As I entered the ring and got Sophie on her mark behind the starting line, my pervasive thought was simply what Jesse had said: *You got this*. From here on out, the dogs were doing all the work. It felt a little surreal as Sophie

Sophistica tore through the course. She was loving every fraction of a second. We both were.

Afterward I saw the numbers on the electronic board. Sophie had carved more than three-tenths of a second off her best time. She had beaten her own record.

Valerie clapped and had tears in her eyes. We exited the ring, and I brought Sophie straight over to Valerie. She shook her fists in the air and gave Jesse a haughty smile. "Great job," he called to her from his front-row seat. Indeed, Sophie Sophistica had won first place in her division.

I felt a little dazed as the twelve- and sixteen-inch classes competed. Valerie's dog was still in first place for Best in Agility. But it was the next height—the twenty-inch classes like Jesse's dog—that almost always won the overall competitions. Mark undoubtedly knew that when he'd lauded the fairness of the computer rankings.

Again, I ignored both runs of Dog Face's two competitors—Border Collies—in the finals. I was in the ring then. Dog Face was ready to race behind the start line. We began. He raced toward the first obstacle and glided over the gate, clearing the rail by several inches. I felt a chill as I led him and directed him. His every movement was so fluid, it was breathtaking.

We were approaching Mark. Dog Face had to dodge around him. Mark coughed, at the very same moment as he had in the preliminaries. I forced myself to keep going through the finish. I was unwilling to embarrass him the way he'd embarrassed me. I glanced up at the time clock.

Dog Face had once again clocked under thirty seconds!

Valerie climbed onto the fence, which was against both the rules and show etiquette. "Mark Singer!" she yelled. "I am writing you up for this! You coughed at a crucial juncture of the race!"

"I couldn't help but cough," Mark said, "and it didn't affect the dog. Look at his time!"

"Nobody's writing anybody up," Jesse said. "Let the results stand."

As the crew reset the jumps for the twenty-four-inch heights, Valerie walked up to me. "Dog Face won. Sophie will take second place."

I didn't bother to note that three more dogs were yet to race. "I'm sorry, Valerie."

"Don't be. You brought out Sophie Sophistica's best race ever. I'd be an idiot to ask for anything more."

The assistant judge handed Mark the iPad with the results. He nodded, looking away from our position near the start line. "In third place for Best Overall Dog: Dancer, a Border Collie owned by June Skyler. In second place, last year's champion, Sophie Sophistica, a Westie owned by Valerie Franks. Winner and new champion, Dog Face, an Airedale owned by Jesse Valadez."

A young man walked up to me just then. "I'm with the Fort Collins Times. I'd like to interview you on agility training...get your thoughts on the Beagle versus the Westie and Airedale that you were controlling."

"Handling," I interjected.

"Right. Do you have a few minutes?" he asked.

"Sure. I—"

"I'm the Westie's owner," Valerie told him.

"You are?" he asked. "Is it okay if I interview Allie, here, about her and the Airedale?"

"Certainly," Valerie said. As she headed toward the exit, she glared at the reporter. Her dogs had come in second place twice now. I began to hope that Jesse's Eeyore lost to Valerie's Westie tomorrow in the Best Terrier category.

Chapter 25

Baxter was unusually tightlipped as we drove to the Fort Collins Fairgrounds early the next morning. "I wonder if there's a betting pool going as to whether or not Davis fires me today," he said after a long silence.

"At least we'll be getting the Terrier competitions done in one fell swoop. Tomorrow will just be the remaining division championships and Best of Show."

"Yep. Just have to see what kind of havoc our homicidal maniac can wreak today and still avoid detection." He gave me a sideways glance. "Do you have any theories as to who it is?"

"Not really. My best guess is Kiki. Or Marsala. I'm assuming Mark was far too busy with judging the agility trials in building two yesterday to have been behind any of the hijinks. And Jesse, Valerie, and Eleanor seem to have nothing to gain by wrecking the show."

"What about Cooper? He has the physical strength and was the likeliest killer."

"True. I just...I hope it isn't him. I feel sorry for the guy. He seems to be trying his best and giving his all but coming up short time after time."

"Yeah. But he could easily be hiding deep-seated rage."

I gave no reply. Baxter was right. Plus, Cooper had fibbed about my having already agreed to have him and not me as Eeyore's handler. But I didn't care to judge him too harshly for that. It's easy to hear what we want to hear, and to want to tip the scales in our favor, especially when we're forced to ask for help. His self-confidence and self-image had to have been severely diminished by the lawsuit and our subsequent financial strain.

A police car was parked in front of the main building. "Damn," Baxter said. "I hope something horrible hasn't happened. Again."

We entered and walked toward the offices in the back of the building.

Jesse and Cooper were having a conversation, both of them with sour expressions on their faces. Jesse saw me and waved me over. I gave Baxter's arm a squeeze and changed courses to join Them.

"Cooper and I have been discussing which one of you should present Eeyore today," Jesse explained.

"And while I'd like to be the handler," Cooper said, "my arm isn't feeling good." He visibly paled as he looked over his shoulder. "Some policemen are here, and I am getting—" He broke off, visibly paling as he looked over his shoulder. He broke off as a pair of police officers were walked toward us with Davis. Davis pointed at us, and the officers nodded and continued their course.

"Allie," Cooper said. "You should present Eeyore."

"I guess that settles that," Jesse said. "Unless, of course, Allie gets arrested." Jesse chuckled a little.

"I wouldn't joke about that," Cooper muttered. "It's like throwing stones inside your own glass house."

"Jesse Valadez?" an officer said.

"Yes."

"Sergeant Howard." He gestured at his fellow officer. "This is Officer Tate. We'd like to talk to you about the murder of Terrington Leach. Can you come down to the police station with us now?"

"Can this wait an hour or two?" Jesse asked. "My dog is about to be competing. I could meet you at my trailer, just a hundred yards or so from here. At—" he glanced at his watch "—ten a.m.?"

The sergeant nodded at the officer. "Ten a.m."

"My trailer is right—"

"We know where it is."

His wording sounded threatening to me, but Jesse showed no reaction.

As they walked away, Cooper let out a sigh that was more like a gasp from having been holding his breath. He chuckled with relief. "Dang. I warned you. Karma."

"Hey. I didn't kill Terrington. I wasn't even near the place. It's probably *you* the police are homing in on. They want to interview me, is all."

Cooper's features had grown stony. "Good luck, Allie." I hope you do a great job, and Eeyore wins. Despite his clueless owner."

"Hey! I'm just telling it like it is. No need to resort to name-calling."

"Sorry. I'm out of sorts." Cooper walked away.

Jesse shook his head. "This is hardly the way I'd like the leadup for Eeyore's first professional show to go...with me in the stands. Or pacing around nearby. On my broken leg. But then, the cliché for performing is always to say, 'Break a leg.' So maybe I'm already lucky." He bent down and gave his dog a hug. "Just do your best, good boy."

There were six other Airedales in the competition. I vaguely recognized two of the other dogs' handlers. To my surprise, Valerie was handling one of hers—probably a brother of Bella, the infamous in-heat dog in last year's competition. As I watched the two in their trip around the ring, I could detect no limp or hesitation in her step. They looked perfectly matched in pace. I was probably the only person in the immediate area who was watching her and not her dog.

The judge, Tamara Barnes, was giving off positive vibes during her up-close-and-personal inspection of Eeyore, which, due to the Airedale size, took place on the floor, not a table. Her facial expressions reflected that she had found Jesse's dog to be particularly striking. Then again, I could be reading her all wrong. For all I knew, she could be noticing graffiti on his fur that I'd overlooked. As Eeyore circled her, I was a little self-conscious of my own footwork, though Eeyore's gait had seemed nice and even. We made our own journey around the ring, then he stood proudly making perfect eye contact with me. He held that position for what seemed like an extra-long time. I looked at the judge. She nodded at me, looking straight in my eyes.

At that moment, I knew my initial take on her had been correct; she had chosen Eeyore as the winner. A few minutes later, we were collecting his enormous blue ribbon. Valerie's dog came in third.

Jesse gave me a big hug and gave Eeyore an even bigger one. I stepped aside and left him to take the praise as he was photographed with the dog while holding up the ribbon.

"Hey, Allie," Jesse called after me. "You're the best!"

"Thanks," I said returning his triumphant smile. He was scheduled to talk to the police in just twenty minutes. There was no way he could be acting so carefree about the upcoming interview if he had anything to hide.

I'd only taken a couple of steps from the ring before I saw Cooper watching me, looking downhearted. I crossed the distance between us.

"I hope you don't feel like you were cheated out of showing Eeyore."

He shrugged. "It was the only decision I felt I could make, under the circumstances."

"I'm sorry."

"Don't apologize. You're not to blame. You're pretty much the only person here who's kind enough to talk to me." Cooper looked as if he'd been crying. "All I did was to try to stop Terrington's bleeding. All I got in return for trying to save his life was to be identified as the chief suspect. I feel like I'm tied up on a railroad track, and a train's heading straight for me."

"I'm sorry, Cooper," I said again. "Why don't you skip the show tomorrow? Go to a movie, or take a drive in the mountains. Something to get your mind off all of this."

"I can't. Kiki hired me to supervise the teardown tomorrow afternoon. She just wanted me to agree to bow out today, but I'm showing the Bull Terrier and the Scottie anyway. We all know Eeyore was the only high-profile dog with a shot of winning Best in Show. He's also the last shot I had at making something of myself. It's like my ex was always telling me. 'Nice guys finish last.'"

I got a lump in my throat as we exchanged goodbyes.

Baxter had mentioned last night that he was meeting with the Mayor of Fort Collins for publicity photos. I knew he'd want to hear about Eeyore's victory. I headed for his office. The door was ajar, so I quietly pushed it open a little farther to see if he was still in a meeting. I spotted Baxter and Kiki in an embrace, with Baxter pushing her away. I could tell by the look of anger Baxter flashed at Kiki that she had kissed him when he wasn't expecting it.

"Allie," he said as I stepped through the doorway.

Kiki's cheeks grew red. "Sorry, Allie," she said. "This...um...this isn't what you think. I was merely giving Baxter a little kiss to thank him for the hard work he's done for my father and me."

"A lot of people have been working really hard to pull off this dog show. I doubt you're kissing anyone else on the lips."

"You should leave, Kiki," Baxter said.

I glared at her.

"I just...I lost my self-control for a moment." She turned and stared into Baxter's eyes, her own eyes pleading. "I can't help myself. I have feelings for you, Baxter."

"They're not reciprocated, Kiki. I'm in love with Allie. You knew that. And my feelings for Allie are never going to change."

I fought down the leap of joy that my heart took at hearing Baxter's statements, wanting to remain stern. "We're a committed couple. Why don't you get that?" I asked.

Kiki snorted. "I don't see a ring around your finger. It's not like I'm trying to break up a marriage."

"We own a *house* together," Baxter pointed out.

"You'd never know that if you were just watching your behavior. I don't see any spark whatsoever between you two."

"Only because you don't *want* to see it," I said. "You're determined to fool yourself."

She stared at the floor, her cheeks red. After a couple of seconds, she straightened. Her eyes misted. "I've made a fool of myself." Kiki swiped at one of her eyes. "Well, I gave it my best shot. As they say, you can't blame a person for trying. I'll stay out of your hair as much as possible from here on out."

"I'd appreciate that," Baxter said.

She left, battling tears.

Baxter and I exchanged glances. "I'm sorry, Allie. I just...didn't see that coming."

"*I* did, but I didn't think she'd be quite that aggressive. But then, you *are* pretty irresistible."

"Animal magnetism?" he asked with a grin.

"Okay. We'll go with that." I looked again at the door, imagining Kiki's inner pain as she crossed the room, worrying about how she'd cope. "She's been defending you from Davis's making you the fall guy. I hope this doesn't undo that."

"Me, too." He massaged the back of his neck. He'd been getting so little sleep. "I can't wait for tomorrow afternoon to come. You were right. I should have turned down the job. It wasn't worth the meager earnings. Whatever happens between now and Sunday evening, this will be a black mark on my resume."

"On the bright side, we're getting to know Eleanor. I really believe that we can bring all of this neighborhood squabbling to an end."

"Or not. It could just get worse. She could decide we were behind the spray paint. And the powder in her Poodle's crate. The same way we hadn't expected her to lash out at us over the cat getting locked in our barn. She has a history of overreacting."

"That's a possibility, too, Bax. But no matter what, we've got each other. We'll handle it."

"True. You're the love of my life. And I don't care if anyone else can sense that when we're together. Just as long as you do."

"The same—"

Someone rapped twice on Baxter's door and opened it. Valerie.

We both took a big step back.

"Sorry to interrupt your...personal moment. There's a photographer who wants to take our photos, Allie."

"Okay."

"Nice suit, by the way. I hope you brought an extra one, in case we get poured upon again. It's always better to be overprepared than unprepared. There's no downside to being ready for whatever comes one's way."

Unless that mind-frame of hers is what makes her so insufferable, I thought.

"I'll see you later," I told Baxter, truly regretting Valerie's timing. "Eeyore won first-place in the Airedales."

"That's great to hear," he said.

After collecting a gorgeous Westie, probably Sophie's brother, Valerie led me to a photography booth near the front door of the building. Jesse was there with Eeyore. The photographer took a couple more shots with me joining Jesse and Eeyore. He waited while Valerie's and my photos were taken.

Valerie thanked the photographer, and we walked up to Jesse. "Well, it looks like both Dog Face and Eeyore will win," Valerie said. "Thanks to your dog causing my Bella to be less than a year out from whelping five puppies, your Eeyore is in an excellent position."

Jesse raised an eyebrow. "To win the Terrier class?"

"Yes. Especially considering that judges are typically loathe to name the same dog best in the division." She patted her Westie. "My Constant Constantine here won Best of Show last year, so he will probably come in second in the Terrier class to your Eeyore.

"By that way of thinking, maybe Eeyore will win Best in Show."

Valerie snorted. "That's too much for an inexperienced dog."

"I'm not so sure. Allida here is something of a natural."

"I agree with you there. But Allie doesn't have the credentials yet to crack into the Best of Show."

"You know what, Jesse?" I said. "I think Valerie is right. It was a true honor for me to win the Airedale grouping with Eeyore. But it was deeply disappointing for Cooper. Furthermore, it would be all the more impressive for the judges to show him with a second presenter. You might want to seriously consider using Cooper from this point on. He needs the work, and he has the credentials."

Valerie shook her head. "That's the wrong strategy. You'd be pulling the judge's attention away from your dog and onto the handler. Cooper has the wrong kind of credentials. He's a murder suspect. No way will the judges award a dog he's showing with Best in Class, let alone Best in Show. If he turns out to be guilty of killing off his arch rival in the ring after he presented the Best in

Show, Fort Collins Dog Club will never outlive that kind of ignoble press coverage."

"You're trying to use negative psychology on me now, aren't you?" Jesse said. "You want to trick me into ditching Allie." He faced me. "Allie, you're still Eeyore's presenter."

Just then I realized Cooper was right behind me. He must have been close enough to overhear our conversation; he was clearly livid.

"So I'm too tainted to present a dog at a competitive round? I'm not innocent until proven guilty? I'm to be shunned until proven guilty?"

"Sorry, Coop," Valerie said. "I always call things as I see them. It's not personal. I would foresee the same outcome for anyone in your predicament. That's just the way things are. Nobody wants to link their name and their dog's name with a longshot who's a prime suspect in a murder."

"In other words, I should help everyone here out and recuse myself from showing my dogs whose owners haven't already shunned me."

"I didn't say that. But that is precisely what *I* would do in your shoes. Furthermore, I would never have set foot in this venue. I care too much about the reputations and experiences of all the dogs and their owners. I think you've been playing the martyr card for too long."

Cooper wore an expression of utter rage as he glared at Valerie. She merely stared back at him, her hands on her hips. Cooper was within an armlength of her. Valerie was not backing down one iota. Without saying a word, he pivoted and stormed out the door.

I sighed with relief. Only then did I realize I'd been holding my breath. "I was afraid he was going to hit you."

"So was I." Her entire body shook as she exhaled. "Maybe I should consider biting my tongue sometimes." She gave me a tentative smile. "It's hard to teach an old dog like me new tricks."

Chapter 26

Later that afternoon, the Best in Terrier competition began. The Skye Terrier was adorable. He had black fur on his huge pointy ears and his muzzle, and light gray, long fur everywhere else. If you squinted at him, his ears looked like the wings of a black bird that had alit on his head. There were twenty different breeds of Terriers in the ring, counting Eeyore. We were arranged from largest to smallest, so Eeyore was going first. It was nerve-wracking to present a dog with Marsala and her Bull Terrier, plus Valerie and her beautiful Westie, competing against me. Those two were the true veterans of the dog-show circuit, and I knew they wanted to continue their reign. Not only did I not have their experience, but it felt like the blind leading the blind. I was presenting a rookie to the ring in a competition with veteran, prize-winning Terriers. Plus, I would be complementing the gait of a dog that took strides longer than mine.

Despite my insecurity and self-doubt, when Eeyore's inspection ended and it was his turn to traverse the ring, my heart suddenly filled with joy. Here I was, having the opportunity to sprint alongside a perfect specimen of his breed in his very first competition. Why feel anything less than bursting with pride at my good fortune? We circled the judge, and she gave me the out-and-back command. Just then, Baxter approached the ring directly across from my position. We beamed at each other.

And so off Eeyore and I went, loping along the oval-shaped fence in a victory lap, regardless of the final results. Eeyore once again posed perfectly. The judge's and my gazes happened to meet. She had an odd look of alarm. I got the feeling she was torn by how impressed she was with Jesse's dog.

We waited for all twenty dogs to have their turn. I couldn't get rid of the thought that the judge had appeared to be conflicted. It became time for the judge to make her cut. I led Eeyore forward when signaled by the judge, and we again circled the ring for a second look along with Marsala's Bull Terrier and Valerie's Westie. I was shaken by the judge's expression as Eeyore strutted past her. I could only hope it was my imagination, but she looked deeply embarrassed.

My heart was thrumming. We were called to the center of the ring. Tamara pointed three at Constantine, Valerie's prize-winning Westie last year. Then she pointed two at Eeyore, not even glancing at him or me, and one at Chardonnay, Marsala's Bull terrier.

"Hooray!" Marsala shouted to the heavens.

Kiki did the honors with the microphone, of announcing the names of the dogs and their owners. She'd seemed especially delighted as she called out Marsala's name.

I met the judge's eyes again. She was blushing, and she immediately averted her eyes. My every instinct was telling me the judge had been forced to choose the wrong winner. I shifted my gaze to Valerie. She was looking at me with sorrow in her eyes. I assumed she felt that her dog had been cheated, yet she shook her head and said, "Sorry."

Limping only slightly, Jesse entered the ring, and I immediately ceded the leash to him, ignoring that he shook his head. He pulled me into a hug. "Will you look at that," he said, still grinning ear-to-ear. "A rookie presenter and a rookie dog took second place in the Terrier division."

I forced myself to smile. "Yep. Pretty cool."

Valerie walked up to Jesse. "Eeyore should have won. He was the best dog, and Allie was the best handler."

She strode out of the ring, without waiting for photos, congratulating Marsala, or saying a word to the judge.

"Huh," Jesse said.

I was getting a lump in my throat. I couldn't bring myself to tell him about the judge's suspicious reactions. It wasn't as if I could prove anything, and if I'd been mistaken about what someone was thinking, it wouldn't be the first hundredth time I'd done so.

Jesse and I congratulated Marsala, who was kind enough to give me a big hug. "You did a great job, Allie. You really had me worried."

I gave Jesse the leash and left the ring. Baxter met me and gave me a quick hug, saying, "Great job, darling. I really thought you had it in the bag."

"So did I. And so did Valerie."

"Eeyore has that x-factor. Still, you can't really argue with the decision," Baxter said. "Marsala's Chardonnay is also an outstanding specimen."

"True."

Baxter, per usual, got a call on his phone. I spotted Valerie, who still looked fit to be tied. Just as I was turning away, I spotted an Airedale puppy on leash near her feet. I gave Baxter a quick, "See you later," as I headed over to talk with Valerie.

"Tamara isn't much of an actor," she told me in lieu of a greeting. "I doubt we'll see her in the ring again anytime soon."

I tore my eyes away from the puppy. "Do you think she accepted a bribe?"

"Yes. Don't you?"

"I'd like to think she didn't."

"Jesse's Airedales are gorgeous specimens. That's why I held back on selling one of the females of Eeyore's brother's puppies."

That was enough of an invitation for me; I knelt and petted the adorable little furry baby. "You mean this adorable puppy is Dog Face's?"

"Speak of the devil, here you are." I stood up. Jesse grinned at me and said nothing. He bent down and petted the puppy. Valerie shook her head, as if annoyed.

"Jesse, I haven't been proud of my behavior for quite a while," Valerie said as Jesse straightened his shoulders. "For what it's worth, our Airedales probably scooted their cages together without assistance. I should have been much smarter than to hire the imbecile who brought Bella when she was in heat and cost me the chance to show her this year."

"She's a fine dog. A real winner."

"She is. And I have something for you. Retribution, at long last." She handed him the leash of the Westie puppy.

"Is this one of Dog Face's puppies?" Jesse asked, looking positively stunned.

"Yes, and she's yours if you want her. I denied you your right to take your pick of the litter. But she was returned to me. The buyers had to relocate in Asia and couldn't have a dog there."

I looked at her in surprise. She'd only just told me that this was a puppy she'd chosen not to sell.

"What's her name?"

"Calliope Can Dew," spelled like the morning 'dew.' But with your track record, I suppose you'll rename her something dreadful like Watch Out Below."

Jesse grinned from ear to ear. "I'll stick with Calliope. Calli for short."

"Good decision." Valerie studied my eyes. "Allie, let me know if you want to handle my agility dogs on a permanent basis."

I was surprised by her offer. I would need a few weeks to decide how I felt about working long-term for her, though. "Okay. Thanks."

She studied my expression, looking slightly cross. "Give it serious consideration, Allie."

"I will."

"For that matter, I'd be happy to hire you to work with my show dogs, as well. I like the way you carry yourself in the ring. You appear to be impressed, and proud to be showing the dog. That's an X factor that not many handlers have."

She had hired Terrington Leach to present her conformation entrees. Curious, I asked, "Do you think Terrington had an X factor?"

"Not exactly. With him, he gave off the impression that he wouldn't deign to present anything below the best in show. It worked for him. But then, he had that male superiority complex. Whereas for *me*, I've grown weary of the whole racket. I need to take off my hair shirt. It no longer serves me."

"Meaning it *used* to serve you well?"

"Absolutely," Valerie said. "I would never have risen above being the neighborhood spinster who raises puppies because she can't have children of her own. You can't be a pushover, and you can't be a shrinking violet. Maybe I went overboard these last couple of years. These days, I'm almost afraid to be nice."

"But...what are you risking by simply being nice? You've already established a solid reputation as *the* go-to breeder for Terriers in Colorado. Do you truly need to maintain a tough-as-nails persona?"

"Yes, Allie. Unfortunately I do. I'll be in my seventies soon. Nobody under the age of fifty even *notices* women in their seventies and up. I can't lose my edge and still have the dog-community's respect I've fought so hard for."

Her answer gave me pause. She walked away before I could formulate a reply.

An hour or two later, I sought a quiet place where I could perhaps stare at the distant mountains and unwind. I desperately needed to sort out my thoughts. For Baxter's sake if nothing else, I didn't even want to tell him about how suspicious both Valerie and I were about bribery. Yet at the same time, I wanted the injustice to be stopped, and the culprits to be punished. I decided to head for the back of the building, some ten-feet away from the wire-fenced property line. As I started to round the corner, I heard low voices and froze, realizing it was Mark and Marsala, not wanting to stumble into a mutual tryst, but also not wanting to desert Marsala if she was in danger.

"Don't you talk to me about bribes," Marsala said, raising her voice. "I'm the one who's well aware of all the lines *you've* crossed. Everyone looks the other way about the Airedale you got from Valerie."

"I didn't get him *from* her. I rescued him from owners that didn't want him. That has never affected my judging!"

"Of course it did! And then you sabotaged *Jesse's* Airedale!"

"And that's what this is *really* about," Mark retorted.

"Shush!" Marsal hissed. "Keep your voice down!"

I could no longer make out what they were saying. I wasn't going to let this continue. I strode around the corner. They both stopped talking and gaped at me.

"Hi, there. I overheard you talking about bribes. Are you two conspiring?"

"Allie," Marsala snarled. "You're like that old commercial for American Express. You're everywhere I want to be."

"Thanks, Allida," Mark said. "I couldn't decide when to call enough *'enough.'* Now you've made the decision for me." He unzipped his ever-present safari vest and held the right side open. A thin, black wire extended from a jacket pocket. The wire led to a black, button-shaped microphone fastened near the top of the zipper. "I've been wearing a wire."

"Wearing a wire?" Marsala shrieked. "What are you? A Narc?"

"No, just a concerned dog-show lover. It's always bugged me...the bribery that went on at this dog show. Ever so slightly, but ever so constant."

"I didn't say or do a single unethical thing to you," Marsala growled, pointing her finger at him as if she wished it were a dagger.

"That's arguable. What *is* as clear as day, though, is that you've been getting special treatment from Kiki for at least two years running, in return for money. It was just your rotten luck that *I* had a crisis of conscience last year and caught you in the act *this* year."

"He's lying through his teeth," Marsala said to me.

Frankly, I was having trouble deciding how to react.

"I'm going to call Davis and Kiki right now." Mark pressed some buttons on his phone. "Davis? It's Mark Singer. I'm having a heated discussion with Marsala outside. Meet us and Allie Babcock in the staff conference room. It's about the activity between Marsala and your daughter. Both of you are going to want to hear my evidence." He promptly hung up and stuffed his cellphone back into his vest pocket.

Marsala gasped. "What are you talking about! Are you out of your mind? I'm not about to go *chat* about this with everyone." She tried to walk past me, but I blocked her path.

"Your dog is inside, Marsala," Mark said. "I'm not above holding him hostage. Either way, you're going to have to answer to the charges I'm filing against you and Kiki. This whole week, I've recorded all of my private conversations with the two of you."

Marsala paled. After a pause, she said, "I guess I have no choice but to defend myself." She looked at me. "Hopefully somebody sane will stop this nonsense before it goes too far."

Meanwhile, Mark had unlocked the back door and was now holding it open. "After you, ladies."

Marsala glanced back at me as if to see if I would lead the way. I decided I could likely outrun

Mark if she decided to make a run for her Bull Terrier, so I brushed past her. The three of us made the short walk to the small conference room, which was empty. Marsala's face had regained its color, as well as its angry expression. She paced in the back of the room like a caged animal. After a minute or two, Davis entered, with Kiki in tow.

"This is an outrage," Marsala immediately said. "You either fire this sham of a so-called judge and issue an apology, or I'm going to sue FCDC for its every last dime!"

"Sit down, Marsala," Davis said sternly. "Obviously we need to hear Mark out before I can take action."

Mark and I took seats and a moment later, so did Marsala.

"I have no idea why I'm here, Daddy," Kiki said. "I have work to do. I can't be—"

"Sit," Davis told her, pointing at a chair. She rolled her eyes and groaned, then plopped down in the designated chair. Davis remained standing and glared at Mark. "Now, what is all of this about? And I'm warning you, it had better be good."

"I discovered that your daughter is taking bribes from Marsala. Marsala tried to be Kiki's go-between in bribing me, as well."

"I did no such thing. I was trying to see if Kiki's sales pitches were true. That's all."

"Sales pitches?" Davis repeated, looking stunned.

"This is ridiculous," Kiki said. "I'm not a judge in the show. *Mark* is. He must be covering for himself. I can't impact a dog's show results or standings. Nobody can bribe me to do anything whatsoever for them."

"Except by aligning yourself with the judges," Mark retorted, "talking up dogs, telling them to do you a favor and overlook this or that. And it's all paid for by increasing the size of the donation on the receipts."

"That's preposterous. The Fort Collins Dog Club has to file reports to the IRS," Kiki said. "I'd never be able to get away with cooking the books like that."

"You can and you have...up until the IRS notices irregularities and does an audit. I've also recorded some interesting statements from Terrington Leach. He was onto you, wasn't he? He bragged to me that you were giving him kickbacks."

"No. That's just the way Terrington is. *Was*, rather. Always bragging about himself. Making himself the star of every interaction."

"You got it all switched around," Marsala said. "*She* coached him. They could look for their favorable judges. She would set up the judges, and he would give her a percentage of his bonus for first place."

Kiki gasped. "She's lying! If any of that was actually true, I'd have been hurting my profits by killing him."

"You got too greedy," Mark said snidely. "And you got yourself in trouble because there were three quality breeders in the Terrier class who were showing their own dogs. Valerie, Jesse, and

Marsala. But then Jesse broke his leg by falling off a dog's teetertotter."

"I didn't kill Terrington. I didn't set off the sprinkler system. I didn't accept bribes from anybody."

"But you put the tack in my shoe," I said.

She shot me a glare. I could see in her eyes that I'd guessed correctly, and she didn't want to turn her attention away from defending the more serious accusations.

"The trouble is, Kiki," Mark continued, "I was already prepared to turn over every dollar you gave me under the table. That's why I recorded everything." He grabbed his tiny recorder from his vest pocket, removed the microphone, and placed them both on the table. He looked up at Davis and slid the recorder toward him. "All you need to do is listen."

"No! It's Marsala," Kiki cried. "She's the one who bribed Tamara Barnes to pick her dog! And I don't know who bribed you to undermine Dog Face's trials. It obviously didn't work, anyway."

"I don't know anything about this," Marsala said. "I simply gave Kiki a check for a charity she set up for ending puppy farms, which also helps honest breeders like me charge a fair price for our dogs. If it's phony so that she can launder money, I want my money back."

"Yet you just won your division," I said. *At Jesse's expense*, I thought.

"Rightfully so! My dog was the best Terrier!"

"Kiki would never do something like that!" Davis cried.

Mark started pushing buttons on his recorder. "Do you recognize your own daughter's voice on this recording?" He held it up.

"*Hi, Marsala. Mark says you wanted to talk to me about donating to a good cause. We can even put it in the name of your dog.*" The voice was Kiki's.

"*Right,*" Marsala's recorded voice replied. "*He was saying something about the chances of increasing my dog's chances of winning.*"

"*Yes, absolutely. We put the name of your dog in the 'in honor of' field, along with his or her status, such as 'winner of Best in Terrier Class at Fort Collins show.' In exchange for a donation of at least a thousand dollars, that is.*"

"*I don't see how that will help Chardonnay, for example,*" Marsala said.

"*I will tell the judges about their increased profile. How they are widely considered the top competitor, for example. Which is true, of course. There is only one in each division that can be a top donor, and to be given extra points…or attention, really, by the judge.*"

"*A thousand dollars? That's awfully steep.*"

"*It's tax deductible. And it's for a great cause that we all want to help along. Puppy mills need to be permanently banned in this country.*"

"*Well, sure. I thought they were already banned.*"

"*Not everywhere. And it's not happening quickly enough. Right, Mark?*"

"Right. We need to promote good breeders like you. Raise your sales. Especially when that money goes to the judges. Like me."

Davis stared at Kiki as if he was seeing her for the first time. "How could you do this to me? To the Fort Collins Dog Club? It's not like you needed the money. Or the acclaim. I gave you and your mother everything you ever wanted."

"You taught me how easy it was to take people's money."

"I taught you how to be a shrewd businessman! I never taught you how to steal and cheat!"

"Of course you did! You taught me that everything was negotiable. That the best side got the spoils. That's all I did. I gave people what they wanted in exchange for what I wanted. Money."

"And you committed tax fraud to do it!"

"Which is what you said you paid your lawyer to do on our family's behalf!"

Mark said, "I knew it. I was right. *She* killed Terrington Leach."

"No, I didn't. That isn't true."

Mark grabbed his phone. "I'm calling nine-one-one."

"This is nuts! Stop it, Mark!" She stepped toward me. "Allie! You're supposedly the Nancy Drew of the dog world. Stop this! Right now! Yes, Terrington and I were partners, and we bilked money out of the attendees. I'd be the last person on earth who wanted him killed."

"Yes," he said into the phone. "I'm Mark Singer, a judge at the dog show in the Fort Collins

Fairgrounds main building. We need a police unit to come and arrest Terrington Leach's killer. Her name is Kiki Miller."

She shaped her hands like a cone and shouted at Mark's phone, "I'm innocent!" She spread her arms. "I also tried to recruit Mark. I knew he'd been crossing the line all the time. Sucking up to young women. Tipping the scale in his judging."

Mark peered at her.

"We both know you tried to sabotage Dog Face's scores!" Kiki cried.

He covered his phone, pressing his meaty hand against the top edge. "To slow him down! I also have it on my tape when *you'd* bribed me to have him win! He did anyway! I didn't want others to think I was in on it with you when I made the recordings public."

Kiki's cheeks reddened. She looked pleadingly at her father. "Daddy, you have to help me. Tell the police I'm telling the truth. Mark, Allie. You saw I didn't have much blood on me. Daddy! You know I'm innocent!"

Davis pivoted and walked away, saying over his shoulder, "I don't know the first thing about you. You're no daughter of mine."

Chapter 27

Baxter and I felt utterly drained as we drove home after midnight. We'd been fortunate enough to get in touch with our part-time employee a few hours earlier, and she was able to feed and tend to our poor, neglected dogs. My mother was always on backup call, as we were for her Golden and Collie, but I would have hated to send her out to Dacona in the middle of the night.

The police did indeed arrest Kiki, and they took Marsala in for questioning as well. Mark left with one pair of officers to give his testimony and file charges. Valerie told me that she and Davis had a powwow in his office; she'd seen him storm out of the conference room. She assured me that Davis gave digital files to the officers that would provide them with all the financial records for the Fort Collins Dog Club and was confident investigators would be able to detect if Kiki was indeed committing fraud and theft. Jesse returned to the Fairgrounds and said that he had spoken with investigators, and they were homing in on the true culprit. Jessie said they'd asked him about bribery and Kiki's involvement. He opined that Terrington had probably been blackmailing her.

The next morning, Baxter and I tried to make up for our dog-owner negligence, while giving ourselves an energy boost with coffee and power shakes. As we drove toward Fort Collins, Baxter patted my knee. "The doors close at noon. This is going to be ten times easier than any day this week."

"Especially for me. Thanks to Eeyore being cheated, I'm a mere spectator for Best of Show honors." I'd also be totally free to watch the remaining Best in Divisions for the Sporting, Working, and Herding Classes. The Hound and Non-sporting winners had already been determined, but I didn't know the results. Thinking of the original Eeyore, I lowered my voice and grumbled, "If it *is* a good morning."

Neither of us spoke for a couple of minutes. "I hope you're adopting Winnie the Pooh's attitude this morning, not Eeyore's," Baxter said.

"You hope that I'll be searching for a honey pot?"

"No," he said with a laugh. "That we can be cheerful, because the hard part is over."

To my annoyance, as much as I wanted to, I didn't agree with that assessment. "I certainly hope it is. And I really do suspect Kiki was the killer. But last night, I kept trying to play out the scene in my head. As far as I know, nobody saw her at the Brunswick Café. Maybe she'd driven into the back parking lot, called Terrington, and asked him to come out and meet her. But, if so, she then had to go inside, enter the kitchen, and grab the knife. The thing is, Baxter, if the murder was premeditated, she'd have brought a knife from home. If it *wasn't* premeditated, what pushed her over the edge? Terrington was inside, arguing with Cooper, waiting for me to arrive. Valerie, Terrington, Marsala, and Mark were inside the restaurant. Who was left to set her off? To make her think she had to murder Terrington that very moment?"

"Maybe some dog owner from one of the other divisions said something about meeting with Terrington. Or maybe he told her he was about to meet—" Baxter broke off, a quick grimace crossing his features.

A shiver ran down my spine. "Me," I said sadly. "Terrington could have told Kiki he was meeting me at the café after all, and that he was going to spill the beans." I hated that possibility. I didn't want to believe if I'd been on time, things might have gone very differently. "She'd have to be cold-blooded enough to drive around the block a couple of minutes later and wave at me as if nothing happened."

Baxter reached over and patted my thigh. "This is why the police are trained to examine crime scenes and suspects. They'll catch whoever is responsible."

"Hopefully, they already have the right person in custody. If so, it's all pretty much over."

"If it *is* a good morning," Baxter said mimicking my own pessimistic tones.

Later that morning, while Baxter was busy with his managerial duties, I was watching the Non-sporting competition. My phone beeped. Tracy had sent me the full video of Bingley's competition. I watched it, grinning at the dog's and my antics in spite of myself. I decided to indulge myself in watching it on Baxter's much larger computer screen. I forwarded it to him, then texted that I'd like to watch the video and needed access to his office. He sent me a thumbs-up emoji.

He was standing and adjusting his computer screen for premium viewing. "Shut the door and have a seat. It's show time!"

"Have you watched it yet?" I asked as we both took our seats.

"Nope. I waited for you. But it's all cued up."

He pressed the play icon. "Whoops," he said a moment later, pressing the pause icon. "This is the video I took of you and Dog Face, during the Jumps With Weaves. I wanted to show you that one, too."

"Cool. Let's watch it first." He started it again, and the screen showed the stands behind the arena as he started to focus in on Dog Face and me. Something in the background caught my eye.

"Wait, Baxter. I saw a flash in the back of the stands."

"Let's back up the video."

"There!" I cried, pointing. "What was that?"

"A cigarette lighter." He studied my gaze. "You're thinking it could have something to do with the sprinklers going off?"

"There's no smoking allowed inside the buildings, or anyplace besides the designated area and the parking lot. So why is someone using a cigarette lighter?"

"Whoever set off the sprinklers was testing their lighter."

"Precisely. Why do that if you're about to watch a competition where you're not allowed to smoke? Why not wait until you're in a smoking area?"

I peered at the still frame. "It looks like a tall man. But he's in the shadows."

"I'll back it up, frame by frame," Baxter said. He did so. The figure with the lighter was moving in reverse out of the shadowy corner of the room. With each second-long image, the man's image became clearer and clearer.

My breath caught in my throat. "Oh, Jeez. It's Cooper. He doesn't smoke."

"Are you sure?" Baxter asked.

"Absolutely. I've never once smelled smoke on his clothing, and I remember distinctly at the Greeley show last spring his mentioning that he didn't smoke."

"The fact that a nonsmoker is toying with a lighter doesn't prove anything, you realize. It's just circumstantial evidence."

"Which adds yet more circumstantial evidence to the possibility that he killed Terrington," I said. "Kiki's extortion and Marsala's bribery might not have had anything to do with Terrington's murder."

"Unless it was Cooper's *sprinklers'* prank that had nothing to do with any of the above," Baxter said.

"Let's call the police."

Baxter sneaked a glance at his wristwatch.

"You know what?" I said. "Let's just watch the recordings later. I'm starting to get too edgy about everything. I'd like to get this phone call out of the way and leave watching the video for when we can relax and enjoy it."

"I can call the police now and—" His phone rang.

I rose. "I'll call and let you get back to work. I'll go outside where it's quiet and nobody can overhear.

"Okay. I'll see you at eleven or so. Ringside." He winked at me as he answered his phone.

I left and scanned the immediate area. For once, nobody I knew was in the vicinity. I made it all the way across the expansive floor and out the front door without anybody stopping to talk to me.

I headed toward the back of the main building, but stopped about two-thirds of the way, not wanting to risk bumping into someone after all. I deliberately kept my back turned to the entrance, thinking I would surely give anyone the distinct impression that I wanted to be alone to talk in peace and quiet on the phone.

I found Officer Tates' direct phone number at work and called. He answered on the second ring. I told him about the cigarette lighter that Cooper had flicked on and off an hour or so before someone had tinkered with the ceiling sprinklers in the other building. The pause afterward was deafening.

"Okay," he finally said. "Anything else?"

"Well, no, but the thing is, Cooper Hayes doesn't smoke. And even if he did, he'd have had to use his lighter outdoors, in the designated smoking areas. After the agility trial was over."

"Right. I made a note of that."

"Okay. I was just trying to be a good citizen."

"Thank you, Ms. Babcock. Don't hesitate to call again if you think of anything else that might be pertinent."

"I won't. Hesitate, I mean. Bye." I hung up, feeling a little foolish.

"Hi, Allie."

The voice was right behind me. Startled, I jumped, and turned around, hunching over as if to ward off a blow to my head. Cooper was standing there, looking at me as if pained by my presence.

"Cooper. Hi. You scared me. I didn't hear you coming."

"So I see. You need to come with me now."

"I can't. I'm about to meet Baxter. We're going to watch the...the Hound competition together. But I can go somewhere with you after that. How about eleven? Before the Best of Show starts?"

"I don't have that kind of time, Allie. And I'm afraid I have to insist." He opened his jacket. He had a silver handgun. The barrel of the gun was jammed under his brown leather belt. "We're going to walk toward my car. You're going to get in the car. Don't scream. Don't run. Otherwise, I'll shoot you, then I'll shoot as many people as I can in the building."

He grabbed my arm and started ushering me toward his car. Now I was praying for someone I knew to see me. Nobody was watching. As we reached his car, I spotted two guards looking at a little girl who appeared to be crying. Cooper clapped his hand over my mouth so fast my scream was muted. He threw me in the car. I crawled to the driver's side to escape but he was aiming his gun at me through the window.

He rounded the front of the car, still pointing his gun at me. I started to cry with fear and frustration. "Please look at me!" I yelled, pounding against the passenger-side window.

Cooper ducked into the driver's seat and slammed the door shut. He put the pistol on the left side of his seat. I wouldn't be able to reach it easily. He started the car. We headed toward the far exit. The seatbelt alarm sounded. He fastened his own seatbelt. "Ironically, I'm going to ask you to buckle up," he said, his voice oddly flat.

I hesitated but then obeyed. My brain was in a fog. None of this made any sense. If I jumped out and ran, would he shoot me in the back? Would he open fire on bystanders?

"Where are we going?"

"You'll find out soon enough."

"Did you kill Terrington? Are you taking me hostage?"

"It's a good day to die," he said. "That was a line in an old movie. *Little Big Man*, or something like that. Dustin Hoffman."

My heart and my thoughts were racing. *How long would it be before anyone even knew I was missing? Dear God. Baxter wasn't even expecting to meet me until eleven! And I'd been stupid enough to be happy no one had seen me leave!*

Cooper pulled onto I-25 and we headed south. Maybe we were heading for Boulder. He was driving the speed limit, unfortunately. No chance of getting pulled over.

My phone rang.

"Leave it!" Cooper said. That was a command in dog-training. *Leave it.* How to stop dogs from eating something they shouldn't. You counter-trained them. You got them to expect a yummy treat from you in exchange for ignoring dead animals or goose poop.

My thought patters were running amok.

"It's Baxter," I told Cooper, hoping that was the truth. "He's looking for me. He's going to know I'm gone, and that something's very wrong."

"You'd better pray he doesn't find us somehow. If you want him to live."

"I want all of us to live, Cooper!"

He snorted. "Once upon a time."

"What does that *mean*?"

He didn't answer.

Minutes later, my phone rang again. I looked at Cooper in profile. He said nothing. I pretended to have a coughing fit as I tried to get my phone out of my pants pocket without his notice.

Cooper held out his palm. "Give it here."

I feigned accidentally dropping my phone, then I kicked it under my seat. I knew that cells could be traced while they were powered on. "I can't reach it," I claimed.

He muttered something under his breath that I couldn't hear. "It will all be over soon, Allie," he said in his strange, flat tones. "Might as well enjoy the scenery."

The minutes and miles passed. A smarter person maybe would have figured out what to do. My brain seemed to be on red alert for so long now that it might as well have blanked out entirely. Cooper drove past the exit for Baxter's and my home sweet home. He passed an exit for Longmont and Boulder. Then a second exit. Then he turned west. We were driving toward the Flatirons. Maybe he was taking us to Baseline Road.

Several minutes later, we were heading west on Baseline. Neither of us had said a word for quite some time. My throat was dry. "Are we going to Chautauqua," I asked.

"Farther than that."

"Flagstaff?" I asked.

He nodded. "We're going to the amphitheater at the top. It's where I got married. And it's where we're going to die."

"I don't *want* to die, Cooper. I've given you no reason whatsoever to be part of your suicide pact."

"It's circular. It's the way the world turns. And our existence on this earth. You started it all...you and your significant other. You put me on this path."

"No, we didn't."

"Baxter took away my self-respect."

"He had nothing whatsoever to do with your being demoted and given the temporary position as a manager in the dog show."

"Damage that happens unintentionally is still damaging."

"But it was Davis Miller who caused that...damage, not Baxter. And not me, either."

He slammed his fist on the steering wheel. "I broke up my marriage because I thought I could make you love me back!"

"What? You.... We barely know each other! You told me you got a divorce almost a year ago."

"And I couldn't get you out of my head all of that time. I did all of this for you. I tried to make myself your boss for your sake. I talked you up to every single Terrier owner, convincing them that *you* would be their best shot at winning. At the time, I thought I couldn't compete in the Terrier class. I thought I was the manager. I got you Valerie. I got you Jesse. I had Marsala all convinced, too."

"That's just...I had no idea. And last year's show, I was already living with Baxter. I never led you on. I *told* you I had a partner."

"I thought you meant a business partner. But none of that matters. You caused my world to crash. You led me along like a dog in a choke collar. I nearly died for you! I was going to try to live off the land. Give away my car. Live in the mountains. I left my keys in the ignition. Then I fell and hit my head and broke my arm."

Finally this made some sense. "Cooper. It's your brain injury. Don't you see? That's what's caused this horrible behavior swing!"

For a moment he looked at me with surprise and understanding in his expression. He returned his eyes to the road. We were driving along Chautauqua now. Both sides of the street were lined with cars, in defiance of parking laws.

"No, it can't be," Cooper stated.

"You killed a man because you're not in control of yourself. It's made you violent."

"Now you're a brain doctor?"

"No, but I know you're nothing like you were a year ago. And I know you won't be the first person to have a radical swing after a concussion."

In truth, the idea of willfully tempting car thieves to steal his car and living in the mountains without proper provisions was a sign of depression, plus it had happened before the head injury. But, still. This was a man who needed help.

"Please, let me help you, Cooper. Let me take the wheel. You need to see a doctor."

He took a gasp of air. He was starting to cry. "It's too late. I need to put myself out of my misery."

"No, you don't. You need to see a doctor. I'll take you to one."

"Then you shouldn't have forced my hand. You shouldn't have poked your nose into the murder."

"You asked me to help prove your innocence!"

He clammed up, his jaw muscles working. Experience had taught me there was no statement or action that people couldn't twist around to suit their own purposes or versions of events. We are all the heroes of our life stories. Right now, Cooper needed me to be the villain. Or maybe the unintended consequence—the collateral damage.

We started up Flagstaff Road, with all its twisting switchbacks. Again, Cooper gulped for air. He was crying. He caught my eye.

"You have no idea what it's like to go through humiliation after humiliation. Terrington destroyed every facet of my life. And the worst part was, he didn't even care. I was nothing to him. He just stole my wife and my girlfriend and my dogs and my career. He turned me into a mockery. And he didn't even know my name."

He started crying so hard I was afraid he couldn't see well enough to prevent us from veering off the cliff.

"Cooper. I understand why you hated him enough to kill him. I really do. But this isn't the way to resolve anything. Are you actually going to kill me to try and escape? You're going to commit two murders? I didn't do a thing to hurt you. And you're not going to escape from this. The police will be all over you."

He was starting to slow the car. "You've always been nice."

"Let me go."

"You'll tell the police."

"The police already know, Cooper. That's why they took you to the station in the first place. You'd be killing me for nothing. Please, Cooper. You're not violent. Your head injury is affecting you. Don't make me die because you hit your head."

He slammed on the brakes. We skidded dangerously close to the edge, but the car came to a stop. "Get out. Now. Before I change my mind."

I did as he said. He took off while I was still shutting the door. By the time I'd taken a dozen steps down the winding road, I heard sirens. I waved my arms. The first police car pulled over and gestured at the others to keep going, while holding up his radio.

"He's at the chapel on Flagstaff. He has a gun, and he wants to commit suicide."

"I'll radio that ahead. Do you want me to get someone up here to get you down? We already blocked the road at the base."

"No, I'll walk down. I'll be okay."

He nodded and drove away. I made a silent prayer that I wouldn't hear any gunshots.

Epilogue

Two weeks passed from my brush with death. I still struggled with flashbacks and nightmares. Baxter helped me through them. I fell more deeply in love with him with every passing day.

An hour after Cooper Hayes let me escape from his car, he was taken into custody. The officers said they found him sobbing and rocking himself in the amphitheater, saying that his head hurt. They managed to convince him to put down his gun. He surrendered peacefully.

Meanwhile, Baxter knew when I hadn't returned to the building that something had happened and someone had forcibly driven me away. He, too, had called Detective Baker and told them he was certain Cooper Hayes had kidnapped me. The police had been able to put a tracer on Cooper's cellphone as well as mine.

For reasons I didn't care to examine, Marsala was allowed to show her Terrier in the Best of Show competition. Her dog finished in third place. Ironically to my mind, the winner was a Beagle.

On the Tuesday following that nearly fatal Sunday, Eleanor knocked on our door with a marvelous peace offering. She had withdrawn her complaints to the county about our dog shelter and convinced everyone that we could be good neighbors in Dacona without regard to the kennel. It was late in coming, perhaps, but she even hosted a gathering for the neighbors stating that they should use us as their dog watchers and even cat watchers. Eleanor turned out to be a public-relations savant. In just a few days, we went from the pariahs of the neighborhood to the local resource for premium care in behavioral training and kenneling.

Baxter and I took several days off to just hang out at home with the dogs. Every day I was regaining a bit of my confidence. This particular Monday morning was no different. I was scheduling clients starting tomorrow. Baxter was busy speaking with breeders and veterinarians about our soon to be better-than-ever dog boarding business. I was surprised to see him at shortly after one when I heard him enter the house. He'd told me he wasn't going to return until three at the earliest.

He grinned at me lovingly when he saw me on the living room sofa. "Hey, Allie. I heard the Humane Society has a couple of new arrivals. Let's go take a look."

"Right now?"

"Yep. I got done early. Perfect timing."

Baxter and I had been going to the Longmont Humane Society on a regular basis lately. He kept telling me that one of these days, we'd find a dog there and just know right away that he or she was meant to be ours.

We made small talk as we drove to the shelter. Baxter seemed to be more talkative and energetic than typical. He must have had a successful time promoting our business. As we parked, he smiled at me and said, "I have a good feeling about this."

"Oh, yeah?"

"Yeah. I get the feeling there's a dog with our name on it just waiting for us."

He was so happy I couldn't have helped but return his smile even if tried. He gave me a kiss, then put his arm around me as we walked to the door. He swept it open for me and we entered.

"Hey, Cindy," he said to the clerk. "We're going to take a look around."

She grinned at him as we passed. We went down the first aisle of cages, with its small and medium-sized dogs. They weren't for us, but they were still worth greeting. The air smelled acrid as usual, but I'd take having the company of dogs over fresh-smelling air anytime. The moment we turned the corner to the next aisle, Baxter said, "Well, look what we have here."

And there he was. Our dog. He was black, maybe with some terrier in the mix, definitely with a black Lab in his gene pool. I glanced at the sheet of descriptions on the door. "Hi, Gus," I said. Gus got up on all fours, grabbed a soft chew toy of some kind, and headed to his door to greet us, his tail wagging eagerly.

Baxter opened the door, and we both went inside Gus's cage. "Hey there, Gus," Baxter said. Gus happily pranced between us, pausing and stretching as we gave him a vigorous rub down. I did a doubletake at his collar and straightened.

"There's some sort of a little pouch on his collar," I said.

"Huh. That's kind of interesting," Baxter said. "Maybe it's got his nametag in there. I just hope it doesn't mean someone already put a hold on him."

"Yikes. I sure hope not."

"I know. The dog feels like he's ours, doesn't he?"

"He sure does." I gave the pouch a little tug, and it came right off. "It's fastened with Velcro." I opened the little flap. I saw something sparkling and took it out. It was a diamond ring. I stared at the ring, dumbfounded.

I glanced over at Baxter. He was down on one knee.

I looked toward the gate. The entire staff was now standing behind us, along with a few people I didn't know, who probably just happened to be here, looking for dogs to adopt themselves.

"How did you do this?" I asked Baxter. I started weeping uncontrollably. "Who puts a ring on a dog at a Humane Society?"

"Me. Because you were right. I knew the moment I saw Gus that he was meant for us. Just like I knew the moment I saw you, that you were meant for me. Marry me, Allie Babcock. Please. I will be the best husband I can possibly be for the rest of our lives."

"Yes," I said.

Baxter hopped to his feet and helped me to rise. He wrapped his arms around me in a deep embrace and gave me the most wonderful kiss of my life, amidst the cheers of the gathered crowd.

Everything sank in at once. I had it all. Finally. Everything I'd ever wanted. It had been worth every minute of the wait.

Note from Allie Babcock

Leslie O'Kane is a dog lover, a certified decorator, a tennis player (though she has a caustic relationship with the net), and a hula-hoop dancer (but keeps bruising herself).

Although Leslie has been a published author for more than 20 years, she has issues with self-promotion and is in a 12-step program to overcome her fear of newsletters, blogs, and publicizing her books through social media.

Please help me push Leslie onto the next step by visiting **LeslieOKane.com** and signing up for her **New Book Alert** or sending her an email at **LesOKane@aol.com**, and, if you are so inclined, "like" her Facebook page, **Leslie O'Kane Books**.

Lastly, if you enjoyed this book, please write a review; apparently such things help authors to sell books and encourage them to write more. If you send a copy of your review to her email she will send you a deeply felt personal thank you.

You can find these books at book retailers of your choice, or at my website, **LeslieOKane.com**.

Made in United States
North Haven, CT
30 August 2024